The Penguin Who Knew Too Much

OTHER MEG LANGSLOW MYSTERIES BY DONNA ANDREWS

No Nest for the Wicket

Owls Well That Ends Well

We'll Always Have Parrots

Crouching Buzzard, Leaping Loon

Revenge of the Wrought-Iron Flamingos

Murder with Puffins

Murder with Peacocks

The Penguin Who Knew Too Much

Donna Andrews

Thomas Dunne Books
St. Martin's Minotaur
New York

This is a work of fiction. All of the characters, organizations, and events portrayed in this novel are either products of the author's imagination or are used fictitiously.

THOMAS DUNNE BOOKS.
An imprint of St. Martin's Press.

www.thomasdunnebooks.com
www.minotaurbooks.com

Library of Congress Cataloging-in-Publication Data

Andrews, Donna.
   The penguin who knew too much : a Meg Langslow mystery / Donna Andrews.—
1st. ed.
     p. cm.
   ISBN-13: 978-0-312-32942-6
   ISBN-10: 0-312-32942-3
  1. Langslow, Meg (Fictitious character) —Fiction. 2. Zoo keepers—Crimes against—Fiction. 3. Women detectives—Fiction. I. Title.
   PS3551.N4165P46 2007
   813'.6—dc22

2007013797

First Edition: August 2007

10 9 8 7 6 5 4 3 2 1

Acknowledgments

Thanks once again to:

The staff at the Reston Zoo in Reston, Virginia, and the Henry Doorly Zoo in Omaha, Nebraska, for answering so many questions about penguins and llamas and lemurs (oh my!). And to Dale Graham of Llamarada, for sharing so much llama lore and letting me meet her llamas.

All the friends and family who listen to me brainstorm, give me ideas, read the resulting drafts, or just help keep me sane while I write: Mom; Stuart, Elke, Aidan, and Liam Andrews; Dana Cameron; Carla Coupe; Ellen Crosby; Kathy Deligianis; Dave Niemi; Phillip and Sophie; Laura Durham; Suzanne Frisbee; Peggy Hanson; Valerie Patterson; Noreen Wald; and Sandi Wilson.

Ellen Geiger, my agent, and Anna Abreu at Curtis Brown, for taking care of the business side so well and letting me concentrate on the writing.

Ruth Cavin, my editor (whose first name really should be "The legendary"); Toni Plummer, her assistant; and everyone at St. Martin's Press. Especially whoever asked, "Hmmm . . . has she ever thought of using penguins?"

And the little blue penguins at the Henry Doorly Zoo for helping me figure out how to say, "Penguins? Yes! As a matter of fact . . ."

The Penguin Who
Knew Too Much

Chapter 1

"Meg! Guess what I found in your basement?"

I looked up from the box I was unpacking to see Dad standing in the basement doorway, his round face shining with excitement.

"A body?" An unlikely guess, but Dad was a big mystery buff—perhaps if I amused him, he'd stop playing guessing games on moving day.

"Oh, rats—you already knew? Well, how soon will the police get here? I need to move the penguins—we don't want them any more upset than they already are."

He disappeared down the basement stairs without waiting for an answer. I abandoned my unpacking to call after him.

"Dad? I was joking. Did you really find a body? And why are there penguins in our basement? Dad!"

No answer. Should I go down to see what was happening, or call the police? Damn! I closed my eyes and counted to ten. Normally counting to ten calmed me, but today it just gave me time to realize how much more could go wrong elsewhere in the house. On cue, I heard the crash of something breaking, followed by a sheepish "Oops!" from my brother, Rob, in the front hall. In the living room, Mother ordered a brace of cousins to move the sofa to yet another location. She'd been at it for an hour, and so far only three pieces of furniture had made it from the truck to the house.

In the dining room, Mrs. Fenniman, Mother's distant cousin and closest ally, was singing an Italian aria, changing pitch every dozen notes, which meant she'd had a few martinis already and we'd have to redo the walls after she'd painted them.

I'd only reached seven when Rob interrupted me.

"Meg? You know that big cut-glass punch bowl? Is that a particular favorite of yours?"

"Don't you mean *was* it a particular favorite?" I asked as I pulled my cell phone out of my pocket. "And no, but Mother was quite fond of it, so see if you can sweep up the pieces before she notices. Broom's over there."

"Right-o."

I dialed 911. I wasn't sure the situation quite warranted 911, but I hadn't memorized the nonemergency number for the Caerphilly Police Department and I had no idea which box contained the phone book.

"Hello—Debbie Anne?" I said when the dispatcher answered. "This is Meg Langslow."

"Meg! How's the move-in going? And what's the problem?"

"Slowly. And the problem is that Dad says he's found a body in the basement."

"Oh, Lord," Rob said. He stopped in the doorway, broom and dustpan in hand, the better to eavesdrop.

"Is he serious?" Debbie Anne asked after a moment. "I mean, if it's just some kind of practical joke—"

"He sounded serious," I said. "And I thought I should call you first instead of wasting time going to look myself, and possibly disturbing a crime scene."

"I'll tell Chief Burke you said so. If it turns out to be some kind of mix-up . . ."

Her voice trailed off. I knew what she was thinking. Quite

apart from the major-league practical jokers in my family, there was Dad, with his well-known mystery obsession.

"If it's a mix-up, I'll call back right away," I said, and hung up.

"Did he really find a body?" Rob asked.

"So he says."

"Don't you think you should have checked before calling the cops?"

"If he was pulling my leg, I'll let him explain it to Chief Burke."

"I still think you should check for yourself."

"I'm going to—want to come?"

Rob, who fainted at the mere idea of blood, shook his head and hurried back to the hall.

I took the stairs to the basement.

The smell hit me first.

Not the rank smell of a decaying body or the tang of newly spilled blood, both of which I'd had a chance to experience while tagging along after Dad—less while he pursued his medical practice, of course, than during his repeated attempts to involve himself in murder investigations, like the protagonists of the mystery books he read by the dozen.

No, this smell was a cross between a barn in dire need of cleaning and a fish market that had lost power for a few days. I deduced that I was smelling penguins. The stench wafted from the unfinished, far end of the basement, the part under the library wing, where the concrete floor gave way to packed dirt.

I also heard muted honking and trilling noises. I followed my nose and ears.

I should have brought a flashlight. This side of the basement was not only unfinished, it was unelectrified. And to get to the far end, where Dad was, I had to traverse a part near the stairs that the pack rat former owner had turned into a perfect warren of ramshackle storage rooms.

"Chief Burke? Is that you?" Dad appeared around a corner, carrying a flashlight.

"He's on his way," I said. "Where's the body?"

"This way!" Dad was grinning with obvious delight at showing off the house's exciting new feature.

Not a feature that had been there when my fiancé, Michael, and I bought the place, I suspected. The rambling three-story Victorian house had been so packed with junk by the previous owner that we hadn't initially realized quite how badly in need of repair it was. But I'd spent several months crawling over every inch of the place, getting rid of decades of clutter, and then several more months supervising the repairs—at least the ones we'd decided we had to do before moving in. For that matter, we'd been living on-site for months—camping out first in the ramshackle house and more recently in the barn while the house was repaired. Surely by now I'd have noticed a body lying around, even in this remote and as-yet unrenovated corner of the basement.

Dad and I emerged from the maze of storage rooms into the larger, dirt-floored open area. A couple of battery-powered Coleman lanterns hung from the ceiling, casting enough light for me to see the room. I didn't spot any penguins, though I could hear and smell them nearby. And I could see an excavation near the center of the room.

"Oh, wonderful," I said. "You didn't just find a body. You dug one up."

Chapter 2

Gazing at the hole, I felt slightly reassured. Surely, if the body had been buried, it would turn out to be an old one after all. Little more than a skeleton.

"Yes," Dad said. "And not even buried very deep. It was remarkably easy to uncover—what were they thinking?"

He shook his head solemnly, as if to express his dismay at the shoddy professional habits of the modern criminal class. Or perhaps at Michael's and my shoddy housekeeping skills.

"It's not as if we're in the habit of tilling the soil down here," I said. "Did you suspect it was here, or did you have some other good reason for digging a hole in the middle of our basement floor?"

"For the penguins," Dad said. "I knew they'd be much happier with someplace to swim. So I was going to put in a pond—one of those preformed plastic ones."

"Of course. A pond," I said. It made sense coming from Dad, who had always had a fascination with water features. He probably loved having the penguins as an excuse. "But why not outside?"

"They're penguins," he exclaimed. "You can't expect them to stay outside in the heat of a Virginia summer! In here, we can give them some air-conditioning."

It would be a neat trick, with this end of the basement not even electrified—I could already see the giant industrial exten-

sion cords snaking through the house. And I shuddered to think
what it would do to our electric bill.

"I started digging yesterday," he went on. "But then I realized
that I didn't know how big a hole I needed. So I went to Flugleman's garden store last night and got the precise dimensions.
And almost as soon as I started work this morning—voilà!"

He pointed to his excavation. I grabbed one of the overhead
lanterns, picked my way carefully to the edge of the hole, and
peered in. I didn't exactly see a body—more like a hand sticking
up by itself out of the dirt. But even though I had refused to follow in Dad's footsteps, becoming a blacksmith instead of a doctor, I had enough grasp of basic human anatomy to deduce that if
the hand wasn't still attached to a body, it had been at one point.
Probably, from the size of it, a full-grown male body.

Though hands could fool you. I glanced down at my own,
which were largish for a woman's hands. Of course, at five feet,
ten inches, so was the rest of me. And my work as a blacksmith
wasn't exactly conducive to maintaining elegant feminine hands.
Mother had long since given up chiding me for ruining them at
the forge. Even Michael didn't pretend to find my hands beautiful, but he had pronounced them capable-looking, and made it
sound like a higher compliment. One of his many positive traits.

Our subterranean visitor's hand, like mine, looked well used
rather than well cared for. Capable. On the large side. And
hairier than most women's hands.

So judging from the hand, our uninvited visitor was male.
And either he worked with his hands, as I did, or he had done
something useful with them in his off-hours.

And he probably hadn't been buried beneath the basement
floor all that long, I realized, with a sinking feeling. Now that I
was closer, I could smell decay, even over the penguin poop. If
he'd been there since the late Mrs. Sprocket owned the house, I

wouldn't have smelled anything at all. Or seen enough of him to make all these deductions.

"How recently did he die?" I asked. "Or can you tell from just the hand?"

"Longer than a day," Dad said. "Or decomposition wouldn't be detectable. And there's no rigor, so presumably it has worn off. But not much longer."

"So we're talking days, not months or years, right?"

"Of course," Dad said. "You could figure that out yourself."

"I hoped I was wrong," I said. "It would be so much easier if we could blame him on the previous owner. Anyway—ow!"

Someone—or something—had goosed me. I stumbled forward, barely avoiding the hand. My foot landed on a soft, warm body that squealed and wriggled frantically out from under me, almost toppling me over onto the hand. I glanced around to see a throng of penguins milling about us.

"Oh, dear, they're loose again," Dad said. "There really isn't any place down here that will hold them. Help me take them outside, before they spoil the crime scene."

"A little too late to worry about that," I said. The penguins had discovered the hand and were poking and nibbling at it with their beaks, though luckily they hadn't decided that it was edible.

"Grab a fish and lure them outside," Dad said, taking a bucket down from an overhead hook and handing it to me.

"Yuck," I said, but I followed orders. I grabbed something cold and slimy from the bucket and headed for the other end of the room, where concrete steps led to a set of old-fashioned slanted metal doors that provided an outlet to the yard. Behind me, I could hear Dad gently shooing the penguins. I barely had time to swing open one side of the door and scramble out before they caught up, nearly knocking me down in their eagerness to get to the fish.

I threw the fish into the yard, tossed a few more after it, and then looked around for a place to stow the penguins before they wandered off to visit the neighbors.

The duck pen. It wasn't as if our resident duck and her adopted ducklings spent much time in it. I opened the gate, dumped most of the remaining chum at the far end, then stood waving a fish as a lure until I had all the penguins inside. Dad shut the gate behind them, and I climbed over the fence to freedom, or at least the absence of penguins underfoot.

"Good thinking!" Dad said as he put one foot up on a rail and leaned his elbows on the top of the fence. The veteran penguin wrangler, resting after a successful roundup. "That should take care of them for the time being."

"For the time being," I repeated. "At least until you can take them back where they belong. And just where is that, anyway? Not in our basement, I assure you."

"The Caerphilly Zoo," Dad said. He had pulled out his hand-kerchief and was mopping his face and the shiny expanse of his bald head. "Patrick asked me to foster them for a while."

"Patrick?"

"Patrick Lanahan. The zoo's owner. It's just until he gets through this bad patch he's having."

"What kind of a bad patch?" I asked. In our family, "bad patch" was a convenient euphemism. It could cover anything from brief cash-flow problems or minor marital discord up to a felony conviction with a sentence of twenty to life.

"Only temporary, of course," Dad said.

"Of course. What's wrong down at the zoo?"

"The bank was going to put a lien on the property. And if he hadn't moved the animals out, the bank might have seized them, too."

"Oh, so these might even be hot penguins," I said. "Great."

"Don't be silly, Meg," Dad said. "The bank didn't want to seize the penguins. What on earth would they do with them if they did? They gave Patrick plenty of time to foster out all the animals before they filed the lien."

"To foster out all the animals? Dad, how many animals did you take, anyway?"

"Only the penguins," Dad said, as if hurt by my distrust.

"Ah. Only the penguins," I repeated. Suddenly the throng of black-and-white forms busily exploring the duck pen for escape routes looked small and relatively harmless. I tried to remember what other animals they'd had at the zoo. Nothing particularly dangerous, I hoped. Still, penguins were better than hyenas, weren't they? And hadn't the zoo had at least one elderly, ill-tempered bobcat? "So you're stuck with the penguins until Patrick can pay his bills?"

"Just until he finishes negotiating an agreement with a new sponsor," Dad said. "Which should be any day now."

He was looking at the empty fish bucket with a slight frown.

"Remarkable, how much fish they eat," he said. He glanced at the penguins, then back at the bucket, and sighed.

"Dad, just how long have you had these penguins?"

"Only two weeks."

"They haven't been in the basement for two weeks, have they?" I asked. I thought I'd have noticed penguins, but perhaps the preparations for the move had made me less observant than usual.

"Oh, no—I've been keeping them over at the farmhouse." Although he and Mother still lived in Yorktown, about an hour to the south, a few months earlier he'd bought the farm adjacent to our new house, partly to save it from development and partly so they could come up to Caerphilly whenever they felt like meddling.

"Why couldn't they just stay there?" I asked.

"With your mother coming up today? I didn't think she'd be pleased."

"And you thought I would?"

"I knew you'd cope better than your mother."

"You mean you knew I'd complain less."

"Oh, look! There's Chief Burke!"

As the chief's car pulled up, Dad hurried out to meet him, visibly relieved that something had interrupted my line of questioning.

"Glad to see you!" Dad exclaimed, reaching to shake the chief's hand as he stepped out of the patrol car. "Though I'm sorry it had to be under these circumstances."

"Just what are the circumstances?" the chief asked. His normally cheerful brown face wore a faint frown. "Debbie Anne had some fool story about you finding a body in the basement."

"Yes—extraordinary, isn't it?" Dad said. "Let me show you."

He made a dash toward the side yard, where the battered metal cellar doors were located. The chief and I followed more slowly, and saw Dad's head disappear into the opening just as we turned the corner of the house. The chief looked at me.

"You've seen this body?" he asked.

"Yes. Part of it anyway—the hand. The rest's still buried."

"Lord," the chief said. "And here I was hoping for a quiet Memorial Day weekend."

He walked over to the basement doors and frowned at them for a few moments. Since the doors weren't doing anything to merit disapproval, I suspected that he wasn't really all that keen on going inside. I glanced down through the doors myself and could see why. Now that my eyes were used to the bright sunlight outside, I could see little more than a few steep steps disappearing into the gloom.

"Chief?" Dad called. "Are you coming?"

"Coming," the chief called. "I don't see what he's in such an all-fired hurry about," he grumbled to me. "Body's not going anywhere, is it?"

"You know how excited he gets about murders."

The chief only rolled his eyes. Then he put one foot carefully on the first step, and I watched his head drop lower with each step until it vanished into the basement.

Should I follow, or stay outside to keep an eye on the penguins?

Chapter 3

Before I could decide whether to test the chief's patience by following him, Sammy, the gangling young deputy who'd driven out with the chief, ambled over to my side.

"I guess the family's all over here today to help you move in," he said.

"A few of them. We're just making a start today—most of them are coming tomorrow."

By which time I hoped to have most of the breakable objects locked up safely somewhere. At least the ones that survived Rob's efforts.

Of course, I knew Sammy couldn't care less about how many of my family were here. He was really wondering about the presence or absence of my twenty-something cousin Rosemary Keenan—or Rose Noire, as she preferred to call herself these days. I took pity on him.

"Let me know if you and the other officers will still be around at lunchtime," I said. "Mother and Rose Noire are planning lunch for the movers, and I'm sure it would be no trouble to feed a few more people."

"Thanks!" Sammy said, smiling happily. "I should go see if the chief needs anything. Could you show anyone else who arrives the way?"

"Will do," I said. Not that the other officers needed directions from me. They all knew perfectly well how to find their way into the basement of what they still called the old Sprocket house. Michael and I were just the city folks who'd spent a pile of money buying the place and fixing it up. Neither of us had actually grown up in a city, but we weren't born in Caerphilly, so we'd probably always be city folks to the locals.

Gloomy thoughts. I wondered how soon Michael would return from his trip to our storage bin. Even a body in the basement wouldn't dim his enthusiasm for our half-renovated Victorian hulk and our future life in it. Right now I could use a little of that enthusiasm.

I was pulling out my cell phone to call him when I saw Dad trudging up the cellar steps, dragging his heels like a grade-school kid on the way to the principal's office. As he stepped out onto the lawn, someone banged the cellar doors shut behind him. Dad looked back reproachfully.

"What's wrong?" I asked.

"He asked me to leave," Dad said, his voice plaintive. "Said he couldn't have civilians at the scene. Civilians!"

"He was being polite, of course. What he really meant is that he can't allow any of his suspects to stay at the scene."

"Oh," Dad said, brightening. "That's true. I suppose he can't. After all, the person who reports finding the body does often turn out to be the killer."

"And someone has to tell the rest of the family that we probably have to halt the move temporarily," I said. "The chief's not going to want us dragging more stuff into what's suddenly become a possible crime scene. Why don't you go inside and break the news to Mother and the others?"

"An excellent plan!" he said. And with his good humor restored, he trotted into the house.

I strolled around to the front yard, nodding good morning to several other officers on their way to the cellar, and sat on the porch, where I could keep a lookout for more new arrivals. I reached into my pocket for the notebook-that-tells-me-when-to-breathe, as I called my humongous to-do list. When faced with a crisis, I clung to the notebook the way a toddler clutches a security blanket. And while finding the body at any time would be a horrible thing, finding it on moving day counted as a real crisis, didn't it?

Especially when Chief Burke started trying to figure out who had buried the body, focusing on the most logical suspects—me and the ever-growing crew of family members showing up to help with the move.

I used the paper clip that served as a place mark to open the notebook to my list of priorities for the day. I hadn't yet crossed off many things—after all, it was barely noon—but already the neat clarity of the list I'd made last night had been sullied with half a dozen scribbled additions and annotations. I was used to that happening when real life and one of my lists collided. Especially real life involving my family. But odds were that Dad's discovery would derail the day's agenda entirely. I turned the page to begin an entirely new list.

But before I even started that, I pulled out my cell phone and hit the first speed-dial button. I felt better the moment Michael answered.

"We're still at the storage bin, loading the truck," he said. "You were right; I really underestimated how long it would take."

He didn't mention the reasons it was taking longer, probably because they were still within earshot—the several cousins and uncles who'd gone with him to help load the pickup and were probably still squabbling amicably about what to load next or how to balance the load. He didn't sound annoyed, either. Amazing.

Of course, Michael uncritically adored my family, probably because he'd always felt deprived growing up as an only child, with a widowed mother and two unmarried aunts as his sole relatives. So far prolonged exposure to the Hollingworths, my mother's clan, hadn't dimmed his enthusiasm for the prospect of marrying into a large, noisy, eccentric extended family. I'd recently realized that was one of my reasons for dragging my heels about marrying the tall, dark, and handsome Michael—the fear that after a year or two with my family as in-laws, he'd suddenly come to his senses and go looking for someone less genealogically encumbered.

I'd finally become convinced that Michael really did enjoy my family—just as Dad, who'd been a foundling, had been overjoyed when, by marrying Mother, he'd gained not only a wife but several hundred aunts, uncles, nieces, nephews, and cousins. Buoyed by this knowledge, I'd agreed to Michael's plan for eloping in the middle of one of my family's legendary outdoor parties. Specifically, the over-the-top housewarming party we were throwing on Monday, Memorial Day, once our move back into the house was complete. Anyone who didn't come to the party couldn't complain about not being invited. We knew that neither of our mothers would be happy that we'd preempted the overelaborate wedding and reception plans they'd begun to cook up, but at least by eloping now we could prevent either mother from doing anything rash, like making large, nonrefundable deposits on any wedding paraphernalia. And maybe they'd both be so relieved to hear we'd finally tied the knot that they'd forgive us.

Just in case, we were taking off immediately on a two-week honeymoon. Probably not enough time for either my mother or

Mrs. Waterston to get over her disappointment at the lack of a big wedding, but enough time for them to calm down and refocus their energies on nagging us about when we were going to provide them with grandchildren. At thirty-six, I wasn't sure if my own biological clock was prodding me, but I knew Michael's mother soon would be.

Maybe two weeks wasn't enough. Maybe Michael should ask the college for a sabbatical so we could take a slow cruise around the world. Though for all I knew, that could be what Michael had planned. He'd made all the arrangements for the honeymoon, and refused to tell me anything. The theory was that I'd have one less thing to worry about on top of the move.

If he thought not knowing where I was going would stop me from worrying—

Anyway, that was The Plan. And it was working—so far. As far as I could tell, my premove and preparty nerves camouflaged any prenuptial jitters, and anyone who noticed Michael's good spirits would simply chalk it up to his eagerness at finally moving into our recently—and expensively—renovated house. I doubted anything my eager relatives could do while trying to help would annoy him. Dad's discovery, on the other hand—

"There's nothing wrong, is there?" Michael asked.

"Well, you might want to put loading the truck on hold for now and come back to the house. There's a slight hitch in our plans. Dad's found a body buried in the basement."

I waited for a few anxious seconds.

"How exciting for your father," he said, finally. "Unless, of course—dare I hope it's something an archaeologist would find more interesting than a doctor? A body left over from the Civil War, perhaps? Or something the Sprockets left behind?"

"I said body, not bones," I said. "Dad says our body, whoever it is, hasn't been dead more than a day or so."

"Damn," Michael said. "Do we know who it is?"

"Not yet."

"That's unsettling," he said.

I knew what he meant. Until we found out who the victim was, we didn't know quite how to react. The somber feeling induced by hearing of someone's death might swell into grief if we knew the victim. Unless it was someone we really didn't like, in which case we might feel a hint of guilty relief. For now, we were in limbo.

"And not to sound too selfish," he added, "but I bet this is going to throw a monkey wrench into things." Into The Plan, he meant.

"Too early to tell," I said. "Why don't you postpone any additional loading for now and come back?"

"Roger. I'll bring Horace."

"Good idea." My cousin Horace was a crime-scene technician back in Yorktown, my hometown, and since the Caerphilly Police Department was too small to have many forensic capabilities, the chief sometimes enlisted Horace's help when a major crime occurred. If Horace was in town, that is; though these days he was almost always in town, since, like young Sammy, he'd also developed a crush on our distant cousin Rose Noire.

"It might take us a while to make sure everything's either securely loaded on the truck or safely locked back in the storage unit," Michael said. "But we'll be back as soon as we can."

"Great."

I put the phone away and was lifting the pen to make some notes when I heard a car door slam. I looked up and saw a woman striding purposefully down our front walk, leading a llama.

Chapter 4

"Hello," I said, while frantically racking my brain to see if she was a relative I should recognize. Not that my family had a monopoly on eccentricity, but calling on people with a llama in tow was the sort of thing many of them would do. And an alarmingly large number of relatives seemed to be arriving early to help with the move, instead of waiting until Monday's giant house-warming picnic.

My latest visitor was short and plump, probably in her forties, with cropped salt-and-pepper hair and a face that would look pleasant if she stopped frowning. It was not a face that rang a bell, though, nor could I remember hearing that any of the family had taken an interest in llamas. I knew I'd never seen the brown-and-white llama before.

The woman didn't answer my greeting until she had reached the porch and had climbed the first two steps. Then she handed me her end of the llama's rope. The llama, fortunately, remained on solid ground.

"I'm sorry," she said. "It's just not working anymore."

I studied the llama for a few moments. Admittedly, I was no llama expert, but it seemed to be working fine to me. It stared back at me with calm, sleepy-eyed reassurance. It looked quite friendly, even warm. I had to remind myself that was just the way all llamas look, and not a valid reason to take the llama's side over the woman's in whatever dispute they were having.

"I've been trying to talk to Patrick for a week and a half now and haven't gotten an answer," the woman said.

I glanced back at the llama. Was Patrick its name, then? Did she really expect the llama to answer? I resisted the urge to inch a little farther away from her.

"And no one's seen him for days," she added.

Ah. Not the llama then. It was quite clearly visible, standing calmly in the middle of our front walk. I repressed the urge to pet its long, soft coat. It wasn't a stuffed animal, and I had no idea whether llamas bit people.

"And when I talked to your father last night, he said that he might be able to help us out. We're already two days late taking off to see our new granddaughter. We can't stay here llama-sitting forever."

Light dawned.

"Oh, I see," I said. "The llama's from the Caerphilly Zoo."

"Patrick said a few days, and it's been two weeks."

Of course. Patrick Lanahan, the zoo's financially inept owner. The one who'd saddled Dad with the penguins. And, apparently, stuck this woman with a llama. If you asked me, she'd gotten the better of the bargain.

"Your father said he had some pastureland that would be perfectly suitable, and if I hadn't found Patrick by this morning, I should bring them over."

Them?

A man appeared at the other end of the walk, shortly followed by second llama. Then a third. Llamas kept popping one by one through the opening in the high hedge that screened our yard from the street until I saw that the man was leading six llamas, roped together like a pack train. As I watched, the third llama in line reached down with his nose and goosed the llama in front of him, which squealed with outrage and leaped into the air. Perhaps I only imagined the look of amusement on the faces of the remaining llamas. Or perhaps these were not merely llamas, but prank-playing juvenile-delinquent llamas.

"Where do you want me to put these?" the man asked.

I thought of several rude and improbable answers, but I suppressed them. I got up and led my charge to the backyard. My visitors and the rest of the llamas followed. I quickly got the idea that leading more than one llama at a time was a bad idea. Even the short walk to the backyard gave them plenty of time for goosing, biting, and kicking each other. At least they weren't spitting, which I'd heard llamas were fond of doing.

"You can put them in here for now," I said, opening the gate to the pen outside the barn. It was a little small for seven llamas, but at least it was in good repair, since we used it for a dog run. I made sure the dog door between the pen and the barn was closed, since I didn't know how Spike, our dog, would react to the llamas when he returned. Well, okay, I knew how Spike would react; he'd try to kill one of them, and at eight and a half pounds, he'd be fighting way out of his weight class. Locked in the barn, he could only bark himself hoarse.

Neither of the llamas' temporary caretakers expressed the slightest concern over the small size of the pen.

"I'll get someone to take them over to the pasture as soon as possible," I added. "We're a little busy right now."

"Yes, I understand you're finally moving in today," the woman said. "Your father said that was why I should drop them off here, instead of at his farm."

Just drop them off with Meg. Yes, that sounded like Dad. The couple turned to go, without expressing any further concern over the llamas' well-being, which struck me as rather callous. It wasn't as if the llamas had deliberately outstayed their welcome.

"Is there any message I should give Dad?" I shouted at the couple's departing backs. "About the llamas?"

Like maybe "Thanks for taking them off our hands"?

The man turned.

"No," he shouted. "But if Patrick ever turns up, you can tell the no-good son of a—"

"George!" the woman hissed.

The man turned away again and they left.

I looked back at the llamas. They were standing clustered by the fence. They didn't look at all upset at seeing their former guardians depart.

I was pondering whether to take them over to the pasture now or wait until someone else was free to do it, when two tall, lean figures came around the corner of the house. Randall Shiffley, the foreman of the construction crew that had been working on our house, and one of his brothers or cousins—Vern, I thought, though I wasn't sure.

I greeted them, a little warily. Had I asked them to come by to do some project? Not that I recalled. We still had dozens of projects inside and out, and we'd probably be hiring the Shiffleys to do the work, but not yet. The place was livable, though far from perfect, and we were looking forward to a few weeks or even months of peace and quiet. Not to mention a few months of not handing the Shiffleys every bit of cash we could scrape up.

Fortunately, Randall got straight to the point.

"We came to talk to your father," he said. "About the rights to the land."

Rights? Dad had bought the farm adjacent to our lot from Fred Shiffley, Randall's uncle. Was there some problem with the purchase?

My face must have revealed my puzzlement.

"The hunting rights," he said. "I went over to the farm the other day to make sure we had everything straight on that, and I got the idea he was trying to avoid talking about it."

"Was my mother there?" I asked.

"Think so."

"That explains it, then. Mother's not all that keen on hunting."

"Ah." He frowned and considered this for a few moments. "How not keen is she?"

"She won't let him use poison on mice. Only humane traps. So he could exile them across the York River. For a couple of years, every time I went home, Dad was trying another brand of humane traps."

"He finally find one that worked?"

"No, most of them should have been marketed as mouse toys. But someone gave them a cat, and he turned out to be a natural mouser. Mother doesn't seem to mind Boomer killing and eating mice—it's his nature."

"I don't suppose she feels differently about deer."

"She shows *Bambi* to all my nieces and nephews every Christmas."

Randall digested this news in silence. He didn't utter the dreaded words "city folks!" in that familiar condescending tone, but he didn't really have to.

"She loathes insects," I said, trying to be helpful. "So if you could convince her that deer aren't actually mammals but large, furry insects . . ."

Randall snorted at that.

"Doesn't seem likely," he said. "And I don't suppose there's any chance you and your dad could convince her that we're actually large, partly bald cats?"

I decided to assume this was a rhetorical question.

"You don't keep after the deer and you'll be kicking them off your doorstep in the morning," Vern added.

I had to admit, I was torn. I didn't share Mother's—and Rose Noire's—sentimental fondness for the deer. I'd seen too much of them since moving out into the country—the deer, that is. Though come to think of it, lately I'd also seen Mother and Rose Noire rather too often. Anyway, I'd gotten better at spotting deer droppings before I stepped in them, and was learning how to minimize the number of deer-borne ticks I had to pick off myself. I hadn't had much time to think about landscaping our yard, so I didn't yet have the typical gardener's grudge against the deer, but I understood the problem the local farmers had, protecting their crops from what they referred to as long-legged rats. So I wouldn't mourn if the deer population took a steep drop—for example, if they all decided that Caerphilly was growing too civilized and migrated, en masse, out to West Virginia.

But the idea of someone shooting and killing deer practically in my backyard made me squeamish. So did the prospect of eating venison, though I had no problem wolfing down a juicy steak or a barbecued chicken leg. In some ways, I was still very much city folk after all. I decided to duck the whole issue.

"You should probably talk to Dad when Mother isn't around," I said. "And make sure Rose Noire's not there either. Or anyone else in the family, for that matter."

"That include you?" Randall said, raising an eyebrow curiously.

"Especially me. I hate trying to lie to Mother, probably because she always sees through me."

Randall nodded. And then frowned and pursed his lips as if trying to decide whether or not to say something.

"Everything else okay?" he asked.

"Just fine."

He and Vern waited for a few moments. I saw Vern glance toward the street, where Chief Burke's car was parked.

"So why's the chief here?" Randall asked finally.

"Oh, Dad found a body in the basement."

"Body?" Randall said. He sounded strangely agitated. "What kind of body?"

Chapter 5

"A human body," I said. "Beyond that, I couldn't say."

"You didn't see it?" Randall asked. He looked relieved. That was curious.

"They haven't finished digging it up yet," I said.

"Bet he found it while working on his penguin pond, then." Randall and Vern snickered.

"You've heard about the pond?" I asked.

"We were down at the feed store last night when he came in," Vern said.

"Sounds like he'd already dug a hole ten times bigger than he needed," Randall said with a chuckle. "Those preformed ponds don't come more than two, three feet deep."

"We could have told him that," Vern said, shaking his head.

"Bunch of damn fool people who had no idea what they were talking about were giving him all sorts of wrong advice," Randall added. "Hope he didn't listen to them, or he'll have the whole house down around your ears before you know it."

Considering how much we'd already paid the Shiffley Construction Company to restore our three-story Victorian white elephant to reasonably sound condition, I hoped he was exaggerating.

I resolved to focus on the positive side of what he'd said.

"Lot of people down at the feed store last night?" I asked.

"Packed," Randall said, with disgust. "They're open late Fridays, you know. All the damned city folks were out, getting ready for the long weekend."

"We wouldn't have gone down there at all on a Friday, but we had a job that came up suddenly, and we needed some supplies," Vern added.

I'd noticed that the Shiffleys, like most long-term residents, often experienced the sudden, inconvenient need to visit the feed store at the very times when it was overrun by the dreaded city folks. If I found something that annoying, I'd rearrange my schedule to avoid it, but the Shiffleys seemed to find a perverse pleasure in being annoyed by the city folks.

Flugleman's Feed Store had been in business for about 120 years, supplying generations of local farmers. In the last several decades, the number of working farms in Caerphilly had declined—though only slightly, unlike some parts of the state, where whole counties of farmland had been built up and paved over. The Flugleman family had responded by expanding its business to include lawn and garden supplies and rechristened it Flugleman's Farm and Garden Emporium.

Flugleman's was also a major stop on the local grapevine. If Dad had been down at Flugleman's, loudly talking about his plans for the penguin pond and seeking advice from anyone and everyone there, within hours the whole county would have known that our basement contained a hole that was already far too deep for Dad's needs—a hole that he would probably have to begin partially filling in this morning before he procceded with his pond construction.

A hole that would look like a godsend to anyone who happened to have an unwanted dead body lying around in need of disposal. Or, for that matter, anyone who wanted to commit a homicide while such a convenient burying place was available.

Chief Burke wouldn't like it much, but I felt relieved to know that my family wouldn't be the only suspects.

"Don't worry," Randall said, patting me on the shoulder. "Everyone knows the Sprockets have always been pretty strange. It'll probably turn out to be some craziness one of them got up to."

"Thanks," I said. I decided not to tell them that the body was at least a year and a half too fresh to blame on the house's previous owners.

"Where'd you get those things from, anyway?" Vern asked, pointing at the penguins.

"You know Patrick Lanahan?"

"The lunatic who runs the Caerphilly Zoo?" Randall said. I got the feeling he wasn't all that keen on Lanahan.

"Is he here?" Vern asked. "Because we really need to talk to him, too."

"Sorry," I said. "If he was here, you'd be welcome to talk to him, as soon as I gave him a piece of my mind about dumping the penguins on Dad."

"The damned scoundrel," Vern muttered. Apparently he took a dim view of Lanahan's foisting stray penguins off on innocent bystanders.

"If he drops by to visit his penguins, could you give us a call?" Randall asked. "We need to speak to him about something. Been trying to track him down for over a week."

"Will do," I said.

"Meanwhile, those things aren't going to be happy for long in that little pen," Vern said, indicating the penguins.

"Unfortunately, I think Chief Burke will put Dad's plans for a basement penguin habitat on hold," I said.

"Why not fence off part of your father's cow pond for them?" Randall asked. "Works for the ducks. And we could run down to

Flugleman's for a couple rolls of chicken wire and some posts. Have it up in an hour or so."

I glanced over at the penguins. They were a little crowded in the duck pen. And the fishy odor of penguin poop was already starting to permeate the yard. The pond was out of sight, and even more important, downwind. Moving the penguins to the pond sounded like a great idea.

Of course, the Shiffleys weren't donating their services. And I suspected that a few rolls of chicken wire and some posts would cost far more than seemed reasonable—like everything else we'd bought for the house. Could our depleted bank balance cover the penguin fence?

Then again, they weren't our penguins.

"Sounds like a great idea," I said. "Dad will be happy to foot the bill—nothing's too good for his penguins, as I'm sure you've already noticed."

"What about your camels?" Vern asked.

"Llamas," I said.

"Look like camels to me," Randall said.

I turned, intending to point out the key differences between a camel and a llama, and found that the Shiffleys were right. We had camels. Two of them, neatly tethered to the barn door. Through the hedge, I spotted a vehicle driving off at high speed—a pickup truck with a horse trailer hitched to the back. Evidently, Dad had also said "Just drop them off today with Meg" to whoever had fostered the zoo's camels.

"We'll be putting the camels in your uncle Fred's old pasture," I said. "With the llamas."

"Probably a good thing to check first that there's no breaks in the fence," Vern said.

"Let's do that now, before we go to Flugleman's," Randall

suggested. "That way, if we need any wire or posts for mending the pasture fence, we can pick them up at the same time."

"Good plan," Vern said.

They both nodded a casual good-bye and turned away.

"I'll let Dad know what we've worked out," I called after them.

Let him know and extract a blank check made out to the Shiffleys, in fact. The Shiffleys paid no attention to me as they strode off to the pasture.

"Meg?"

I looked up to see Sheila D. Flugleman, the current manager of the feed store. Speak of the devil.

"I see you have all the zoo animals here!" she said. "How nice!"

"Not all of them," I said. "Just the llamas and camels and penguins."

"Well, it's a start."

"And an end, I hope. We're moving in today, in case you hadn't noticed. We don't need all these animals underfoot. You wouldn't be dropping by to offer to foster some, would you?"

"Oh, I wish I could, but my dog is so territorial. It really wouldn't work."

"So how can I help you?" I asked. It sounded more polite than "What the hell are you doing here if you're not coming to take any animals off our hands?"

"Do you mind if I collect the . . . um . . . droppings?"

"Droppings?"

"From the zoo animals."

"Why?" I asked. Not that I had any objection to someone removing the animal droppings that were already starting to appear, and would doubtless continue to accumulate steadily as long as the animals were with us. If Sheila had offered, matter-of-factly, to help us out by cleaning up after the animals, I'd have assumed she was a zoo volunteer with a strong stomach and an admirable sense of altruism.

But the furtive look of eagerness on her face made me nervous. That and her obvious reluctance to explain. What could she possibly want with the droppings? Was she some kind of dung fetishist?

"I sell them," she said at last.

"The droppings?"

"I'll show you." She raced back over to her truck and opened the cab door. I followed, and watched as she rummaged through the contents of the passenger seat and the floor.

"Here it is!" she exclaimed, handing me something around the size of a five-pound flour sack.

It was a heavy paper bag printed in bright colors with pictures of various exotic animals—I spotted lions, tigers, elephants, zebras, giraffes, and monkeys. And blazoned across the front in a typeface that would have looked at home on a vintage Grateful Dead poster was the word "ZooperPoop!"

"You've probably seen it on sale at the store," she said.

"Yes, I have." I refrained from saying that I hadn't decided whether it was the silliest thing I'd ever seen or the most disgusting. I'd assumed the gaudy little bags languished on the shelves until someone needed a gag gift for a gardener. Possibly a gardener he wasn't really all that fond of. "And you've run out of the . . . raw materials?"

"Our supply is dangerously low," she said. "I've been trying to call Patrick for over a week now, to ask why the zoo is locked and where the animals have gone. I saw the Eldens passing by the store with the camels in their horse trailer, but I was helping someone check out, and by the time I got out to my car, they'd disappeared. But they were heading this way, and I remembered your dad talking about the penguins when he was in last night, so I took a chance and came out here."

"That was a lucky break," I said. And at least now I knew who to thank for the camels. "So people really buy that stuff?"

"I can't keep it in stock. Patrick's animals really don't produce an adequate supply."

Possibly the first time anyone had made that complaint about penned animals.

"I've started negotiating with the Clay County Zoo to augment the supply."

"I didn't know Clay County had a zoo," I said. "Though I suppose I should have guessed that if we had one, they'd want one too." Caerphilly and Clay counties were such bitter rivals—in everything from high school football to the agricultural competitions at the state fair—that I was almost surprised to find the border between the two guarded only by back-to-back dueling signs telling motorists going in either direction that they were now leaving the most beautiful county in Virginia.

"Well, it's not much of a zoo," she said, in the condescending tone most Caerphillians used when speaking of our less fortunate neighbors. "Not really much more than a glorified petting zoo. But it would be, technically, zoo poop."

"And is there some special virtue to zoo poop that makes people pay a premium for it?"

"Not really," she said. "It's the cachet. It's different—exotic! They can tell their friends they feed their prize azaleas nothing but ZooperPoop!"

"I'm not that fond of my azaleas," I said, eyeing the price tag. Short of the filet mignon I'd fixed for our Valentine's Day champagne dinner, I couldn't remember the last time I'd fed Michael and myself something that expensive.

"It mostly sells in upscale garden stores. I only keep a few bags at the store for when the rich people from town come out. So can I get on with it?"

"Be my guest," I said. "The llamas and camels really should be moved to the pasture next door as soon as someone has the time to do it."

"Right," she said. "I'll look there for them next time."

I'd been hoping she'd volunteer to do the moving, but perhaps I should have just asked outright instead of hinting. She grabbed a shovel and a pair of buckets from the back of her truck and trudged toward the temporary llama pen. I returned to my seat on the front porch.

"That damned Smoot here yet?"

I turned to see Chief Burke standing in the doorway behind me, frowning out at the road.

"What's a Smoot?" I asked.

"Dr. Smoot, the new medical examiner," he said. "We've got the body excavated enough to move it, if he'd just show up to pronounce."

Dad appeared just behind the chief.

"If you're getting impatient—," Dad began.

"If I'm getting impatient, I'll call Smoot to find out where the hell he is," the chief said. "Thanks all the same."

"Do you have any idea who the deceased is?" Dad asked.

"You know he won't tell you," I said. "But if you're curious, I bet I could make a pretty good guess who our uninvited guest is."

"And who would that be?" the chief said, looking rather smug, as if he didn't think my guess was likely to be on target.

"Patrick Lanahan."

"How the hell did you know?" the chief asked, scowling.

Chapter 6

"She's right?" Dad asked. "It is Patrick? Amazing!"

"You're darned right it's amazing," the chief said. "And I want to know how she knows."

"Not because I had anything to do with putting him there," I said.

"Then why did you think it would be him?"

"I must have talked to half a dozen people this morning who haven't seen him for days," I said. "And it's a small town, so while I suppose it's possible for two people to mysteriously go missing, it's unlikely, so odds are he's the one."

It sounded weak—more like good guesswork than anything else—but after a moment the chief nodded. Which meant I didn't have to tell him my second, more self-centered reason for guessing that the body was Lanahan's: that right now, if I tried to think of someone whose death was likely to cause me the greatest number of problems, Patrick Lanahan would probably head the list. Who knew how long the penguins, llamas, and camels would be with us?

Or for that matter, how many other people Dad had already told that they could drop off their unwanted animal visitors with me?

I felt a momentary pang of guilt. I didn't particularly like the fact that my first reaction to hearing about the death of another human being was annoyance at how it would inconvenience me. I made a silent vow to learn more about Lanahan when I got the chance. Maybe he'd turn out to be a wonderful person who cared deeply about his animal charges and had done much to make the world a better place. A philanthropist who'd made profound contributions to preserving endangered species. Or at least a decent guy who hadn't deserved whatever had happened to him. For the time being, though, I felt a strong but unreasonable grudge against him.

I realized that Chief Burke was frowning at me.

"How well did you know Lanahan?" he asked. He was holding his little notebook. And unlike my notebook, in which I tried to capture everything in the world I needed to remember, the chief scribbled in his notebook only when someone said something that might turn out to be evidence.

"Not at all," I said. "I've met him, but I can't say I know him. Though I had every reason for wanting to keep him alive."

"Why is that?" the chief asked.

"With him gone, who knows how long we'll be stuck with the penguins and llamas?"

"Llamas?" Dad said. "How exciting!"

He scurried toward the backyard, presumably to commune with the llamas.

"And camels," I called after him.

"Send Smoot down when he gets here," the Chief said again, and disappeared back into the house.

A minute later, just as I was lifting my pen to scribble in the notebook, Michael drove up in our truck. I could see my twelve-year-old nephew Eric in the passenger seat, holding Spike, our furball of a dog. A small clutch of cousins sat in the truck bed. Cousin Horace leaped out before Michael had completely stopped, and sprinted for the house.

"You think the chief can use me?" he shouted.

"Probably. Down in the basement."

He waved and continued on into the house.

Michael was close on his heels, but instead of dashing into the house, he enveloped me in a reassuring hug.

"Are you all right?"

"I'm fine," I said. "More exasperated than anything else. The chief hasn't said we need to stop the move."

"But odds are he will, as soon as he thinks about it."

The other three cousins who'd been helping load the truck followed him.

"Anything useful we can do?" one asked.

"Not at the moment," I said.

"You okay?" another asked.

"I'm fine," I said. "Maybe you could go in and see about Mother and Dad, though."

"Roger." They all hastened inside. No doubt they realized that Dad could tell them all about the body, and that if Mother was around, she'd have coerced someone into fixing refreshments.

"So just how did your father find this body?" Michael asked, taking a seat beside me.

"He was digging a hole in the basement—the dirt floor part under the future library. To put in a pond for the penguins."

"Why was he putting the penguins in our basement?"

"Beats me," I said. "He was—wait. You knew about the penguins?"

"I knew he had them over at the farm," Michael said, looking slightly sheepish.

"And you didn't tell me?"

"I didn't think it was all that important. Especially since I told him there was absolutely no way we could take care of any animals. What with the move and all."

"He seems to have forgotten that part. People are starting to drop by and leave animals here."

"Perhaps he misinterpreted me," Michael said with a sigh, "and assumed that as soon as we'd moved in, we'd be happy to have animals."

"Even so, he's jumping the gun, letting people bring them today," I said. "And already—where's Eric?"

"Putting Spike in his pen."

"He can't do that!" I said, jumping up and racing toward the backyard. "It's full of llamas."

I could hear Spike barking somewhere in the backyard as I ran, and I feared the worst. Fortunately, when I turned the corner, I saw that Eric was still gazing at the llamas in rapture while Spike, predictably, was straining at the end of the leash in his attempt to attack them. Dad, of course, had disappeared.

The llamas were humming. It was a curiously soothing sound, but not being a llama expert, I had no idea if they found Spike's antics cute, or if the humming was a battle cry that indicated they planned to knock down the fence and trample him.

"Why don't you take Spike into the barn," I suggested. "He can stay there until we move the llamas into the pasture."

"Cool," Eric said. He began tugging Spike toward the barn, still looking back at the llamas.

"Fascinating," Michael said. He, too, was staring at the llamas.

"They'd be just as fascinating and a lot happier if someone took them to the pasture," I suggested.

"Okay," Michael said. Still staring. Damn.

"The Shiffleys are checking the fence to make sure there are no holes in it, but I can't imagine it's gotten too bad. It's only been a few weeks since their uncle Fred moved his cattle out."

"I'll get your dad to help."

"Good idea," I said. "I thought he was back here, but perhaps he's gone inside to tell Mother about the llamas."

"I bet he knows what they like to eat," Michael said while gazing at the llamas. "That could be useful—it would help us keep them toward this end of the pasture till the Shiffleys have finished inspecting the fence."

I watched as he strode off to the kitchen, still glancing back. The fact that he was already thinking about treats for the llamas was something I'd worry about later.

"Excuse me."

I turned to see someone peering around the corner of the house. Probably in his thirties, average size, with rather ordinary features. Completely unremarkable, in fact, except that his suit appeared to be several sizes too large for him. His hands were all but hidden in the overlong sleeves. The pants cuffs were turned up slightly to keep him from stepping on the bottoms, and from the mud stains and fraying on the cuffs, he hadn't always remembered to do so.

He was carrying something—holding it behind his back. Not another animal, I hoped. Then he came all the way around the corner, and I realized that it was a black doctor's bag. Aha! No doubt here was the overdue medical examiner.

Chapter 7

"Dr. Smoot," I said. "Welcome."

He shook my offered hand shyly.

"Where is the . . . ?"

"In the basement. I'll show you."

I led him to the entrance, pulled up one metal door, and ostentatiously stood aside, to show that I knew my place, and wasn't even interested in peeking into the basement. Nice try, but I should have saved my efforts.

"Down there?" Dr. Smoot whispered.

"That's where we keep the basement."

"It's very dark."

I noticed he was edging slightly away from the door.

"Yes, unfortunately that end of the basement's not electrified yet," I said. "I could get you a flashlight."

"And very small."

"It gets bigger inside."

"I'm not sure that helps," Dr. Smoot said. "Great empty echoing caverns of blackness."

"It doesn't echo," I said. "And it's not empty—Chief Burke is down there, and Sammy, and my cousin Horace, and I forget how many other officers."

"I'm sorry," he said, starting to back away. "I just can't do it. Tell Burke I'm sorry."

"Don't tell me: you have claustrophobia."

"They didn't tell me the body was down in a basement!"

"Why don't you come up to the kitchen and have some coffee?"

"No! Not indoors!" Smoot shouted.

Probably better to stay outside anyway. If Dad found out Dr. Smoot was too claustrophobic to descend to the scene of the crime, he'd volunteer again to fill in at the crime scene, which would only annoy the chief more.

"Or just sit and rest here for a bit," I said. "I'm sure you'll feel better."

"You can't make me go through that door!" he said, backing away faster.

"No, of course not." I grabbed his elbow and led him away, toward some lawn chairs. "Do basements in general bother you, or just dark ones?"

"It's the doors mostly," he said. He sat down in one of the chairs and mopped the sweat off his face with one voluminous sleeve. "Those damned ominous outside doors."

They didn't look particularly ominous to me. I certainly didn't like them—they were covered with flaking green paint, and whenever I saw them I remembered that one item in my notebook was to assess whether we should strip the old paint, sand off the rust, and repaint them or just put in new doors. Annoying, yes, and doubtless expensive, but ominous? Still, who was I to criticize someone else's phobia?

"Would a normal stairway work better?" I asked aloud.

"You have a stairway to the basement?" he snapped. "Why didn't you say so?"

"This way's shorter. But if you'd rather do the stairs . . ."

"Show me."

I showed Dr. Smoot in through the back door. To my relief, we passed Dad and Michael on their way out.

"Off to move the llamas," Dad said, waving gaily.

"Llamas?" Dr. Smoot echoed.

"They're outside," I said, quickly, in case he had a phobia about them as well, and led the way to the kitchen. It was empty, except for Rob sitting in one corner reading a comic book. He glanced up with a faint frown on his face, as if we were interrupting some important bit of work. For all I knew, it was work. After three decades of cruising through life on his charm and the blond good looks he had inherited from Mother, Rob had finally found his vocation. These days he made an obscenely good living coming up with bizarre ideas that his staff of programmers could turn into computer games. Compared to some of his sources of inspiration, comic books were pretty normal.

"Mother and the rest went over to the farm," he said, burying his nose back in the comic book. "They'll be over later with lunch."

"Thanks," I said. "Basement's this way," I added to Dr. Smoot, throwing open the door.

He glanced through the opening. I was relieved to see that he didn't panic, but he seemed to be waiting for me to lead the way.

Chief Burke would have to put up with me, apparently. I grabbed a flashlight and obliged.

Dr. Smoot nearly lost his nerve when I opened the door from the finished part of the basement into the unfinished part, with its maze of small rooms. I eventually cajoled him into moving again, but only after he grabbed my arm with both hands, and from the unsteadiness of his steps, he probably had his eyes closed.

"It's only a few more steps," I repeated. I tried to say it loudly enough that Chief Burke would hear me and relieve me of my recalcitrant charge, but apparently the chief was arguing with

Sammy. I could hear their voices, the chief's mellow baritone alternating with Sammy's nervous tenor, and occasionally I saw sudden flashes of light.

When I got closer, I saw that the light came from Horace, who was slowly and methodically laboring with a small trowel to uncover the rest of the body, pausing every few minutes to wield his digital camera.

"I've brought Dr. Smoot," I said.

"You could have sent him," the chief said. "We can take it from here."

"Don't desert me!" Smoot wailed, tightening his grip on my arm until I was worried that he'd cut off the blood circulation.

"Dr. Smoot was a little worried about the . . . um . . . footing down here," I said.

"You didn't tell me the body was in a basement," Smoot moaned.

I heard whispering.

"That's all right then," the chief said, in a falsely hearty voice. "Sammy, why don't you go help the doctor?"

Smoot welcomed Sammy's help—I breathed more easily when one of Dr. Smoot's hands detached itself from my bruised forearm. But it took both of us to coax him over to the side of the hole, and he stood there for the longest time with his eyes pressed tightly shut, breathing deeply.

Since I was standing there anyway, I leaned over to peek into the excavation Horace was making. If I hadn't known it was Lanahan, I might not have recognized him at first. Alive, he had been handsome in a beefy, football-player way. Now, his features looked pale and puffy, and the faint, rather dashing scar on one cheek stood out more. But it was Lanahan. My eyes drifted down to his chest. For a moment, I couldn't quite decipher what I was seeing, and then it all fell into place.

"Good grief," I said. "Is that an arrow in his chest?"

"You're not supposed to see that," the chief snapped.

"Fine," I said. "Am I not seeing what I think I'm not seeing?"

"Horrible," Smoot muttered. "Great dark echoing caverns of blackness."

Since he still had his eyes closed, I didn't think he was referring to the arrow.

"Technically it's a crossbow bolt," Horace said.

"Is he going to be all right?" the chief asked.

"I thought you said he was dead," Smoot said. "Why did you bring me down here? If he's alive, any old doctor would do."

Sammy and I looked at each other. Sammy shrugged.

"He looks pretty dead to me," I said, in my most soothing voice. "Dr. Smoot, why don't you just open your eyes and pronounce him officially."

"And then Meg will lead you right out," the chief added.

"Isn't he supposed to do some investigating?" I asked. "I mean—"

"We can worry about that down at the morgue," the chief said. "Let's just get him to pronounce so we can move the body."

Smoot pried one eye open, gazed down at the body, and moaned. "Yes, he's dead," he said, screwing his eyes shut again. "What a horrible place to die!"

"Don't worry, he didn't die here," I said as Sammy and I began to lead Smoot away from the excavation.

"How do you know that?" the chief demanded.

"I think we'd have noticed if someone was down here playing bows and arrows in the middle of the night," I called over my shoulder. "And it would have to have been the middle of the night—after Dad knocked off digging for the evening, which couldn't have been that long before Flugleman's closed, and before we all got up to begin the move, which was maybe five this morning."

"Hmph," the chief said.

"I'll get the door," Sammy said. We'd been leading Smoot toward the cellar doors he hated so much—my plan was not to let him open his eyes till he was nearly outside. It worked—he took one look at the open doors, uttered a squeak, and ran outside.

A second later, we heard a crash, a scream, and what sounded like peals of maniacal laughter.

"What the hell was that?" the chief snapped.

I followed Smoot up the cellar steps and looked around.

"Ah," I said. "The hyenas have arrived."

Chapter 8

"Were you expecting hyenas?" the chief asked.

"Evidently."

There were three of them, in a cage so large that I doubted whoever had delivered them could possibly have gotten it into a pickup truck. Which meant I could probably figure out who the hyenas' previous hosts had been by checking the list of local residents with access to a flatbed truck.

The hyenas were pacing up and down in their cage, snarling at one another occasionally, their eyes glued to Dr. Smoot, who was lying facedown on the lawn, panting and whimpering.

"Good Lord," the chief said. "You'd better get him inside before the buzzards show up."

"I'll ask Dad to look after him," I said, stepping out of the basement.

"Good idea," the chief said.

"How long has Dr. Smoot been medical examiner?"

"Acting medical examiner," the chief corrected. "About two weeks. We needed someone in a hurry when old Doc Hartman died."

From his frown, I suspected Dr. Smoot's tenure as acting medical examiner would be a short one.

"When your father's finished with Smoot, ask if he'd mind

stepping down here for a minute," he said finally. "There might be one or two medical details Smoot didn't catch."

"Roger," I said.

From the chief's scowl, I could tell how painful the request had been—at a guess, somewhere between having a root canal and being bitten by fire ants. Dad's desire to be involved in a real, live murder investigation had annoyed the chief more than one time already.

Chief Burke backed down the stairway and slammed the cellar doors shut behind him.

I started toward the pasture to look for Dad, but as I was passing the back door, the front doorbell rang.

"What now?" I muttered, but I trudged up the back steps, through the kitchen, and down the hall to answer it.

On my way, I ran into Rose Noire, heading upstairs.

"Meg, if it's okay, I'm going to borrow some of your clothes to wear while I take care of the animals."

I glanced up. No, the ankle-length India print skirt wasn't practical for chasing after camels, and if I owned anything as beautiful as her turquoise blouse, I wouldn't take it within a mile of the penguins.

Of course, the skirt and blouse weren't exactly suitable for helping us move in, either, but I'd already decided that last night's herb-smudging ceremony was Rose Noire's major contribution to our move. If she was busy with the animals, she wouldn't be trying to fix the house's feng shui in the middle of the move—for that, I'd happily sacrifice any number of clothes.

"Plenty of old T-shirts and sweats in the closet," I said. "But I have no idea what box my nicer clothes are packed in, so if you're not careful, I might steal your blouse and skirt for the party."

"It's a deal!"

But the skirt would probably be too short on me, so I still needed to find the box soon to have something other than jeans and a T-shirt to wear for my own wedding.

Not something I needed to worry about just yet.

I put on my polite hostess face before opening the door. After all, maybe it wasn't another Friend of the Caerphilly Zoo looking to foist yet another animal on us. Maybe this time it would be someone dropping by to help with the animals. Take a few home.

Not that I was holding my breath.

I swung open the door and saw a tall, slightly stooped elderly man standing on the doorstep with his back to me. He looked as if he had dressed for a safari—olive green cargo pants, muddy hiking boots, a brown shirt, and a khaki fishing vest, its dozen pockets bulging with unidentified bits of gear. He had a pith helmet tucked under his left hand, and had probably just taken it off—his untidy white mane had a bad case of hat hair. He kept looking down at something he was shuffling in his hands, and then glancing up at the landscape. An odd figure, but he didn't seem to be carrying or leading any stray animals, so my welcoming expression grew a bit more sincere. I cleared my throat, in case he hadn't noticed the door opening.

And then he turned around and my jaw dropped. I'd seen that craggy, deeply tanned face before. Of course, so had anyone who had habitually watched *National Geographic* specials over the last four decades, to say nothing of the Discovery Channel and Animal Planet. What possible reason could a world-famous zoologist and conservationist have for showing up on our doorstep?

"Montgomery Blake," he said, sticking out a gnarled, weather-beaten hand. "You must be Meg Langslow."

So it really was him, or a damned good impersonator. Still

tongue-tied with surprise, I shook the offered hand, and my star-struck awe gave way to irritation as I realized that Blake was one of those men who saw shaking hands as a contact sport. I reacted the way I usually do. Blacksmithing has made my hands a good deal stronger than most women's, so I returned his death grip, with interest. I noted with some satisfaction the wince he couldn't entirely hide, and then immediately felt guilty. Blake must be at least ninety. I should be marveling that he still had so much strength, not getting sucked into some macho competition.

"You have a firm grip for a woman," he said.

Considering what I'd tried to do to his hand, that was a little like saying that King Kong was tall for a chimp. And what was I supposed to answer: "Thanks—you're pretty strong yourself for a senior citizen"?

I settled for "Thanks."

"I like that in a woman," he said. "Must be the blacksmithing."

I suppose some people would have been flattered at the notion that someone so famous was taking an interest in them. It only made me nervous.

"Here," he said, shoving forward the wad of papers he was now holding in his left hand. A bunch of envelopes and flyers. I took them and glanced at them, puzzled, until I realized that he'd just handed me our mail. Which he'd apparently been studying while waiting for me to answer the doorbell.

"How come that jerk's got you on his mailing list?" he asked, his finger stabbing at one of the flyers. "Surely you're not even thinking of voting for him. His environmental record's unspeakable."

"I'll keep that in mind when I have a chance to study our mail," I said. The nerve of the man! If I'd been caught going through someone's mailbox, I'd have been mortally embarrassed— and here Blake was hectoring me about the contents of mine. I took a deep breath and kept my voice neutral. "Can I help you with something?"

"Is Dr. Langslow here?" he asked. "They told me over at the farmhouse that he might be."

"He's in the backyard with the hyenas."

"You have pet hyenas?" he asked.

"I hope not," I said, and led the way through the house.

Chapter 9

We found Dad and Eric in the kitchen. Dad was wringing out a damp cloth. Evidently he'd already met our new guest—he greeted Dr. Blake with enthusiasm.

"Blake!" he exclaimed. "Come to help with the animals? Splendid! You can see to the hyenas while I take care of my patient."

To Blake's credit, he didn't balk—just followed Dad out into the yard and strode over to the hyena cage while Dad helped Dr. Smoot into a nearby lawn chair and applied the hot compress he'd brought from the kitchen.

"Ah!" Blake said, with satisfaction, circling the cage to inspect its occupants. "*Crocuta crocuta!*"

"What's that?" Eric asked. Ever alert to sources of entertainment, he had tagged along at Blake's heels.

"The spotted hyena," Blake said, in his best on-camera voice. "Their scientific name is *Crocuta crocuta*. Three reasonably good specimens here. A trifle underweight, but we'll soon have them back on a proper nutritional program."

"Stand back from the cage, Eric!" I said. "We don't want you becoming part of the hyenas' nutritional program."

"Would they really eat me?" Eric asked. He sounded a bit nervous—perhaps because all three hyenas were staring intently at him.

"Oh, yes!" Blake exclaimed. "They're quite efficient predators."

"There now," Dad was saying to Dr. Smoot. "What's the trouble?"

"In the wild, of course, they prey mostly on the larger herd animals," Blake went on. "But they're opportunistic feeders."

"Vampires," Dr. Smoot said.

"Nonsense!" Blake exclaimed. "Hyenas aren't vampires, or even pure scavengers. True predators. Intelligent ones."

"I meant in the basement," Dr. Smoot said.

"Are there vampires in the basement?" Eric echoed.

"There are no vampires in our basement," I said. "Only police."

"Yes, why are the police in your——," Blake began.

"That's where my claustrophobia started," Dr. Smoot broke in, sounding rather cross at having his confession interrupted. "With my big brothers doing their vampire thing in the basement."

"Their what?" Blake asked, frowning.

I didn't say anything, since I was busy banishing the image that had appeared in my mind: a cluster of Smoots dangling upside down from the rafters of our basement, their oversized suits hanging down in soft, pendulous folds.

"Their vampire thing?" Dad echoed.

"For Halloween," Smoot said. "They would dress up in long black capes with bloody fangs, and hide in the cellar, and when they heard smaller kids walking by, they'd burst through the cellar doors shrieking, to terrify them. Doors just like that!" he added, pointing to our harmlessly rusting cellar doors.

"Wow," Eric said, in that uncertain voice he often used when even he could tell that grown-ups were behaving weirdly.

"Why are the police in your basement?" Blake asked, after a moment.

"Horrible," Smoot muttered.

"We've had a murder there," Dad said.

"No we haven't," I said. "Someone buried the body there, but

I'm sure he was murdered someplace else. Which reminds me—Dad, Chief Burke wondered if you could give him the benefit of your medical knowledge. Since, um . . ."

I glanced at Dr. Smoot, who was still sitting in our lawn chair muttering "Horrible! Horrible!" at random intervals.

"Oh, right!" Dad said. "No problem. Someone keep an eye on Smoot while I'm gone."

The hyenas, true to their reputation as efficient, intelligent predators, had already given up watching Eric to concentrate on Smoot. Fortunately he had his back to them and didn't seem bothered.

"So whose body is buried in your basement?" Blake asked.

"They haven't finished digging him up yet," I replied, and then I cast around for a way to change the subject. "So is it true that hyenas have an instinct for spotting the weakest members of a herd and targeting them?"

"All predators do," he said, glancing at Smoot. "Even the human ones. Especially the human ones. We should probably move them someplace quieter," he added, looking back at the hyenas. "Having people around is apt to upset them."

"And vice versa," I said. "Maybe we could put them at the far end of the yard, behind some of the outbuildings."

"I'll need some help moving them," he said.

"Michael's down at the pasture with the llamas," I offered, pointing out the direction.

"That would be Professor Waterston?" Blake asked. "Your fiancé?"

My suspicions came back full force. It wasn't that I wondered how he knew these details—if he and Dad had both been spending a lot of time at the Caerphilly Zoo, Dad had probably told him all about us. But most people just nod, smile, and forget details like that. Why had he remembered them?

"That's right," I said aloud. "Why don't you take the camels down there, and I'll look for the Shiffleys."

"The what?"

"Shiffleys," I said. "Two-legged predators of the genus *Contractor*."

Blake chuckled, and went to collect the camels. Eric came out of the kitchen with a glass of lemonade and handed it to Dr. Smoot. Thoughtful of him—lemonade or hot tea, depending on the season, was Mother's remedy for anything that might be upsetting us, so even members of my family who didn't like either beverage instinctively tried to pour them into anyone around us who seemed upset.

"Keep an eye on Dr. Smoot," I told him. "I'm going to find the Shiffleys."

I strolled around to the front of the house to look for the Shiffleys' truck. I found Randall Shiffley squatting beside a cage that had appeared on our front lawn.

"What's in this one?" I asked as I squatted to check it out.

"Some kind of short-tailed rats," he said, with mild distaste.

"Well, rodents of some kind," I said, peering at the occupants of the cage. To me, they looked more like overgrown hamsters with slightly mold-tinged fur, and they were peacefully nibbling on some peaches. "Did you see who left them?"

"Nope," Randall said. " 'Nother hit-and-run animal dump."

"Speaking of which, could you and Vern help us move the hyenas?"

Randall did a brief double take, then resumed his usual look of imperturbability.

"Sure thing," he said. "Soon as Vern gets back."

"Where's he gone?" I asked. Not, I hoped, to Flugleman's just yet, since we might not have come to the end of the animal arrivals.

"Walking off a fit of temper. He'll be fine when he gets back. Leastways I hope so."

"What's he mad at?"

"Me," Randall said. "I said something he took the wrong way. He's touchy these days."

I stared at him in astonishment. What could possibly have happened to undermine both Randall's normally calm manner and the Shiffleys' impenetrable facade of family unity?

"Yikes," I said. "What's he so touchy about? I wouldn't want to put my foot in my mouth."

Normally Randall wouldn't have told me. Of course, normally he wouldn't even have said as much as he already had. And even now, he frowned for a few moments before speaking.

"You heard about Charlie's problem?" he asked.

I pondered that for a moment. Like my family, the Shiffleys were a large and colorful clan, so I wasn't at all sure who Charlie was, much less what medical, moral, legal, psychiatric, or other woes had befallen him.

"Which one is Charlie?" I asked finally.

"Vern's middle boy. If you haven't heard anything about it——"

"Then you're in luck; you can tell me the real story, before I hear any unfair and distorted rumors."

Randall chuckled as if to say that he knew exactly what I was doing, but he launched into his story.

"That Lanahan fellow from the zoo has filed charges against Charlie. For supposedly shooting one of his fancy gazelles."

"And Charlie didn't shoot it?"

"Well, yeah, he did, but it wasn't his fault. Damned thing had gotten out of the zoo and was just wandering around the woods like an ordinary deer."

"I see."

"It wasn't Charlie's fault!" Randall said, almost shouting. "It was hunting season——crossbow season——and Charlie had a permit, and he was hunting on his daddy's land, and it's not like he was careless."

"Of course not," I said. "Did you say crossbow?"

Chapter 10

"Yes, Charlie's good with a crossbow," Randall said, with a touch of pride. "Takes more skill than hunting with a rifle."

"I'm sure it does." I was trying to push away the memory of Patrick Lanahan's body, still half buried in our basement, with a crossbow bolt sticking out of the chest.

"He could see it was a deer," Randall went on. "He didn't know till he shot it that it was one of Lanahan's fancy imported ones. Little bitty thing about fifteen, sixteen inches tall."

And Charlie had mistaken it for a full-grown deer? Maybe Lanahan was right to be suspicious.

"What did he do?" I asked aloud.

"Came and told his daddy and me, and we took the carcass over to Lanahan. Tried to apologize and make restitution, even though the confounded thing was trespassing at the time. Lanahan behaved like a total jackass."

"He didn't understand that it was an accident?"

"Lanahan insisted it wasn't—he said Charlie must have made a hole in the fence and lured it out. Which was pretty damned stupid. Why would he deliberately shoot a scrawny runt like that? We're not trophy hunters. We hunt to put meat on the table."

"And there wasn't much meat on the gazelle?"

"That evil little dog of yours would have a hard time making a meal of it," Randall said. "But try telling Lanahan that. He's filed charges. Won't listen to reason. That's why we'd appreciate it if you let us know if he shows up here—he's got to sooner or later, right? To do something about the animals."

I opened my mouth to explain how unlikely it was that Patrick Lanahan would show up to reclaim his animals, and then thought better of it. Chief Burke wouldn't appreciate me spilling the beans. Especially not to someone who might be a suspect. Or at least the brother of one suspect and the uncle of another.

"I hate to think of that miserable bastard ruining Charlie's future," Randall said.

"Surely once Chief Burke investigates the charges it will be all right? Charlie will be cleared."

"We can't count on that," Randall said. "And we sure as hell can't count on it happening in time."

"In time for what?" I asked. But just then Vern appeared, and Randall frowned and shook his head, as if to warn me against continuing the conversation in front of Vern. Since Vern seemed his usual calm, unflappable self, I didn't want to rock the boat. Randall and I both pretended to be keenly interested in the cage of rodents.

"Pasture fence is fine," Vern said. "Anything else we should do before we head off to Flugleman's?"

"She's got some hyenas she wants moved," Randall said. "You want us to take these rats out back, too?"

By the time we reached the backyard, Montgomery Blake had rounded up Michael and several of Chief Blake's officers and cajoled them into hoisting the hyenas' cage onto some kind of wheeled chassis—probably another piece of leftover farm equipment from one of the sheds. He greeted us with enthusiasm.

"More new arrivals!" he exclaimed, and strode over to look at the cage with an energy that belied his age. "Aha! Acouchis!"

"Geshundheit," Randall said.

"No, that's their name," Blake said, peering into the cage. "The acouchi. South American rodent. Note the greenish sheen of their fur."

"It's supposed to look like that?" Randall said, crouching down beside Blake. "I just thought they had mange or something."

I sat down on the back steps, leaving Blake to enthuse about the acouchis to his new audience. Before too long, he'd recruited the Shiffleys to his moving crew, and the hyena cage went slowly rumbling off toward a more distant part of the yard.

The chief joined me on the back steps to watch it go.

"You tell anyone whose body we have down there and what happened to him?" he asked.

"No, not even the Shiffleys, who appear to be quite knowledgeable about crossbows."

"Lot of people around here are."

"I had no idea it was legal to hunt with a crossbow."

"Used to be illegal unless you were disabled," the chief said. "General Assembly opened it up to everyone in 2005. Makes for a longer season—there's an early bow season before the regular hunting season begins. And they say crossbows are easier than regular bows. Lot of people taking up crossbow hunting these days."

"Lanahan file charges against many other crossbow hunters?"

The chief didn't answer, and from the expression on his face, I decided not to push it.

"You expecting any more animals?" he asked.

"I hope not. Why?"

"Truck just pulled up by the pasture," he said, and went inside.

He didn't have to sound so smug about it. I decided to stroll down to the pasture. Maybe give the latest animal dumper a piece of my mind.

Chapter 11

Since there was still a murderer on the loose, I looked over the lanky, jeans-clad new arrival carefully before I got close. He didn't appear to be carrying any animals, or, for that matter, a crossbow. He had parked his pickup truck by the fence and had gotten out to look at the llamas. He had propped his forearms on the top rail of the fence and was leaning on them, shoulders and head drooping dispiritedly. The llamas were humming softly at him.

"Can I help you?" I asked.

"Probably not," he said. He turned around, revealing a face so lugubrious it made his body language seem upbeat. "I'm Jason Savage. Caerphilly Animal Welfare."

He stuck his drooping right hand in my direction diffidently, as if most people turned up their noses at the thought of touching it.

"Great to see you," I said. I grabbed the hand and shook it briskly. The Animal Welfare Department! Why hadn't I thought of calling them already?

"Um . . . thanks," he said, frowning at his hand as if I'd done something to it—which was ridiculous; I hadn't been trying to imitate the Montgomery Blake death grip.

"You've come to take away the animals, I presume," I went on, trying for a tone of businesslike regret.

"People aren't usually that glad to see me," he said. Oops—perhaps I'd sounded too eager.

"Well, most people probably aren't putting the welfare of the animals above their own selfish interests. I understand that you're only doing your job. We've got the rest of them up at the house."

"More llamas?" he asked, sounding anxious.

"No, that's all the llamas. But we've got penguins, hyenas, and some kind of rodent, last I looked."

"Oh, Lord," he muttered.

"We'll miss them, of course, but we have to think of the animals. We haven't really got enough room to take care of them."

"You've got a lot more room than we have," Savage said. "Count your blessings."

"I beg your pardon?"

"It's a small county. We've only got a small shelter. We can't house more than a dozen dogs or cats at any one time, and that's if some of them get along well enough to share a cage."

"Can't you call a neighboring county?"

"Most of them are calling all the time, trying to dump animals on us," he said. "I might be able to take some of the smaller animals if I can get rid of a few dogs. You wouldn't like a beagle or two, would you? Got some very nice beagles."

"Thanks, but the last thing we need right now is a puppy."

"Oh, they're not puppies," he said. "Full-grown beagles. They'd be—let's see—three years old now. Housebroken. Fully trained. Raised them myself from puppies."

"At the shelter?"

"We don't have much turnover," he said. "I'd recommend taking all four—that way they'd entertain each other much of the time."

"All four?"

"Or how about a collabrador?" he suggested, no doubt sensing my lack of enthusiasm for beagles. "Nice collie-lab mix. Probably has good herding instincts—get along well with your llamas."

"We have enough dogs," I said. "And they're not our llamas. Are you telling me there's nothing you can do?"

"When we're full up, like now, what we usually do is get one of the nearby farms to take the overflow. Since they're already settled in at a farm, I don't see any reason to worry about them."

"That's it? You're not going to do anything about our animal problem?"

"I'll go up to the house and check on the other animals," he said, pulling a small notebook out of his pocket and beginning to scribble in it. "You said penguins, hyenas, and what?"

"Some kind of sniveling rat," I muttered. I confess, I was hoping he'd take it personally, but he just nodded and jotted something in his notebook.

"I'll check them out and let you know if you need to do anything differently for their welfare."

With that, he turned and trudged toward the house. Great—not only was the Animal Welfare Department not going to take any of our unwanted animals, but now it was going to nitpick how we took care of them. Shaking my head, I turned back to lean against the fence as he'd been doing. Maybe contemplate the llamas until I calmed down a bit.

And contemplating the llamas was curiously calming. Though I was a little annoyed that they'd stopped humming.

"So how come Mr. Savage from the animal shelter gets humming and I don't?" I said aloud.

"Maybe they like you," Michael said. I started slightly when I realized that I'd been so focused on the llamas that I hadn't noticed him coming up to lean on the fence at my side. "Apparently humming can be a sign that they're unsettled in some way," he added.

"Oh, if that's the case, far be it from me to unsettle the llamas."

"Unless it's a mother llama humming to her cria," Michael went on.

"Her what?"

"Cria. Baby llama. And you know the whole thing about them spitting on people?"

"Yuck," I said, taking a couple of steps back from the fence. "I'd forgotten about that."

"Don't worry," Michael said. "They usually spit only at each other—it's part of establishing the pecking order. If a llama's been properly socialized, with other llamas, he'd spit on a human only by accident, if the human got in the middle of a llama fight. Or maybe if he was really mad at the human."

"So how do we know these llamas have been properly socialized?"

"They haven't spit at anyone yet. Tried to kick Spike when he got into their pasture, but that's perfectly understandable."

"And if I told your mother you'd said that, do you think she'd take Spike back?" Spike was technically Michael's mother's dog, though we'd had him on semipermanent loan ever since her allergist had recommended a trial separation.

"I expect she'd sooner take one of the hyenas," Michael said. "They're smarter than dogs, you know."

"Hyenas?"

"Llamas. The Peruvians have been breeding them for intelligence for centuries. Basically, they eat the stupid ones."

"I've been at parties like that," I said. "So you've been reading up on llamas?" The idea alarmed me. Since childhood, I'd known that bringing home stacks of books on a topic was a danger sign that a new enthusiasm had seized Dad. By the time I'd recognized the same symptoms in Michael, it was a little too late to change how I felt about him.

"Well, not yet," Michael said. "There hasn't been time. But Blake's been telling us all about them."

"I can imagine," I said. "I can hear him from here."

We both turned and glanced back at the house. Randall and Vern Shiffley, along with several of Chief Burke's officers and a handful of my relatives, were gathered around something in the middle of the lawn. Blake, standing on a picnic table bench, was lecturing his makeshift student body.

"Officious old goat," I muttered, turning back to the llamas.

"You don't seem to like Dr. Blake much," Michael said. "Any particular reason?"

I was opening my mouth to protest that I liked Blake just fine when I suddenly realized it would be a lie.

"No, I don't," I admitted. "Don't ask me why. I'll watch myself. Be extra polite to him and all that."

"Odd," Michael said. "That's just what your mother said a minute ago. She doesn't seem that keen on him, either."

So it wasn't just me! I felt a surge of relief.

"Well, after all, he's spoiling Dad's fun, or hadn't you noticed?" I said. "Dad's usually the one who gets to give the wildlife lessons."

"That's why you dislike him?"

"I don't *dis*like him," I said. "But I don't trust him. What's he doing here, anyway? Why isn't he off in the veldt or the tundra or the bush somewhere, rescuing something in front of a camera?"

"Supposedly, he's here to rescue the Caerphilly Zoo," Michael said. "Not sure whether he's going to donate the money Patrick needs or find him some other donors or maybe take over the zoo—your Dad was a little vague on what Patrick is expecting. Or maybe it's Patrick who's being vague. But whatever it is, sounds like a good idea to me. Soon as Patrick shows up and they can work things out, our animal problems will be over and we can move full speed ahead on The Plan."

"I wouldn't count on it," I muttered.

"You haven't changed your mind," Michael said, looking ashen. At his tone, all the llamas stopped grazing and lifted their heads to stare at us. "We've got the license and the plane reservations and——"

"No, I haven't changed my mind, and there's no threat to The Plan," I said, raising my voice slightly to be heard over the humming of the llamas. "But I wouldn't count on Montgomery Blake solving all our animal problems anytime soon."

"Why not?"

"How long has Blake been in town?"

"A few days—why?"

"Blake shows up, Lanahan goes AWOL, and the next thing we know, Dad's digging up bodies in the basement."

"Bodies! Have they found more than one?"

"No, just the one," I said. "But one's enough. I gather Chief Burke hasn't announced whose body it is."

After a moment, Michael's face turned from puzzlement to dismay.

"You think it's Patrick Lanahan's?"

"I've seen it, remember?" I said. "I had to drag Dr. Smoot into the basement. It's Lanahan all right."

"Damn," Michael said. "He seemed okay, Patrick. Your father's going to be pretty upset. He'd been spending a lot of time with Patrick, working on the zoo. And what happens to the zoo? It could take a while to sort that out."

"Let's just hope Lanahan was organized enough to make a nice, straightforward, uncontestable will. One that spells out quite clearly what happens to the zoo and the animals."

Michael burst out laughing.

"Patrick?" he said. "Organized? You really didn't know him that well, did you?"

"So much for that hope."

"Seriously, if he'd been at all organized, things would never have gotten so bad at the zoo to begin with, and we wouldn't have all these animals underfoot."

He was looking rather resentfully at the camels. I thought the camels were getting a bum rap—after all, so far they hadn't been any more trouble than the llamas. But I didn't expect him to blame the llamas, who were humming gently and wearing expressions of warm sympathy and heartfelt regret.

"Don't worry," I said. "I'm sure Dad and the rest of the family can take care of the animals till we get back."

Michael frowned slightly. No doubt it was dawning on him that if Dad was capable of trying to stash a baker's dozen of penguins in our basement while we were still in residence, there was no telling what lunacy he might commit if we left the house undefended for two weeks while the denizens of the Caerphilly Zoo were still homeless.

"I'll talk to him," he said.

"And say what? 'Please don't tick Meg off just when she's finally agreed to marry me' won't work, obviously, unless you've given up all hope of keeping our planned elopement secret."

"I'll think of something," he said. "Meanwhile, I came over to let you know that your mother has arrived with lunch."

"Excellent."

"And Rose Noire wanted me to tell you to hurry up if you're taking her class. She's starting right after lunch."

"Her class? What's she teaching this time—more aromatherapy?"

"Massage and acupressure for animals."

"I'll pass."

"Oh, come on. She claims it does wonders to calm and mellow animals. Think how useful that would be with Spike."

"I'd sooner massage one of the hyenas."

Chapter 12

As we strolled back to the house, I mused that I wouldn't mind watching Rose Noire's class—at least if I could talk her into demonstrating on Spike. But since childhood, Rose Noire had always assumed that "I'd rather just watch" meant that you needed a little more coaxing. And I suspected she was planning to have her pupils practice on some of the sheep that had, as usual, wandered over from Seth Early's pasture across the street. So if the class was starting after lunch, I'd eat and run.

We found Mother presiding over a buffet table, looking tall, cool, and elegant in one of her summer party dresses, not a single strand of improbably blond hair out of place. Mrs. Fenniman and the other family members who'd actually done the food preparation scurried back and forth from the kitchen with plates and bowls. Someone had moved one of our picnic tables to the far end of the lawn, apparently so Chief Burke and his officers could discuss the case privately while eating their lunches.

At least two members of the investigation team were paying little attention to the discussion. Sammy and Horace kept glancing over at the part of the lawn where my cousin Rose Noire was whiling away the time until her planned class began by ministering to Dr. Smoot.

The M.E. was still sprawled in one of our Adirondack chairs, looking picturesquely frail. He had a compress over his eyes and a steaming teacup in one hand, and Rose Noire appeared to be trying to light some sort of incense at his feet.

"I see Rose Noire has found a new victim for her aromatherapy," Michael said. "At least she's doing it outdoors."

"She knows I'd kill her if she tried it in the house again," I said with a shudder. Several weeks before, in a well-meaning attempt to add a note of romance to Michael's and my harried life, Rose Noire had sneaked into the house on Friday afternoon and burned an excessive amount of what she claimed was aphrodisiac incense. Unfortunately, Michael had turned out to be allergic to something in the incense, so instead of a romantic weekend we had suffered through what we both still referred to as The Big Sneeze.

"At least Smoot doesn't seem to mind," Michael said, shaking his head.

"I think he's enjoying the attention," I said.

Seth Early, who owned the sheep farm across the road from our house, was also casting hostile stares at Dr. Smoot. I sighed. I hoped Rose Noire wasn't accidentally recruiting Dr. Smoot to her legion of suitors. It was bad enough with Sammy, Horace, and Seth Early infatuated with her.

As I watched, Mr. Early stood up, walked over to a small clump of sheep, and began pummeling one of them, frowning savagely. I opened my mouth to protest, and then realized that he wasn't just relieving his anger—he was giving the sheep a back massage. And the sheep was happy. It had closed its eyes and was leaning toward him, while the other sheep shuffled about nudging and shoving it as if impatient for their turn.

Yes, definitely a good idea to leave before the animal-massage class began.

Nearby, Montgomery Blake was sitting at the head of another picnic table, with something on his shoulder—a small gray animal, halfway between a cat and a monkey, with a long black-and-white striped tail. Another of the somethings was sitting on the table, holding a slice of apple in its slender paws and nibbling at it.

"Let me guess—lemurs?" I murmured to Michael.

"Got it in one. Ring-tailed lemurs, to be precise."

One of the lemurs turned my way, revealing enormous yellow eyes with black rings around them, like a raccoon's. In a zoo, I'd have found them unremittingly cute, but this was our backyard, and the lemurs seemed to be consuming an impressive amount of fruit. Odds were they'd be producing an impressive amount of raw material for Sheila Flugleman, and didn't lemurs live in trees?

"Uh . . . Meg?" Rob sidled up with an apologetic look on his face.

"What's wrong?" I asked.

"There are some reporters here."

"Tell them to go away and stop bothering us."

"Oh, it's okay—they don't want to bother us," he said. "They want to bother the chief."

"Great," I said, "Go tell him."

"Couldn't you tell him?" Rob said. "He always yells so when he thinks someone is interrupting his investigation."

"What makes you think he won't yell at me just as much as at you?" I said. "In fact, he'd probably yell even more at me."

"Yeah, but you're used to it."

I sighed with exasperation. Rob was probably right. I was more used to getting yelled at, and it bothered me less than it would him, but that didn't mean I liked it. I headed over to the chief's table. But before I got there, I spotted something that let me off the hook.

"Too late," I said, to no one in particular. "Here they come."

A pack of reporters was just rounding the corner of the house.

In the lead was the bubbly blonde who, rumor had it, would be deserting the local TV station any day now for a job at one of the Richmond stations. Close on her heels was a far more polished-looking blonde who already worked for one of the Richmond TV stations. A chic African American woman from the Caerphilly radio station followed at a more stately pace, as if to suggest that the real excitement couldn't possibly begin until she arrived anyway. The two TV cameramen trotted along next, each following his designated reporter, while bringing up the rear was a disheveled young man from the student newspaper, who seemed to be paying more attention to his distinguished colleagues than to the event that had lured them here.

The chief looked up and scowled.

"As if we didn't have enough damned hyenas already," he muttered. Then he put on his bland, no-comment face and stood up to meet the press. The cameramen deployed their cameras, and all three women thrust microphones in the chief's face.

"Chief Burke, can you confirm—," the local blonde began.

"When will you release the identity—," the Richmond blonde said at the same time.

The radio reporter just made sure her microphone was in the thick of the pack, while the journalism student began scribbling wildly with one hand while trying to aim his digital camera at the chief with the other.

"Welcome, ladies and gentlemen," the chief said in his rich, mellow baritone. "I see you've saved me the trouble of calling a press conference. We're here to investigate the discovery of a dead body. The deceased was Dr. J. Patrick Lanahan, thirty-seven, the founder of our beloved Caerphilly Zoo. Dr. Lanahan's next of kin have been notified, and for the time being, we're treating the death as a homicide."

"For the time being?" I heard Dad mutter beside me.

"If he finds a suicide note I, for one, am not buying it," I whispered back.

"I regret to say that's all the information I can give you at this time," the chief said. The reporters started shouting more questions, but the chief raised his voice and talked through them. "However, I'm sure you'll all be excited to learn that Dr. Montgomery Blake, the world-famous naturalist and a friend of the deceased, is here today, and would like to say a few words about the sad plight of the animals from the Caerphilly Zoo."

I wondered if Blake and the chief had planned this for when the reporters showed up or if Blake was just normally quick on his feet. He strode over with the lemur still perched on his shoulder, shook the chief's hand as if they were old school chums, and then turned to the cameras with that familiar benevolent smile. The fact that the lemur had grabbed a double fistful of his white mane and was holding on for dear life somehow looked charming rather than silly.

I wasn't in the mood to listen to speeches. I saw Mother going into the kitchen, and I decided to join her. So I heard Blake's short but glowing tribute to the fine work Lanahan had done at the zoo, followed by a few noncommittal words about his hope that some way could be found for this fine work to continue. Blake was well launched on an impassioned description of the plight of endangered species by the time I ducked through the kitchen door.

"So—you think he did it, don't you?"

Chapter 13

I turned to find that the student reporter had followed me inside.

"Come on, I know you suspect Blake," he said.

Was my reaction to Blake that obvious, or was that just a reporter's trick to make me talk?

"I'm sure I have no idea who's guilty," I said. "What makes you think I suspect him?"

"The way you were frowning when he started speaking. What have you got on him?"

I glanced outside where Blake was still orating.

"It's called canned hunting," Blake was saying. "Basically, it amounts to trapping animals in an enclosure and allowing so-called hunters to shoot them at will. There's no real skill or sport involved. . . ."

It sounded despicable. Blake was right to fight it. And he was on the side of the angels when it came to endangered species. A staunch conservationist. Why did I find him so easy to dislike? And so easy to suspect?

"I don't have anything on him," I said. "I approve of his work. I've given money to his foundation. But I hate listening to speeches—even ones I agree with. Now shoo."

The reporter reluctantly shuffled outside again, and went over to join the crowd around Blake, who was still talking, and feeding the lemur a slice of peach. Through the screen door, I could see that Blake was keeping his face as close as possible to the lemur to make sure he stayed on camera. After all, Blake might be famous, but the lemur was a lot cuter, and endangered to boot.

"Good riddance," Mother said with a sniff. "I don't see why everyone is making such a fuss about that annoying Dr. Blake anyway."

"Especially considering how he's spoiling so much of Dad's fun," I said.

"And that young man does have a point," she said. "Dr. Blake could be a suspect. I think you should check him out. We don't really know why he's here, now do we? Is the Caerphilly Zoo really the kind of project he'd normally spend his time on?"

"I'm sure the chief has already thought of that, Mother," I said. "For all we know, he's already identified the murderer."

"That would be nice," Mother said. "And if he hasn't, I'm sure you and your father will help him out. We don't want this unfortunate business to spoil all your lovely plans for the weekend, now do we?"

I was momentarily startled—Mother was absolutely the last person in the world Michael and I wanted finding out about The Plan. Had she guessed?

Probably not; I realized she was probably only referring to the move, and the giant Memorial Day cookout and house-warming party we had scheduled for Monday. The party we planned to duck out of early, so we could race over to the Clay County courthouse to tie the knot as quickly, simply, and privately as possible. I'd already mentally composed the note we were going to send back to our guests: "Thanks for coming to our wedding reception. We've already taken off for the honey-moon. Have fun while we're gone, and don't break too much."

But I hadn't committed it to paper, and I'd been extremely careful not to say anything that might give her the slightest clue.

Had I been a little too careful? Dad liked to brag about my marvelous detective ability, but if I had any skill in that area, it was Mother I'd inherited it from.

The best defense is a strong offense, they say.

"You're up to something," I said. "What is it?"

Mother assumed her most innocent look, and just then the chief strolled into the kitchen.

"If you folks want to carry on with your moving, that's fine with me," he said. "As long as you stay out of the basement. And if you don't mind, I'd like to sneak the body out this way, while the reporters are all fawning at Blake's feet."

"Sneak him out?" Mother asked. "Why do you need to sneak?" Not one of her favorite words—she was fond of saying that if it would embarrass us to see something we did in a photo on the front page of the *Daily Press,* we shouldn't do it.

"Maybe it's foolish of me," the chief said, "but I just don't approve of seeing pictures of a murder victim all over the newspaper or the TV screen—not even in a body bag. It's just not seemly. But I haven't had much luck bringing the damned press around to my point of view, so all I can do is try to sneak the body out when they're otherwise engaged. So if you don't mind, while Blake's still going strong . . ."

"Be my guest," I said. "I'll go out front and sound the alarm if one of them appears. And if they do show up before you can get him out, maybe we could sneak him out under cover of the move."

"I'll watch the back door, and then tell the family we're starting work again," Mother said. I could tell from her face that she approved of the chief's scruples.

The front yard was blissfully empty. No reporters, no family members, and no stray animals.

"All clear?" the chief asked from inside the front door.

"All clear," I said, and stepped back to give them plenty of room. The chief supervised as Sammy and Horace wheeled a small gurney out, picked it up to go down the front steps, and then scurried over to our driveway, where they deposited the body bag in the back of a pickup truck.

"Isn't that Michael's truck?" I asked, startled.

"He's going to drive us," the chief said. "Mort down at the funeral home says the hearse blew a rod, and he doesn't know when the garage will have it running again."

"And if anyone asks," Michael said, striding out onto the porch, "I've gone into town to fetch a load of the stuff I've been keeping in the corner of my office. Which is exactly what I will be doing after we drop Patrick off at the funeral home."

"And I'm going over to the storage bin to get the move going again," I said. I went inside to get my own keys. Out on the porch, I overheard the chief giving Sammy orders.

"Don't tell any of those confounded reporters that I'm over at the zoo, you hear? If they ask, Horace and I went into town for some equipment, and I'll be back directly. And call me if anyone finds that damned Shiffley kid!"

Damned Shiffley kid? Had Charlie Shiffley already popped to the top of the chief's suspect list? Or was he just the only suspect unlucky or unwise enough not to be immediately available for questioning?

Chief Burke's job, not mine, I reminded myself. My job, for now, was to get the move finished.

And that's what I did for the rest of the afternoon. I put myself in charge of the crew loading the stuff from our storage bins into the trucks. It was hot, sweaty, muscle-aching work, but at least it kept me away from the house. I didn't have to watch Sammy's epic battle to keep the reporters from infiltrating the basement. I could try to forget about the fact that Mother was arranging and rearranging everything, probably in ways that had nothing to do with what Michael and I had planned. If any more animals arrived, I didn't have to deal with them.

It was dusk by the time I arrived back at the house.

Chapter 14

I felt an irrational surge of relief when I pulled up in front of the house and found it still standing and apparently quieter than it had been during the afternoon. Silly of me—someone would have found me to share the news if anything really exciting had happened, like a house fire or the arrival of a troupe of performing bears.

There were still a few vehicles parked along the roadside. The chief's sedan and one of the patrol cars. A few others, but they might belong to relatives showing up annoyingly early for Monday's party. And with any luck, most of them had gone over to visit Mother and Dad at the farmhouse for the evening. Peace and quiet reigned.

But I did spot one visitor. He was down by the pasture, leaning on the fence, gazing at the llamas. Not the Animal Welfare guy, though—the newest visitor was tall and stocky. I strolled down to see what he was up to.

He turned when he heard me approaching, and stuck out a thick, callused hand.

"Ray Hamlin," he said. "Proprietor of the Clay County Zoo."

"Meg Langslow," I said. "I've heard of your zoo."

I didn't mention that most of what I'd heard was condescending. And I found myself wondering if he would normally have struck me as foxlike, or if I was starting to think in animal metaphors. His copper red hair was combed back in a manelike fashion, perhaps to disguise a thinning spot on top, and his face had a quizzical, lopsided look, as if he'd been about to say something sardonic and got stuck midway, with one eyebrow perpetually crooked a little higher than the other.

"So, you folks in the market for an ark?" he said. He wheezed a couple of times with laughter, and then the wheeze mutated into a cough, which gave me time to restrain my irritation. At least three other people had made the same joke at various times over the course of the afternoon.

"We do have a lot of animals, yes," I said. "And more arriving all the time. More than we're really equipped to handle. I was planning to get in touch with you to see if there was any possibility you could take some of them. At least in the short term."

"Hmm," he said, frowning at the llamas. "I have several llamas already."

"You don't have to take the llamas if you don't want to," I said. For the time being, the llamas didn't require much more than a little pasture space. I could think of other animals whose departure was a higher priority, animals that were a lot more trouble to have around. The hyenas, for example. And the penguins.

"Nice llamas, of course," he said. He cocked his head to one side and continued to scrutinize the llamas, as if unwilling to reject them completely before figuring out if they were superior, in some subtle way, to the llamas he already had. I'd seen my nephew Eric, at a younger age, wearing the same expression one Halloween, trying to decide whether the benefits of rummaging through a proffered goody bowl were worth letting go of the candy he already had clutched in both sticky little fists.

"Most of the ungulates aren't really a problem, anyway," I said.

"The what?" he said, frowning.

"Ungulates. Hoofed animals."

"Oh, ungulates," he said, as if correcting my pronunciation, though I couldn't tell a difference between my pronunciation and his. "Yeah, the herd stock isn't a problem. It's the carnivores you've got to watch."

More wheezing.

"Exactly," I said. "And we've got a few of those, too."

"I don't suppose you have a list of the available animals," Hamlin said. "I have a general idea of what he had, of course, but I haven't visited him in quite a while. I don't know which ones I'd want to take on."

"You don't seem to be getting the point," I said. "We're not offering you a chance to cherry-pick the Caerphilly Zoo to fill in the gaps in your own collection. Some of these animals probably require special care that we have no clue how to provide. In the short term, we need someone who is qualified to foster them. We're talking animal welfare here."

"Yes, the animals' welfare comes first, naturally," he said quickly. A little too quickly, and he didn't sound all that sincere. I began to have second thoughts. Did I really want to entrust the health and safety of our animals to this man?

Of course, if even I was starting to think of them as "our animals," finding them a new home had become especially urgent, before Michael and Dad completely forgot that the menagerie didn't belong to us. And just because he rubbed me the wrong way didn't mean Hamlin was unkind to animals.

"Once everything is settled, I'm sure we can work closely with you to find a permanent home for all the animals. Determining which ones you feel would benefit from living at your zoo and which ones would be better off at another facility."

He frowned again, and then his face cleared. He'd got the

message. Help us out of this crisis, and maybe you will get a chance to cherry-pick Patrick's collection after all.

Though I wasn't promising anything. And luckily, the animals weren't mine to promise.

"I'll still need to know what animals you have so I can arrange spaces for them," he said. "If you can get together a list, I can start working on freeing up as much space as possible. The Clay County Zoo's still pretty small—I wasn't a trust-fund baby like Lanahan. But we'll do what we can."

"That's fine," I said. I felt relieved. Partly because I'd made progress toward getting someone to take the animals off our hands. And, contrary as it sounds, partly because I'd have a little more time to vet him before entrusting the animals to him.

I'd get Dad to check him out. For that matter, if Dr. Montgomery Blake insisted on hanging around, maybe I could guilt-trip him into helping check Hamlin out. Blake seemed a lot less gullible than Dad.

Or maybe just a lot less nice. He and Hamlin should get along splendidly.

I felt a momentary pang of guilt. Why was I being so quick to suspect the worst of Blake? Apart from his slightly officious and overbearing manner, he hadn't really done anything wrong. I pondered my distrust for a few moments without coming any closer to an answer, except that my gut instinct told me Blake wasn't exactly what he seemed. I resolved to keep an eye on him.

I headed back to the house. The yard was quiet, apart from an occasional noise from one of the animals that hadn't settled in for the night. All the humans had gone inside—except for Dr. Smoot, who had returned to the Adirondack chair. But he wasn't actually sitting in it—in fact, he, too, appeared to be settling down for the night.

Chapter 15

I stood, hands on hips, surveying Dr. Smoot's arrangements. He had appropriated a couple of pillows from the porch swing. He'd placed a plastic garden bucket upside down to the left of the chair, to serve as a table. On the bucket, he'd arranged a box of tissues, a paperback copy of *Scaramouche,* and a flashlight. And he'd taken off his shoes and socks and was walking around barefoot, holding a glass of water and brushing his teeth.

We were used to relatives showing up for an afternoon visit and staying for a week, but I'd never laid eyes on Dr. Smoot before today.

I went over to talk to him.

"So, is there anything you need?" I asked, in my most cheerful, helpful hostess voice.

"Yes, actually there is," he said, and began taking off his pants.

"What the—," I began, and then I realized that he wasn't disrobing. Beneath the baggy gray pants he was wearing tan Bermuda shorts.

"What a relief!" he said, echoing my thoughts. He pulled off his tie and began unbuttoning his shirt. I watched with fascination as he pulled it off, revealing a faded Duke University T-shirt.

"Could I have a coat hanger?" he asked. "I don't want to spoil my work clothes."

"Um . . . right," I said. "You're planning to sleep here? Wouldn't you be more comfortable—"

"Not inside!" he shrieked, turning pale.

"No, of course not," I said. "Here's better. Plenty of fresh air."

"I'm sorry," he said. "After a fright like I had today, I find it hard to go into any confined space again for a while."

"How long a while?" I asked.

Dr. Smoot looked at me with reproachful eyes.

"I understand," I said quickly. "It's just—wouldn't you be more comfortable in familiar surroundings? I mean, where do you sleep when this hits you at home?"

"In the backyard," he said. "In my hammock. Yes, that would be more comfortable, but I just can't face the car."

He shuddered dramatically.

"Yes, that would be a problem," I said. "Perhaps if you—"

"Even with all the windows open, a car's way too small right now. I just need to rest here for the time being. If the car's in the way, I'd be happy to give you the keys so someone could move it."

"The car's fine where it is," I said. "Have you ever considered getting a convertible?"

"I'm fine," he said.

"Michael has a convertible," I said. "It's amazing how free and unfettered you feel, driving around in a convertible."

"I don't want to be a bother."

"One of us could run you home in the convertible if you like."

"I wouldn't want you to go to that much trouble," he said. "Just a coat hanger. And maybe a light blanket, if you have one."

I gave up and went inside to fetch a coat hanger. I found Michael, Dad, Eric, and Dr. Blake sitting around the kitchen table, eating chocolate ice cream.

"Aunt Meg, do you want some ice cream?" Eric asked. Dad waved the scoop invitingly.

"What's wrong?" Michael asked, putting down his spoon.

"Dr. Smoot plans to camp in our backyard tonight," I said, heading for the hall. "I'm going to take him a coat hanger for his suit."

"No you're not." Michael caught me by the arm and steered me back to the table. "You're going to have some ice cream. I'll deal with Smoot."

"He'd like a blanket, too, if we have one," I said. Michael nodded, and disappeared into the front hall. I sat, thinking I was too tired to eat, but after I'd stared at Michael's ice-cream bowl for a few seconds, I decided it looked appealing after all.

"So, getting back to the opossum," Blake said. I glanced over and saw that he was, indeed, holding up a small, sleepy-looking possum. "Do you know what else is interesting about it?" He was using that determinedly cheerful voice people often use when talking to young children, so I deduced that he was speaking to Eric. But Eric was at least half a dozen years too old for that kind of voice, so I also deduced that Blake hadn't had much contact with children.

Either of Eric's older brothers would have called Blake on it, but Eric was a remarkably good-natured kid. He merely shook his head.

"They have an opposable hallux!" Blake said. "Do you know what that is?"

"Big toe," I said through a mouthful of ice cream.

Dad beamed at me.

"Good guess," Blake said.

"Wasn't a guess," I said. "Dad taught us all about possums. We had plenty of them around the house when I was growing up."

"It's illegal for private citizens to keep them!" Blake said, in the booming tones of a fire-and-brimstone preacher denouncing fornication.

"Not if you're a licensed wildlife rehabilitator, which Dad is," I said. "It's perfectly legal." I was tired, but I restrained myself from sticking out my tongue and saying, "So there!"

"Well, that's all right then," Blake said. Rather grudgingly, I thought. "Anyway, the interesting thing—"

"Hey, Meg!" My brother Rob came in, carrying an empty ice-cream bowl. "There are a couple of Sprockets here to see you."

"That's all we need," I muttered.

"What's a Sprocket?" Blake asked.

"The people we bought the house from," I explained, scraping up a last bit of ice cream. "Edwina Sprocket, the former owner, left equal shares in her estate to all her nieces and nephews, or to their children if they were already dead, which meant that before we could buy the place, we had to get each and every one of them to approve the terms. Over a hundred in all."

"That must have been difficult," Blake said.

"Difficult? It would have been difficult if they were reasonable people," I said. "And they're not. It was well-nigh impossible. But I thought we'd finally finished with the Sprockets. Did they say why they were here?"

"Um . . . not really," Rob said. "They just asked for you."

"Figures," I said. "I'll go see what they want."

The two Sprockets were typical—short, pale, and rather mousy, with peeved expressions on their largely chinless faces. They looked for all the world like large white rats who'd temporarily taken human form. I was half inclined to ready a cage for them, between the hyenas and the acouchis. They'd have made perfect casting for Cinderella's coachman and footman.

"Rutherford Sprocket," one of them said. "And this is my brother Barchester."

"How do you do?" I said. "Can I help you?"

"We came about the body," Barchester said.

Chapter 16

"What about the body?" I asked.

"We've come to identify it."

"He's already been identified," I said.

"Oh," Rutherford said. "That seems highly irregular. But I suppose we can claim it for burial."

"You'll have to ask Chief Burke," I said. "I'm sorry—I didn't realize Dr. Lanahan was a relative of yours."

Though it would certainly explain Lanahan's feckless behavior with the zoo.

"Dr. who?" Barchester said.

"Lanahan. Patrick Lanahan. That's who the body is."

"I don't see how that could be possible," Rutherford said. "Who is this Lanahan person, and how did he come to be buried in our great-uncle's cellar?"

"He is—or was—the owner of the Caerphilly Zoo, and I have no idea how he came to be buried in the cellar. And it's our cellar now, so unless Dr. Lanahan's a friend or relative, I think it's really our problem."

"But it wasn't your cellar when he was buried there," Barchester said. "Twelve years ago, it was Uncle Plantagenet's cellar."

"And last night, when someone buried a body in it, it was our cellar," I said. "Look, I think we must be talking about two completely different dead bodies here."

Rutherford sighed the impatient sigh of a man trying to explain an elementary concept to someone who is proving unaccountably dense.

"We came about the body of our great-uncle, Dr. Plantagenet Sprocket," he said. "We heard that you had unearthed a body in the basement, and we assumed that the remains of our unfortunate relative had finally come to light. Are you telling us that someone else has already claimed the deceased?"

"I don't know about claiming, but someone else has already identified the body," I said. "This Plantagenet Sprocket— you said he was your great-uncle, right? Married to Edwina Sprocket?"

"Yes," Rutherford said. "The shameless hussy!"

"We never trusted her," Barchester said, shaking his head. "Not from the minute he brought her home." Which was pushing things a little—neither of them looked over forty, and Edwina Sprocket had been in her nineties when she died. Still, presumably he was using the word "we" out of solidarity with the distrustful Sprockets of generations gone by.

"How old was he?"

"When he met his untimely end—," Barchester began.

"When he disappeared," Rutherford corrected.

"Are you disputing that he met an untimely end?" Barchester said, turning to scowl at his brother.

"No, but it isn't proven in a court of law," Rutherford said.

"As you like," Barchester said, through gritted teeth. "At the time when he allegedly disappeared and met his untimely end."

"He didn't allegedly disappear," Rutherford snapped. "We know damn well that he disappeared. It's the untimely end that's alleged."

"Was he in his thirties?" I put in, to cut short this typical Sprocketish bickering.

Both Sprockets turned to glare at me.

"Of course not! He was over eighty when he disappeared!"

"Sorry," I said. "Our stiff's too young to be your uncle. In his thirties, according to the chief. And as I said, they've identified him already as someone else."

"They've found the wrong body," Rutherford said, shaking his head.

"It was the only body there to be found," I said. "Now if there's nothing else you wanted . . ." I gripped the doorknob, to suggest that perhaps it was time for them to leave.

"Where's Chief Burke?" Barchester said. "I think we need to talk to him about this."

"Be my guest," I said. "He's in the dining room."

If I were a nicer person, I'd have warned them that the chief was trying to wrap up what had already been a long day and probably wasn't in a good mood. They probably wouldn't have paid any attention though. They marched over to knock on the dining-room door and were admitted by a yawning Sammy.

"I'm going to bed," I announced to no one in particular.

I stumbled upstairs and down the hall to the master bedroom. After a look of longing at the still-disassembled king-sized bed leaning in pieces against the wall, I topped off the air in the inflatable camping mattress and strolled into the bathroom. Technically, the brightly colored snake in the bathtub wasn't in my way, but odds were I'd have forgotten about it overnight, and I didn't want to run into it when I stepped in to shower in the morning, so I relocated it to the tub in the hall bath. One of the guests would probably find it, but most of them hadn't been invited to arrive this early anyway, so I didn't see that they had much room to complain. Then I brushed my teeth and collapsed onto the air mattress.

I heard Michael come in and do the same thing. So much for a romantic first night in our newly renovated home.

I was almost asleep when a bloodcurdling scream jolted me wide awake.

"What the hell was that?" Michael asked.

"I think someone found the snake I put in the hall bath," I said.

"Why did you—never mind. That came from the backyard, not the house."

The screaming had subsided into muted wails, and I could also hear voices, and someone laughing. I stumbled over to the window overlooking the backyard. Rob, wearing a black cape and a smear of stage blood around his mouth, was sprawled on the ground just outside the cellar doors, laughing hysterically. The wailing appeared to be coming from a small cherry tree. Dad, Horace, and Rose Noire were standing beneath the tree, saying soothing things to it.

The Adirondack chair was empty.

"Ah," I said. "Rob was helping Dr. Smoot relive childhood memories."

"Serves him right for telling everyone about his damned trauma all day," Michael muttered.

Rob's laughter died down—not that he'd stopped, but he'd reached the point where he only had the breath to utter an occasional, barely audible squeak. But just about then, the hyenas kicked in, more than making up for his silence. Chief Burke burst out of the back door, strode over to the cherry tree, and stood looking up at it with his hands on his hips.

"Get a grip on it, man!" he bellowed.

I heard another scream at closer range.

"Now that was definitely the snake in the hall bath," I said.

Michael groaned, and pulled a pillow over his head.

I followed his example.

Chapter 17

Normally I manage to ignore dawn. But most of our guests, two- and four-legged alike, seemed intent on greeting it with loud, enthusiastic cries of one kind or another. I could hear the hyenas chuckling in the barn, the penguins honking in their pen, Spike barking furiously from somewhere inside the house.

I strolled over to the window and glanced out. Several sheep were grazing in the backyard, accompanied by a stray llama. Apparently Mrs. Fenniman was trying to clear the sheep out of the yard—she was prodding one in the rump with her enormous black umbrella, but the sheep seemed oblivious.

The lemurs were on top of the penguin coop, sitting on their haunches, their front paws on their knees, eyes closed, heads tipped back, apparently basking in the morning air.

It almost looked as if they were doing yoga. Down on the lawn Dr. Smoot had assumed much the same pose. I deduced that at some point someone had coaxed him down from the cherry tree, and he'd spent the rest of the night in the Adirondack chair.

Sheila Flugleman popped out of the penguin coop, carrying her trusty buckets toward the front of the house. Nice to see someone was on the job. The penguins occupied a cage with wheels on the bottom, rather like a small, bare-bones version of a circus wagon. The cage looked brand-new, and reassuringly sturdy. Dad had probably enlisted the Shiffleys to build it. As I watched, Dad clucked to the donkey hitched to the front of it, and the wagon rolled slowly off toward the pasture.

Was the donkey from Lanahan's petting zoo? Or had Dad used the penguins' transportation needs as an excuse to acquire more livestock?

The sheep suddenly raised their heads and trotted briskly off to my right. The llama followed them, though not with-out a few glances over its shoulder. A few moments after the sheep vanished, four wolves appeared. On leashes, luckily—apparently Rose Noire and Horace were taking them for a walk. And talking to them, nonstop. I couldn't hear what Rose Noire was saying. Probably trying to convert them to a mindful vegetarian lifestyle. Judging from how eagerly they strained against their leashes, I didn't think she'd have much luck.

I glanced over to see that Michael was still fast asleep. He'd probably succeeded better than I had in tuning out the hyenas during the night. I threw on some clothes, grabbed my notebook, and headed downstairs.

Before I even hit the stairs, I heard bustling below. I peeked over the banister and saw several pieces of furniture milling indecisively around in the hallway. Our dining table, and all of its chairs. I leaned a little farther out and saw that they weren't moving under their own steam but on the backs of a squad of my larger cousins and nephews. Mother's voice rang out.

"Well, if the chief is going to be difficult, we'll just have to put them in the living room till he's finished," she said.

The table and chairs obediently turned and trooped through the archway from the hallway into the living room. I ventured down the stairs. Mother was standing in the archway frowning.

"Meg, dear, do see if you can convince the chief to be reasonable," she said when she spotted me. "He won't let me take any of the furniture into the dining room."

"He does have a murder to investigate," I pointed out.

"But it's not as if the rest of the world can come to a grinding halt while he does it," Mother said. "I don't see the problem with letting us into the dining room for half an hour to set up the furniture. Now I can't arrange the living room, either."

I could see why the chief was balking. With Mother in charge, half an hour would be more like three—she'd insist on rearranging everything five times. It would drive the chief bananas. I wasn't looking forward to witnessing or participating in it myself. Perhaps I could find an excuse to spend much of the day somewhere else, doing something indisputably important.

"And we have hundreds of people coming on Monday," she said.

"They know we've just moved in," I said. "They won't expect us to have everything perfect."

"They'll expect us to make an effort," she said, with a withering look.

"I'll talk to the chief." And I would—though probably not about reclaiming the dining room just yet.

"Thank you, dear," Mother said, smiling. She glided into the living room, ready to goad her crew into action again.

"And see what you can do about getting rid of all these animals," Mrs. Fenniman said, following Mother into the living room.

"Easier said than done," I muttered, but not loudly enough that they could hear.

Something hit me on the head. Something soft, wet, and

sticky. I grimaced, and carefully scraped whatever it was off the top of my hand.

A chunk of mushy yellow fruit.

I glanced up to see a sloth, hanging from the chandelier. It appeared to have fallen asleep in the middle of eating an overripe peach.

"That's it," I said. "I'm out of here."

"Not permanently, I hope," Michael said, looking down over the banister.

"No," I said. "But I'm going to hunt down Dad and make him tell me exactly what animals the damned zoo has. So we'll know what to expect, and can start finding new homes for them."

"Good idea," Michael said. "Meanwhile, rumor has it the multitudes are clamoring for breakfast, so I think I'll get cracking."

I set off to find Dad.

As I passed through the kitchen, I found Montgomery Blake there, stirring an odd-smelling concoction he was cooking on the stovetop. A treat for one of the animals, no doubt. I reminded myself to cut him some slack. After all, he really did seem to love animals. I waved at him as I went by.

Out in the yard, Rose Noire had pulled up a picnic bench beside Dr. Smoot's chair and was talking to him with an earnest expression. Dr. Smoot looked anxious. Which was good—anxious was a reassuringly normal reaction to one of Rose Noire's little chats.

"I can understand what a traumatic experience that was," she was saying. "But I think you need to find a way to free yourself from the shackles of your unhappy past and move on."

For my part, I would be happy if Dr. Smoot could free himself from our Adirondack chair and move on back to town, and I wasn't sure how anything Rose Noire might have planned could possibly do any good. But in the interest of family harmony, I kept my face neutral.

I needn't have bothered. Smoot's face expressed every bit of doubt I felt, and more.

"You think I haven't tried?" he said.

"Yes, but you haven't really had any help, have you?"

Smoot's face suggested that maybe he didn't really want help. Especially not help that came accompanied by the kind of ghastly herbal teas Rose Noire was always trying to foist off on people. Dr. Smoot was holding a half-full mug of one of her brews, and from the little puddle in the dirt beneath the chair, I suspected only the first sip of it had gone down his throat.

"Now here's what we're going to do," she went on. I left them to get on with it. Maybe if Rose Noire came up with a sufficiently bizarre plan of action, Dr. Smoot's claustrophobia would ease up just enough to let him get into his car and leave. I made a mental note to ask her where she'd put the wolves before I found out by accident, and continued my search for Dad.

No sign of him in the barn, but just as I was about to leave, I heard a scuffling noise at the far end. With so many animals on the premises—not to mention a murderer still at large—I didn't think unexplained noises should be left unexplained, so I went over to check it out.

Chapter 18

I breathed a sigh of relief when all I found was Rob, crouched by one wall, behind some half-empty boxes.

"Avoiding Mother's work detail, I see," I said.

"I was just reading," he said, assuming an air of virtue that wouldn't have fooled Eric.

I glanced down. He didn't seem to be holding a book, or even a graphic novel.

"Reading what?"

"This," he said, indicating the closest box.

"You're reading one of the moving boxes?"

"It's not technically a moving box."

"No, technically it's the box our air purifier came in," I said. "And you're reading the side that's written in French."

"*Purificateur d'air HEPA ultra silencieux,*" he said. "Yes."

"I didn't know you read French," I said.

"I took it in high school," he said.

"Yes, but I didn't realize it took."

"I'm beginning to realize what I've been missing," he said. "The romance of the Gallic language."

"Have you met a French girl?" I asked. "Or just been watching too many Truffaut films?"

"I mean, some of the words are just the same as English," he said. "*Eliminer* is 'eliminate,' for example. And 'pollen' is *le pollen*. Bo-ring! But just when you think it hasn't got any mystique—listen to this: it also eliminates *'la fumée, la poussière, les spores de moisissures, et les squames de chats.'* Doesn't that just sing to you? *Squames de chats!*"

"No, probably because I know what it says," I said. "Smoke, dust, mold spores, and cat dander."

"Cat dander? *Squames de chats* is cat dander? You see—it loses all the glamour when you translate something out of French. I'm so disillusioned."

"*Je suis desolée* to have been the cause of your disillusionment," I said. "If you're going to brood about it, why not go outside and look useful while you're doing so. Keep Mother happy."

Rob sighed heavily and got to his feet.

"I thought you, at least, would be supportive of my self-improvement efforts," he said.

"I don't suppose you know where Dad is?"

"Of course! I'll show you."

He set out at a brisk pace—unusual for the normally languid Rob. And he glanced back over his shoulder at the house once or twice. I deduced that Mother must have a grueling list of tasks for her minions to perform.

After a few minutes we arrived at the former cow pond, which now housed our duck population and the visiting penguins. If I hadn't known the way, I could easily have found it by following the happy trillings and honkings of the penguins as they rediscovered the joys of a life aquatic. I hoped the weather stayed cool enough for them to stay outside—at least until we figured out how to rig up an air conditioner for their coop.

Dad had brought a lawn chair with him and was sitting just outside the fence, watching the penguins frolic. Rob threw himself down on the grass nearby. Eric and Spike were standing by the edge of the fence, so Spike could growl menacingly at the penguins at close quarters. The penguins mostly ignored him.

"So, you're shirking Mother's furniture-rearrangement detail, too," I said, plopping down beside them.

"I think your mother has plenty of help for that," Dad said.

"I'm also shirking Dr. Blake's animal-care detail," Rob said. "He said something about worming the hyenas this morning."

"The hyenas?" Dad said. "Are you sure?"

"That's what he said." Rob shrugged.

"I can't imagine why he thinks that's needed," Dad said. "You're sure that's what he said?"

"Maybe it was a joke," I suggested.

"Sounded serious to me," Rob said. "Maybe I'm mixed up about what he's doing, but it was something to do with the hyenas, at any rate. That's why I'm out here. I want nothing to do with the damned hyenas."

"I haven't seen any sign of worms," Dad muttered.

"Maybe he's done tests," I said. "Can't you tell from their dung?"

"Fat chance getting any dung," Rob said. "With that silly woman from the garden store cleaning up after the animals every five minutes."

"I think he's overreacting," Dad said. "The poor things are unsettled. They're in a new, unfamiliar environment. They're not getting as much exercise as they need in that temporary cage."

"And they're short of sleep, as anyone staying at our house last night could tell you," I put in.

"I know those hyenas a great deal better than he does, and I don't think there's anything wrong with them that a return to a suitable environment wouldn't cure," Dad said. "Blake should be out working on that, not underfoot upsetting the animals with unnecessary medical procedures."

"Well, what are his qualifications, anyway?" I asked. "Is he a vet?"

"He's a world-famous zoologist," Dad said.

"Are we really sure?" I asked, as a sudden thought hit me. "Do you know where he got his degree from? I mean, is he really a trained zoologist, or does he just play one on TV?"

"Oh, dear," Dad said. "You know, I've never checked on that. What if he's like those radio psychologists? You know, the ones who give advice even though they aren't really therapists."

"Don't worry," I said. "I'll look him up."

"Google him," Rob said with a shrug.

"I would have already," I said. "But we packed our computers up a few days ago, and Kevin won't be here to set them up again until tomorrow. But I'll stop by the library sometime today and do it."

"It's easy to see who the real sleuth is," Dad said, beaming at me. "It never occurred to me that he might not be the real thing. And this could explain the murder—what if Patrick found out that Blake was a phony!"

"And Blake killed him to cover up—that's possible," I said. "But let's not jump to conclusions. We don't yet know that he's a phony."

"We don't know he *isn't*," Dad said.

"I think we'd know if he was," I said. "Remember, he's a human gadfly, always on TV denouncing some corporation for its rotten environmental record."

"I happen to agree with him on most of those issues." Dad looked stern.

"So do I, but not everyone does," I said. "And as famous as he is, don't you think someone would have outed him if he was a phony? But I want to see just what his background is."

Including whether he'd ever been suspected of knocking off anyone for cruelty to animals.

"Meanwhile, there's something else I need to do," I went on. "We can't just sit around waiting for Blake to rescue the zoo."

"Especially if he turns out to be a fraud," Dad muttered. Blake must really have gotten to him.

"So," I said. "You're pretty familiar with the Caerphilly Zoo, right? What kind of animals they have and all that?"

"Oh, yes," he said. "Very familiar. I'm over there all the time."

"Great," I said, pulling out my notebook-that-tells-me-when-to-breathe. "Let's make a list."

"A list? Why?"

"So we'll know what to expect over the next few days, if we can't get the fate of the zoo straightened out. What animals people are going to try to dump on us. And how many."

After a long pause, I looked up from my notebook.

"Well, there are eight or nine penguins."

"Thirteen, actually. Count them."

"If you can get them to stand still long enough," Rob said, waving at the pond where the penguins were busily diving in, swimming around, climbing out, chasing each other around, and then diving in again.

"I'm also aware of how many llamas, camels, hyenas, lemurs, acouchis, and sloths we have," I said. "Let's concentrate on animals who aren't here yet."

"Oh, dear," Dad said.

He frowned as if concentrating deeply. I tapped my pen impatiently against the notebook.

"That's tough," Dad said.

I knew perfectly well that what was stumping him was not the number and identity of the animals at the zoo. He'd been spending an inordinate amount of time there in the past few months. He probably knew not only what animals Lanahan had, but all their names, nicknames, medical histories, and favorite foods. What he couldn't decide was whether it would be a good thing or a bad thing to tell me the full extent of the menagerie that might be headed our way.

"Tell you what," I said, snapping my notebook shut. "You think about it. Scribble down a list and get back to me later today."

"Roger!" Dad said, suddenly cheerful again. He hurried off.

"Wouldn't count on getting that list anytime soon," Rob said with a snicker.

"Want to bet?"

Chapter 19

Rob accompanied me back to the house. I was relieved to see that Blake and his foul-smelling concoction were gone, and Michael and Rose Noire had begun fixing breakfast. Michael was frying bacon and sausage while Rose Noire was slicing up a small mountain of apples, peaches, pears, grapes, and melons into a fruit salad.

"So what other wildlife are we expecting?" Michael asked.

"I don't know yet," I said, plucking a few slices of bacon from the plate where they were draining. "Dad wasn't exactly forthcoming."

"Oh, dear," Michael said. "I have a bad feeling about that. He must know the answer would upset you. I could try to pry it out of him if you like."

"Don't bother," I said. "There's more than one way to skin a cat."

"Oh, Meg," Rose Noire said, closing her eyes in horror. "That's such a horrible, violent expression. I do wish you wouldn't use it."

"Don't worry," I said. "It's only an old saying. No actual cats will be skinned during the course of today's wildlife-rescue activities. Or for that matter, in the murder investigation. Not by me, at any rate. After all, I probably won't have much time to worry about it until after we finish the unpacking."

"Division of labor," Michael said. "You work on the murder and a new home for the animals. I'll see to the unpacking. We don't want to delay . . . the party or anything."

"I can't leave you to handle the unpacking all by yourself," I protested.

"All by myself? You mean the two dozen of your relatives who are already here will be leaving soon, instead of being joined by dozens more? Damn. I was looking forward to bossing them all around."

"You're right," I said. "You see to the unpacking. I'll worry about murder and the menagerie. Is Chief Burke around today?"

"He's appropriated our dining room for his command center," Michael said.

I snagged a slice of toast and went to the dining room. The door was open, and I could see Chief Burke sitting in one of our folding chairs, frowning down at some papers on the card table that served as his desk. When he didn't look up after a few moments, I knocked on the door frame.

"What now?" he grumbled.

"May I interrupt you for just a minute or two?" I asked.

His eyes flicked up at me, though he didn't raise his head. I could see he was trying to give the impression of being much too busy to waste any time on me.

"I want to visit the Caerphilly Zoo," I said.

At that, he lifted his head and sat back.

"Why? You must have at least half the animals here already. Just wait a day or two and you'll probably have the whole collection."

He laughed heartily at this. I tried to laugh along, but I wasn't sure my effort looked authentic.

"Well, that's why I want to visit the zoo," I said, as the chief's chuckles subsided. "Dad seems to have extended an open invitation to anyone who's fostering any of the zoo's animals that if they get fed up, they can come over and dump the animals on us. And I need to know just how many animals that might eventually be. And even more important, what kind of animals."

"Your father can't tell you?"

"He seems to be having trouble remembering."

"You ever consider that it might be a deliberate case of amnesia," the chief said, trying to suppress a grin. "Like maybe he doesn't want you to know how bad it could get around here."

"I'm positive it's deliberate," I said. "He thinks if I know how bad it could get, it will make me madder. And it probably will, for a few minutes, but in the long term, the more I know about how many of what kind of animal we might get stuck with, the better I can cope."

"And visiting an empty zoo will help you cope?"

"An empty zoo full of carefully labeled pens and cages. If I take an inventory, at least I can figure out what animals were there."

"How were you planning to get in?" the chief asked. "I got Mr. Thorndyke from the bank to let me in yesterday afternoon, but he's locked up again and gone off to his beach house for the long weekend."

"If Lanahan's gazelles can get out and wander over to the Shiffleys' woods, I'm sure I can figure out a way in," I said. "Unless you have an objection."

I took the chief's growl for grudging permission.

"Speaking of which, Randall Shiffley sounds pretty worried about his nephew," I said. "Have you really arrested Charlie Shiffley for killing that gazelle?"

"It wasn't a gazelle, it was something called a dik-dik," the chief said, frowning again. "Looks a lot like a deer, only they don't get more than a foot and a half high. And no, I haven't arrested Charles. Recommended that they take him in for an eye exam, if he couldn't tell that thing wasn't a full-sized deer, but arrest him? No. Not from want of nagging from Patrick Lana-han, but I don't take orders from anyone on how to do my job. He told me last week that if I didn't arrest the boy he was going to file a civil suit against the Shiffleys, and I told him to go right ahead, and good luck finding some kind of evidence to show the jury, because my officers sure can't."

"Then I guess the Shiffleys aren't too upset about Lanahan's death. No Lanahan, no civil suit."

The chief scowled.

"Not that it's any of my business, of course," I added.

"Have fun at the zoo," the chief said, and bowed his head over his papers. And then as I was leaving the room, he spoke again.

"And in case you haven't read the papers this morning, we haven't yet revealed how Dr. Lanahan died. So I'd appreciate your continued silence about it."

Did I detect a faint note of gratitude in his tone?

"Can do," I said.

The chief returned to his papers. I assumed I was dismissed.

Chapter 20

I emerged from the dining room to find Eric waiting in the hall.

"Aunt Meg, can I come with you to the zoo?"

"It's not open," I said.

"But you're going."

"Yes, but I'm going to snoop, not to see the animals. The animals are all here, remember?"

"Can't I snoop too? We could be like the Hardy Boys!"

I sighed. Apparently Dad was having an influence on Eric, too.

"Tell your grandmother where you're going," I said.

"I could just tell Grandpa."

"Grandpa will forget five minutes after you tell him," I said. "Tell Grandmother. And hurry back."

I was hoping he'd get distracted and lose interest, but by the time I'd fetched my purse, car keys, and a few other oddments I might need, he was back, leading Spike. I was about to protest that we didn't need Spike, but then I stopped myself. Eric was spending a lot of time with Spike. Bonding with him. Was there a possibility he'd bond so well that he'd want to take Spike home with him?

The idea cheered me up enormously. When Eric began singing "Old MacDonald's Farm" on the way to the zoo, I joined in with enthusiasm.

We'd gotten as far as "Old MacDonald had some sloths" and

were arguing amiably over what noise the sloths made when we emerged from a small stretch of woods and spotted the entrance to the zoo. It wasn't deserted, as I'd expected—in fact, there was a small group of people milling around in front of it. I stopped the car to figure out what was happening before going any closer.

"You said the zoo was closed," Eric said in an accusing tone.

"I did and it is," I said. "I have no idea who they are and why they're here."

But as I watched them, I realized why. Two dozen men and women had gathered in a rough semicircle in front of the zoo gate, carrying picket signs. Most were young and clad in jeans and dark green T-shirts with the words "Save Our Beasts!!" printed on the front. They were looking up at one young man who was standing on a bench with his back to the road, making a speech. He had long dark hair, a ragged beard, and wildly flashing eyes, making him look rather like a modern-day John the Baptist, or possibly a sixties radical made young again. The back of his T-shirt even had a picture of a clenched fist, the well-known logo of the Black Panther movement.

When I began driving closer, however, I realized that the fist was a paw, covered with grizzled fur and sporting long claws. Several rank-and-file protesters turned to whisper to each other, and I could see that the backs of their T-shirts bore the same logo. Then they began waving their signs up and down. I could see that the message on one side was "Animals Are People Too!" with "Let My Creatures Go!" on the reverse.

Rose Noire didn't seem to be among them, so either she belonged to another, rival animal-rights group or she'd made the ultimate sacrifice, passing up an opportunity for a protest to help us move. Or perhaps she felt, as I did, that it was a little strange to have a protest twenty miles from town, outside an empty zoo with no audience other than random passersby—and right now, Eric and I were the only onlookers, apart from a young man who was documenting the event with a bulky, old-fashioned Beta video camera parked on his shoulder.

I recognized the cameraman as one of Michael's film students, using the predictably functional but obsolete equipment available from the college. I decided he might not appreciate my interrupting his work by waving or saying hello.

My arrival seemed to spur the demonstrators on to new enthusiasm. As their leader continued to harangue them, they interrupted him more frequently with shouts and cheers.

"Aunt Meg, why are they all so upset?" Eric asked.

"They don't believe in zoos," I explained. "They want us to turn all the animals loose."

"Even the hyenas?" Eric asked, wide-eyed.

"Especially the hyenas."

I parked by the side of the road, as if we'd come to watch the festivities—but far enough away that the film student would have a hard time getting us in his picture. I wondered if the demonstrators would leave anytime soon so I could get into the zoo without being seen, much less filmed.

"Is this a protest rally?" Eric asked after a minute.

"Yes. Why?"

"So this is what Mom and Dad used to do when they were in college?"

"Sort of," I said. "Only the ones your parents were in were much larger. And for . . . different causes."

I had been about to say more important causes—war, racism, and civil liberties—but that wasn't fair. Cruelty to animals was arguably just as important a cause. And while I had a feeling I'd probably disagree with many of the odder beliefs held by members of Save Our Beasts, what little I'd found out about Patrick

Lanahan made me think that perhaps if he were still alive I might be inclined to join their protest.

The whole business of farming out wild animals to untrained volunteers, for example. Was the man a complete idiot, or did he realize what a bad idea this was—for animals and humans alike—and not care?

Of course, if I were going to start an animal-rights group, I think I'd have worked a little harder on the name. Did they enjoy being called the SOBs?

Just then, the film student hoisted the camera off his shoulder and waved to the protesters. He turned and began walking toward a small nest of cars parked a little farther along the road. The protesters took his departure as an at-ease command. They put down their signs, and most of them sat down cross-legged on the grass in front of the zoo. A couple of them pulled out picnic baskets and began passing out water and sandwiches.

The leader strode over to my car and inspected us with narrowed eyes. Spike, who had been growling softly since we arrived at the zoo, took an instant and arguably quite rational dislike to him and began barking and lunging toward him, even climbing into my lap to get closer to his prey. I made sure Eric had a tight hold on the leash and rolled down my window.

"How would you feel if someone put a heavy collar around your neck and dragged you around at the end of a rope?" the chief SOB asked. He had to shout over the racket Spike was making.

"If I were in the habit of picking fights with dogs ten times my size and running out into traffic, I hope I'd be smart enough to realize that the leash was for my own protection," I said. "And I should point out that I haven't inflicted a muzzle on him, even though he's in the habit of biting passersby with no apparent provocation."

The leader jerked back the hand he'd been extending in Spike's direction. Disappointed, Spike subsided into soft but menacing growls.

"Vicious animals are usually made that way through systematic abuse by humans," the leader announced with a scornful look. Well, two could play at that game.

"I've never understood the narrow-minded tendency most people have to judge animals by completely inappropriate, anthropocentric standards," I said. "Calling a dog vicious, for example, merely because he acts in accordance with his own predator instincts, instead of behaving in a way we find convenient."

The leader opened his mouth as if to retaliate and then thought better of it. Possibly because the film student had changed his mind about leaving and came over to eavesdrop.

"So did you just come out to mock our demonstration, or was there a good reason you came out here?"

Under the circumstances, I thought mocking their demonstration seemed pretty reasonable, but I stifled the impulse to say so.

"We were just passing by on our way to somewhere else and stumbled on your demonstration by accident," I lied. "I confess, I was a little surprised at finding a demonstration outside an empty zoo. You did know it was empty, right?"

"Yes, but the evil it represents continues unchecked!"

"Besides," the film student put in, "they'd already arranged for me to come and film them today."

The leader shot an exasperated glance at him, but the film student just stood there, calmly observing us. He wasn't filming, but he gave the impression that he'd be happy to if we provided more pyrotechnics.

"Since your group is here, I have a question for you," I said. "Are any of you qualified and willing to help take care of some of the animals recently liberated from their vile imprisonment in the Caerphilly Zoo?"

"You're asking us to become their new jailers!" the leader shouted. His followers looked up at his voice, but they didn't interrupt their picnic to join us.

"No," I said. "I'm asking if any of you could take temporary responsibility for the welfare and happiness of even one of the beasts you're trying to save. After all, if the zoo closes permanently, you'll probably be at least partly responsible—"

"What do you mean, responsible?" the leader shouted. "Are you accusing us of killing Lanahan?"

"I'm not accusing anyone," I said—though I was definitely keeping him high on the people who might deserve the accusation. "But someone killed him, and can you be absolutely sure your campaign against the zoo had nothing to do with it?"

"That's ridiculous!" he exclaimed. "You can expect to hear from my attorney; that's absolute libel!"

"Slander, not libel," I said. "It's not libel unless I write it down. But I'm sure your attorney can explain that to you."

The leader stormed off, still sputtering. One of his followers tried to placate him with a sandwich, which he rudely refused.

Mother would have assumed his guilt immediately. Of course, Mother would probably find it easier to forgive a well-bred murderer than a rude saint. Still, I had the feeling that if Chief Burke wasn't already investigating the leader of the SOBs, he should do so immediately.

"Who is that guy?" I asked the film student.

Chapter 21

"Shea? He's the president of Save Our Beasts," the student said. "You think he'll try to sue you?"

"He might," I said. "Then again, he might just be a law student, going through that difficult litigious phase. I remember it hit my brother around the middle of his first semester."

"Sounds like Shea," the student said. "Got an amazing talent for ticking off the people who already agree with him, so it's no wonder he's having trouble winning converts. SOB used to be a much bigger group before he took over."

"Are they just opposed to zoos in principle or was Patrick Lanahan doing something particularly bad?"

The student shifted uneasily.

"There have been rumors that he wasn't feeding the animals properly," he said. "And skimping on their medical care. Given how broke he was, sounds plausible. I can't prove it, though, and he's certainly run up pretty huge bills with the vet and the feed store. And I certainly can't prove the rumor about canned hunts."

"Canned what?"

"Canned hunts—you haven't heard of them?"

I remembered Blake saying something about them when he was talking to the reporters, but I didn't remember what he'd said, so I shook my head.

"It's barbarous," he said, his voice becoming heated. "You take a bunch of animals and pen them up someplace—they usually call them game ranches or hunting preserves—and charge people a stiff fee to come in and shoot where they can hardly help killing something. Some of them guarantee a kill."

"What kind of animals?" I asked.

"Depends on the operation," he said. "Sometimes it's native species—deer, elk, even bear. Virginia outlawed it years ago, except for a couple of places that were already in operation, and they're only allowed to use various kinds of pigs, goats, and sheep. But in some states, they bring in exotic animals to shoot at. Some of them bought from overpopulated zoos."

"So is that why the SOBs are picketing—they think Patrick was selling off unwanted animals to be killed?"

The student nodded.

"Shea even accused Lanahan of running the hunts on his land—which would be totally illegal in Virginia, of course, and I'm not sure anyone takes that seriously. But even selling the animals to a game ranch—that wouldn't be illegal, but it would still be pretty awful. I mean, these are animals that are used to being around humans—they don't have the same fear of humans real wild animals have, so they're a lot more vulnerable, and when you pen them in and let the hunters set up right where the animals have to come to eat or drink—"

"I get the picture. If Lanahan was doing that—well, I can't imagine my father getting involved with him."

"Unless he was trying to investigate him," the student said. "That's what I was thinking of doing—work my way into his confidence to get the real scoop."

"Yeah, that sounds like something Dad would do," I said with a sigh. But was it something he'd do without trying to enlist me? I'd worry about that later.

"So where are the animals, anyway?" he asked. "I was hoping to film them while I was out here, but they all seem to be gone."

"Out at our house," I said. "At least some of them are, and every time I turn around, someone dumps another batch off with us. If we can't figure out something else to do with them, in a day or so we should have the whole zoo reunited."

"Cool," the student said. "Hey, I could go there and film them. I mean, if you and Professor Waterston don't mind. . . ."

"Film away," I said. "And make it as much of a tearjerker as possible—the poor helpless animals, orphaned by the savage murder of their protector, abandoned to the mercies of anyone generous enough to volunteer to care for them."

"Sounds much more interesting than the protest," he said. "Maybe I'll just use the SOBs as local color in a report on the plight of the animals. I think I'll head over there now."

"You're not staying to lunch with the protesters?" I asked.

"I'm not much on tofu and bean sprouts," he said, grimacing. "And Shea gets on my nerves after a while. A really short while. See you later."

"Oh, one more thing," I called after him. "Is Shea his first name or his last name."

"First," the film student said. "Or maybe middle. He goes by Shea Bailey. Sounds more like a fancy restaurant than a name to me. You checking up on him?"

"Why, you know any dirt on him?"

"No," he said, handing me a card. "But if you find any . . ."

"I'll keep you in mind," I said.

He returned to his car and drove off a minute later. I glanced over at Shea and the other protesters. Most of them seemed to have eaten, but now they were lying about, sipping their water and enjoying the sunshine. Perhaps they were waiting for another news crew, or another, more sympathetic passerby, to renew their demonstration.

"Are we going into the zoo now?" Eric asked.

"I think we should come back when they're not here," I said, indicating the protesters. "We don't want them following us in and spoiling our visit, do we?"

Eric shook his head. I started the engine, managed a tight three-point turn without squashing any demonstrators, and headed home.

I was tempted to try sneaking into the zoo by a back way. There were a couple of dirt roads that looked promising, but since I had no idea where the zoo property began, I decided not to wander off into the woods yet. Better to find a map.

"You want to go to the library for story hour?" I asked Eric. The Caerphilly Library had a nice collection of county maps.

"That's for little kids," Eric said, wrinkling his nose. "I'd rather go back and see what new animals we've got."

So I went by the house to drop off Eric. Call me an uncaring aunt, but I hoped he'd be disappointed. However, a lot more cars had arrived during our unsuccessful scouting expedition to the zoo. Most of them probably belonged to relatives, showing up much earlier than expected, but there might be a few disgruntled animal foster parents in the lot.

As Eric ran off to inventory the livestock, I spotted Mother through the living-room window. From her gestures, I deduced that she was still giving orders to her volunteer movers. I decided to sneak in the back door for a cold drink before setting out again.

As I strolled around the side of the house, I found myself wondering if the relatives held a solution to the animal problem. Surely given the hosts of family members who'd be showing up today, tomorrow, and Monday, we could find a few willing to foster the various animals until the future of the Caerphilly Zoo was assured. Especially if I got Mother to talk them into it. For that matter, knowing my family, odds were I could find permanent homes for many of the animals if I just—

"Mwah-ha-ha!"

I jumped as a sinister black-cloaked figure leaped out from behind a hydrangea, baring long, bloodstained fangs and flexing fingers armed with impressive clawlike fingernails.

"I vant to drrink your blood!" he intoned in a deep, guttural voice.

"Oh, very impressive, Dr. Smoot," I said. "I see you and Rose Noire are working hard at overcoming your phobia. How's it going?"

"Very well, thank you," he said, in a more normal voice. He grinned, which looked peculiar in a face painted fish-belly white, except for a few streaks of flesh color where he'd rubbed the makeup off scratching his nose. And he had trouble talking through the fangs without lisping. "I confeth," he went on, "I thought it wath a crathy idea at firtht, but I'm really thtarting to get into it. It'th—very empowering."

"That's good," I said. He not only lisped—he drooled slightly. I started to sidle away, hoping to avoid hearing much more. It always made me nervous when people in therapy wanted to tell me about their psychological problems. Wasn't that one of the main reasons for doing therapy—being able to talk over your problems confidentially with a trained mental health professional? Someone whose first reaction wouldn't be, "Whoa, he's a few ants short of a picnic"—or at least someone with a vested interest in not blurting it out loud. If just talking to any old passerby would help, why do therapy?

Of course, the fact that I was thinking of Rose Noire's bizarre plan as therapy made me even more nervous than did Dr.

Smoot—who was babbling on about how it had felt, leaping out of bushes to scare people all morning. No wonder he hadn't gone home yet. Odds were most of my family hadn't minded a bit, and with them around, he probably fit in better here than he had anywhere in his life.

"That's great," I said. I began backing up in earnest. "Just keep it up and I'm sure you—"

The ground under my feet disappeared.

Chapter 22

"Are you all right?"

I don't think I lost consciousness, but I was too stunned to speak for a few seconds. Then I looked around. I was in a grave. A hole three feet wide, six feet deep, and—

Okay, maybe not a grave. It was about fifteen feet long. So either it was a grave for, say, two professional basketball players who insisted on going head-to-head in the afterlife, or it was more like a trench.

Still, not someplace I wanted to be lying, gazing up at an anxious, drooling faux vampire hovering solicitously over me.

"Can you give me a hand out?"

He frowned for a moment.

"No," he said. "I'm not that far along yet. I'll get thomeone."

His face disappeared. I stood up and tested all my limbs. Nothing seemed broken, despite the six-foot fall.

So why was there a trench in our side yard? Some utility problem? The gas came in the front, and the septic field was out back, so neither of them was apt to be involved. And the phone and electrical wires weren't buried. And, last I'd heard, cable didn't come out this far. What was going on? I began pacing up and down the trench out of sheer impatience.

Dad's head popped over the side of the trench.

"Are you all right?" he asked.

"Fine."

"Stay where you are."

As if I could go anywhere. I was about to start pacing again when the end of a ladder thumped down at the far end of the trench. I ran over and scrambled up and out of the trench.

"There you are," Dad said, beaming at me. "Randall Shiffley's gone off to fetch some of that yellow caution tape they use around construction sites, which should help a lot, but in the meantime, you've got to watch out for the trenches."

"Trenches? There are more than one of them?"

Evidently there were. Looking out over the side yard I counted ten of them, all neatly parallel, all three feet wide and spaced three feet apart. The area between the house and the barn was more than half filled. In a couple of places, boards had been placed across the trenches to make paths. I noticed that the last four trenches were only half as long as the rest, although they were visibly growing toward regulation size even as I watched.

"What is going on?" I said. "Are we digging in to resist an invasion? Or perhaps we've already had the invasion—someone dropped off a batch of giant moles?"

"It's the Sprockets," Dad said.

"The Sprockets?"

As if on cue, Rutherford Sprocket's head appeared in one of the trenches, gradually rising until I could see that he was pushing a wheelbarrow.

"It's quite ingenious," Dad said. "They figured out that if they leave a dirt ramp, it eliminates the need for a ladder, and makes it much easier to haul the dirt off."

Rutherford trundled his wheelbarrow load of dirt across the remaining undisturbed part of the side yard, emptied it onto a giant dirt mound there, and then vanished back into the hole again.

"Who the hell told the Sprockets they could ruin our yard?" I exclaimed.

"They said you did."

"They what?"

"It's for a good cause," Dad said quickly. "They only want to find their great-uncle Plantagenet's body. They said they told you all about it."

I strode over to the edge of the first trench, put my hands on my hips, and took a deep breath.

"Stop digging immediately!" I bellowed.

Heads popped up out of the trenches all over the yard, like startled prairie dogs. Several dozen heads, most of them belonging to members of my family. I assumed the few unfamiliar faces were auxiliary Sprockets recruited by Rutherford and Barchester, though for all I knew they could be my own relatives— distant ones lured by the promise of a larger-than-usual party this weekend, or perhaps newly acquired relatives by marriage. I noticed at least two Shiffleys, and made a note to triple-check the next few invoices from the Shiffley Construction Company, to make sure we didn't get billed for their digging services.

"Everybody out of the trenches!" I shouted at the sea of heads. "No more digging!"

Most of the diggers obediently began climbing out of the holes and scuttling away. The two Sprockets didn't move. I made my way over to the hole they were crouching in, leaping over each of the intervening trenches far more easily than I could have if I weren't so riled up.

"Out!" I said, pointing toward the road.

"But we're looking for Great-uncle Plantagenet," Barchester whined.

"I don't care—get out!"

"We only want to—," Rutherford began.

"Out! Now! Or I'll start filling those holes with you still in them!"

The two grudgingly dropped their shovels on their wheelbarrows and trundled them up the ramps. I dogged their heels until they'd loaded their tools in their car, and every so often, if they seemed to be slowing down, I bellowed "Out!" again. Quite cathartic, and I felt infinitely better as I stood by the side of the road, arms crossed, face still arranged in a severe frown, and watched them drive away.

"Good job," Rob said, joining me. "Although if I were you, I'd have made them put the dirt back."

"I just wanted them out," I said.

"Got that point."

"When Mother's finished with the visiting relatives, I'll get them to fill in the trenches."

"Hey, why waste all that digging?" Rob said. "Wouldn't take that much more effort to put in a pool."

"I just want the yard back."

"Suit yourself," Rob said. "I'm going to see what Dr. Smoot is up to."

Randall and Vern Shiffley returned and began roping off the entrenched area with yellow caution tape. And not a moment too soon—a small convoy of cars and SUVs had pulled up and begun to disgorge another flock of cousins. Most of them were carrying covered dishes, all of them were gawking up at the newly painted house, and none of them, of course, were watching their feet. If not for the Shiffleys' efforts, the trenches would have taken a heavy toll on the guest list and the supply of provisions. But after milling about aimlessly exclaiming over the trenches for a few minutes, they all wandered toward the front door or took the long way to the backyard, around the far side of the house.

Vern nodded absently and strode off toward the edge of the yard, where he pulled out a cell phone and turned his back. Randall came over to stand by me.

"That should take care of it," Randall said. "Nobody could miss all that hazard tape."

"You underestimate my relatives," I said. "And how wild tomorrow's party will get."

"Tomorrow's party? You mean today's party won't get all that wild?" he asked, indicating the swarms of relatives setting up in the yard.

"This is tomorrow's party," I said. "They're getting an early start on it."

He nodded.

"By the way," I said, glancing over to make sure Vern was still absorbed in his phone call. "You said that you couldn't count on Chief Burke clearing Charlie in time. In time for what?"

Randall hesitated for a few moments and glanced at Vern.

Chapter 23

I controlled my impatience and waited for Randall to speak.

"Charlie's a smart kid," he said finally. "Good at math. College material. Wants to be an engineer. And he's a good athlete, too—Virginia Tech offered him a football scholarship, so he can go without racking up a lot of debt. Only they hadn't quite signed the contract when Lanahan started making such a stink about his damned gazelle, and the college has been backpedaling."

"I see," I said.

"I can understand how they feel," Randall continued. "I wouldn't want a kid around who could deliberately steal that gazelle and shoot it out of pure meanness. It was a stupid mistake, yes, but a mistake. Charlie wouldn't hurt a fly, only the longer the stink about the gazelle went on, the less the college people seemed to believe that."

"Well, that shouldn't be a problem anymore," I said. "I gather Chief Burke wasn't ever that keen on trying to prosecute Charlie—no real evidence. With Lanahan gone, the whole thing will probably drop."

"Yeah," Randall said. "But if you think the college doesn't want a sneak thief and a poacher, how do you think they feel about a suspected murderer?"

"Surely they don't really suspect Charlie?"

"No more than anyone else who knows how to use a crossbow," he said. "But no less, either. So we need to get this murder investigation wrapped up as soon as possible."

"I'm sure Chief Burke is doing his best," I said. "He'll find out the truth."

"Someone has to," Randall grumbled.

Why did people always look at me when they said things like that?

"I thought you were going over to the zoo to count cages or something," he said.

"I did," I said. "But there was an animal-rights protest going on, so I decided to come back after they were gone."

"After they're gone? If you mean the SOB people, they've set up camp there, you know," Randall said. "I heard they were planning to stay there all summer, and without Lanahan to make a fuss, odds are they will."

"Oh, great," I said. "So much for getting into the zoo anytime soon."

"You could sneak in the back way," he suggested. He paused to grab a small fallen branch and snap off a six-inch-long stick. Then he squatted beside a small patch we'd apparently missed when sowing grass seed and began scratching in the dirt.

"Here's Lanahan's property." He marked out a rough rectangle in the middle of the dirt patch. "Front gate's here—" two slash marks across one of side of the rectangle "—and here's the road to town—" a long line that disappeared into the grass.

"Okay," I said. I had squatted down beside him, the better to see the map, though my ankles were already wobbling.

"Here's Vern's land, and our cousin Duane's," he said, marking two smaller plots along one side of the zoo—the left side, looking from the road. "You see a small dirt road leading off into the woods a little ways before you go to the zoo gate?"

"I think so," I said. If it was the same dirt road I was thinking of, I'd made a mental note of its location, wondering if it might offer a back way into the zoo if the Save Our Beasts protesters were still marching there when I returned.

"That marks the property line between Lanahan's land and Duane's," Randall said. "And farther back, between Lanahan's and Vern's."

"Check," I said. Nice of Randall to help me out—but I found myself wondering if he had some ulterior motive in showing me the back way to the zoo.

"All this belongs to the Bromleys," he said, indicating the area behind and to the right of the zoo with broad sweeping strokes of the stick, as if indicating that the Bromleys' rolling acres continued well into the grass and possibly beyond the barn. "Timberland. Pines for pulpwood. And old Jase Bromley doesn't rent out the hunting rights."

"Annoying, I'm sure."

"Wasn't a big problem, long as we had Uncle Fred's farm," he said, in a suspiciously innocent tone. "But if there's no hunting there, how come we hear gunshots sometimes?"

"Poachers?" I suggested.

"Could be," he said. "But right here's where Charlie shot that fancy gazelle," Randall said, jabbing the stick into the ground.

I studied the spot he indicated. It was clearly on Vern Shiffley's land, but near the point where his land, Mr. Bromley's, and the zoo grounds all met.

"When it happened, we first thought the gazelle had wandered over from the zoo property. There's a fence, but Lanahan never bothered much about keeping it in repair. But then we remembered the strange goings-on at Bromley's. And Bromley's fences have been falling down for years. There's stretches where there isn't even a fence between Vern's land and Bromley's. Just

Bromley's 'Posted: No Trespassing' signs, and most deer don't pay much attention to those."

"But what would the gazelle be doing on Mr. Bromley's land in the first place?" I asked. My wobbling was getting worse, and I almost fell right in the middle of the Bromleys' acreage, so I put a hand down to steady myself.

"You ever heard of canned hunting?" Randall asked.

"Not until recently."

"There you go," Randall said, as if that solved everything.

"You think Lanahan was running canned hunts?"

Randall nodded.

"And he was doing it on Mr. Bromley's land," I continued. "So there wouldn't be any evidence that animals were being killed on the zoo property."

"I wouldn't put it past him."

"With Mr. Bromley's cooperation?"

"That I wouldn't know."

Or maybe just didn't want to say, since Mr. Bromley, unlike Patrick Lanahan, was from an old local family.

"Whether Mr. Bromley knows or not, this gives him a possible motive for the murder," I said.

"Motive, yes," Randall said. "But no opportunity. Broke his leg about ten days ago, and last I heard he was still in the Whispering Pines Nursing Home being rehabilitated."

"Okay, then he's out, but plenty of people around here disapprove of canned hunts. The Save Our Beasts people, and maybe Montgomery Blake."

"Hell, we disapprove of them," Randall said, shaking his head. "Most real hunters do. We hunt for sport and to put meat on the table, not just for trophies. What's the sport in shooting an animal that has no chance of escaping? And most of those clowns don't aim for the head or the vitals—they aim for someplace that won't spoil the trophy, which means that the animal dies a slow, painful death. You ask me, these game ranches should be outlawed, and if Lanahan was involved with that, I'm not sorry to see him go. But we wouldn't try to kill him over it. We were just trying to sic the law on him."

"Sic the law on him? You mean you reported your suspicions?"

Randall nodded.

"Chief Burke didn't do anything?" I asked.

"He's been trying," Randall said. "But I don't think a city fellow like him knows how to go about it. He had that deputy of his, young Sammy Wendell, skulking around the woods, trying to catch whoever was doing it."

"And Sammy didn't have any luck?"

"You ever heard Sammy crashing around in the woods? No self-respecting poacher's going to hang around long enough for Sammy to catch him. Besides, Bromley's land is half in Caerphilly County and half in Clay County, and the Clay County sheriff has a peculiar lack of interest in the whole problem. I'll give Burke one thing: he works hard and he's honest."

By my count, that was two things, but I just nodded and studied the map some more, to make sure I had the location of the convenient dirt road firmly in mind.

And my mind was busily turning over the implications of what Randall had said. Which seemed to confirm what I'd learned from the film student. While Lanahan, the improvident zookeeper, might be annoying, it was hard to imagine anyone killing him. But Lanahan, mild-mannered zookeeper by day and evil organizer of canned hunts by night—he'd probably have a whole pack of people after him.

If there were canned hunts, and if Lanahan was involved. After all, given what had happened with his nephew Charlie, Randall might not be the most impartial judge of Lanahan's character.

Meanwhile, Vern had finished his phone call. He looked our way, and Randall, with a nod of farewell, went over to join him.

I studied the map for a few more minutes, than scuffed the dirt till I'd erased it. I wasn't sure why—after all, I had Chief Burke's permission to visit the zoo, or at least his grudging tolerance.

But it occurred to me to wonder what the chief thought of the accusations against Lanahan. I went into the house to see if the chief was still occupying our dining room or if he'd been displaced by some new four-legged arrivals.

Chapter 24

I found the chief still ensconced in the dining room, though he'd moved the table he was using as a desk so it wasn't directly beneath the chandelier where the sloth was hanging. Sloths, actually; now there were two of them. Dad and Montgomery Blake were also there, haranguing the chief about something. Rather, Blake was haranguing and Dad was standing by, with an anxious expression on his face. The chief looked even more irritated than he usually did in the middle of a case, so I decided to see if interrupting him would help.

"I have some information for you," I said, joining the trio. "Did you know that the Save Our Beasts people have been picketing the zoo?"

"Save Our Beasts?" the chief echoed.

"It's an animal-rights group," Blake said.

"I guessed as much," the chief said. "But which one? What with the college and all, we have several of them operating in town. I hope they're not nutcases who think we should let the wolves and grizzlies roam freely in their original habitat, whether or not there are thousands of people living there now."

"I think these nutcases may have a legitimate beef," I said. "They think Lanahan was arranging canned hunts."

"It's an outrage!" Blake boomed. "No civilized society should tolerate it. The very idea—"

"Cut the editorial," the chief said.

"How can you condone this barbarous behavior!" Blake shouted. Despite his advanced age, he had a good, strong orator's voice. Through the window, I could see people outside in the yard looking up to see what was wrong.

"I'm not condoning anything," the chief said, interrupting Blake. "I spent thirty years trying to keep the good citizens of Baltimore from slaughtering each other. It's left me with a strong repugnance toward violence of any kind. And a strong respect for the law—"

"Canned hunting's illegal in this state," Blake said.

"And Lanahan was innocent until proven guilty," the chief said. "My officers searched every inch of the zoo grounds, looking for evidence of wrongdoing. And when we couldn't find any, I called state game wardens and U.S. Fish and Wildlife agents in—they couldn't find anything either. So either Patrick Lanahan was a hell of a lot smarter than any of us, or maybe the rumor was just that—a rumor."

"So this has nothing to do with Patrick's murder," Dad said with a sigh.

"I wouldn't go that far," the chief said with narrowed eyes. "Regardless of whether Lanahan was a saint or a sinner, anyone who's all fired up about how he treated animals has a definite motive for his murder."

With that, he stomped off.

"He means me, of course," Blake said. "Won't be the first time I've been persecuted for my beliefs."

He strode off, head high.

"Pretentious old goat," I muttered. Unfortunately, I didn't mutter softly enough.

"Meg!" Dad exclaimed.

"Sorry," I said. "But Blake really gets on my nerves for some reason."

"He does good work," Dad said. "Really he does."

But his tone sounded ambivalent. Was he still worrying about whether Blake was a fake? Or was I, perhaps, not the only member of the family who was starting to find Blake hard to take?

I strolled outside. It occurred to me that now might be a good time to talk to Blake—while he was still worked up about the canned hunts, and perhaps not as much on his guard as usual.

But I lost him in the crowd—how many relatives had we invited, anyway, and were they all going to show up a day early? I made my way to the side yard, where, thanks to the trenches, it was a lot quieter. I ducked under the yellow tape and stepped over half a dozen of the trenches until I stood in the middle of the side yard. I decided I liked the vantage point. I could see more newly arriving cousins trotting up the road from their increasingly distant parked cars. I could see the growing swarm who had already arrived setting up food and drink in the backyard. And they could see me, and we could wave back and forth at each other, but it was peaceful out here in the trenches, and if anyone tried to sneak up on me, I'd see him a long way off.

Luckily no one did except Michael, who appeared at the edge of the yard and, after glancing curiously at the trenches, began making his way across them to where I stood.

"Giant moles?" he asked.

"Close," I said. "Sprockets. Searching for their long-lost and presumed suspiciously dead great-uncle Plantagenet."

"Edwina's late husband, the botany professor? I thought he'd disappeared while on an orchid-collecting expedition to the Amazon."

"That's the Sprocket party line, but apparently a dissident minority think he's buried in our basement."

"Then why are they digging out here?" Michael asked, studying the excavations.

"Police won't let them in the basement," I said. "I assume they're warming up for an attempt to tunnel in. So how's the unpacking going? You're not overdoing it, are you? Do you need my help?"

"Don't worry," he said. "We have more than enough help. We'll have everything unpacked, assembled, and put away long before nightfall."

"And we'll be six months finding our stuff," I said. "But never mind."

"By midday tomorrow they'll all be having so much fun they won't notice when we sneak away."

"By midday tomorrow they wouldn't even notice if the house got up and walked away," I said. "If you don't need me, I'm going to find Mother and put her in charge of organizing a work detail to fill in the trenches. Though Rob suggested maybe we should just dig some more and plan to put in a pool."

"A pool," Michael said. He wiped the sweat off his forehead and looked around at the trenches with greater interest. "That's an interesting idea."

"Just tell the relatives what you want," I said. "Meanwhile, after I talk to Mother, I'm going back to the zoo."

"Is this a detective mission or an animal-welfare mission?"

"It's a saving-Meg's-sanity mission," I said, giving him a quick kiss. "Later."

I found Mother with Rob and Eric, down at the penguin pond. Eric was plastered against the chicken-wire fence, avidly absorbing every detail of the penguins' behavior. Mother was standing upwind, holding a sun parasol over her head and a small linen bag of Rose Noire's potpourri to her nose. Rob was sprawled in Dad's lawn chair, sipping lemonade.

"I'm sorry, Eric," Mother was saying. "But the penguins can't stay forever."

"But see how happy they are here," Eric said.

"I can't imagine anything would be happy living in a stench like that," Mother said, shuddering. "Meg, isn't there something you can do? Bathe them, perhaps?"

"Mother, they spend all day swimming," I said. "They don't need bathing."

"Perhaps if the water were cleaner," Mother said.

"It's a pond," I said. "How are we supposed to clean it?"

"I think they like the smell," Rob said, strolling up. "Just stay upwind and it's fine."

"That's a matter of opinion," Mother said, inhaling her pot-pourri.

"If they were staying longer, perhaps we'd worry about their hygiene," I said. "But this is just temporary, remember?"

"That's true," Mother said. Her expression brightened.

"But why can't they stay?" Eric said. "They're perfectly happy here."

"They're not our penguins, remember?" I replied.

"I'm sure they'd be much happier somewhere else," Mother added. "In a real zoo."

"Or back in the Antarctic where they originated," I said. "I expect they find the Virginia summers rather warm."

Mother sighed in sympathy and fanned herself a little more briskly.

"Oh, no," Eric said. "They like it here. Dr. Blake says if they were back in the Antarctic they'd get eaten. By killer whales and leopard seals. He said there's nothing a leopard seal likes better than a fat, juicy—"

"Speaking of Dr. Blake," Mother said, loudly. "Have you made any progress in figuring out who killed poor Patrick?"

"Is that a non sequitur, Mother?" I asked. "Or merely a subtle way of conveying your suspicion of our eminent visitor?"

"I'm sure you'll find out, dear," Mother said.

"I'm working on it," I said. "Meanwhile, when our helpful legions of family movers have finished with the unpacking, could you steer a few of them to the side yard, to deal with all those holes the Sprockets have been digging?"

"Deal with them how?" Mother said. "Your brother was suggesting—"

"Aunt Meg, look," Eric called. "The penguins are fighting."

Chapter 25

"Oh, no, dear," Mother said. "The penguins aren't really fighting. I'm sure they're only pretending."

Rob, who'd been taking a sip of his lemonade, spluttered and snorted most of it out again, and had to be pounded on the back.

No, the penguins weren't fighting. Apparently this was their mating season. One penguin—presumably male, though I suspect only another penguin would really know or care—had scrambled atop another penguin. He flapped his stumpy banded wings furiously. He paddled his tiny feet as if trying to outrun an army of leopard seals. And he trilled and cooed with impressive ardor. Unfortunately, he didn't seem to be accomplishing anything.

I couldn't tell whether the female penguin was sabotaging his efforts in some way or whether he was merely overexcited and inept, but he kept falling off. Sometimes to the left, sometimes to the right, occasionally backward, and once, rather spectacularly, forward, giving himself a painful-looking bonk on the head. In his defense, I noted, the female was almost perfectly round and her wet feathers looked rather slippery. For that matter, the male penguin was fairly round and slippery himself.

So maybe he wasn't all that effective, but I'd give him an A+ for persistence. And while the other penguins seemed completely uninterested in the spectacle, Rob was literally rolling on the ground, uttering the occasional shriek of laughter when he got his breath. Spike seemed to be having a great time barking at the whole thing, but Eric was watching with a puzzled frown on his face.

"What is he doing to that other penguin?" he asked.

"Meg, dear," Mother said, giving me a look that clearly told me to do something before Eric asked any really embarrassing questions. So far, Mother had always successfully delegated the job of explaining anything birds-and-bees related to someone else, and she clearly wanted to keep her record intact. And I had absolutely no desire to explain hot penguin sex to Eric.

"I'm going back to the zoo to snoop around some more," I said. "But I don't want anyone to know I'm there, so if anyone asks, cover for me, okay?"

As I'd hoped, this distracted Eric slightly from his fascination with the penguins.

"That's nice, dear," Mother said.

"Of course, I'm probably going to have to crawl under the fence or pick the lock in the gate or something."

"Shouldn't you take someone else along," Mother suggested. "To, um . . ."

"To serve as lookout? Who—Rob? He'd just fall asleep or something."

"I could help, Aunt Meg," Eric said.

"Hurry up, then," I said, looking at my watch. "I want to get this over with as soon as possible. Mother, while I'm gone—"

"Deal with the holes in the yard," she said, nodding.

"Maybe we'll see the SOBs again," Eric said as he picked up Spike and headed for the house.

Maybe I should have explained that remark to Mother, but I just left her with her mouth open and followed Eric.

I thought perhaps I'd lose Eric to the side yard, where some of the smaller cousins were using the trenches as the setting for a giant water-gun battle. But after a few curious glances, he turned his back resolutely on the fray and scampered on ahead of me to the car.

As we neared the zoo entrance, I slowed down and scanned the road to my left until I spotted what I hoped was the dirt road Randall had drawn on his map.

"I thought we were going to the zoo," Eric protested when I turned down it.

"We're sneaking in the back way," I said.

"Okay," he said, settling back in his seat. He didn't protest. He didn't even ask why. Was that a bad sign? Was he picking up too many misguided notions from his mystery-mad grandfather?

Or for that matter from his nosy aunt?

I shrugged, and studied the landscape by the side of the road.

Obviously, one of Lanahan's major expenses when he set up the zoo had been the fence—an imposing ten-foot-tall chain-link barrier. But either he hadn't gone for top-quality materials, or time and the elements were hard on fencing. In several places, trees had fallen on the fence, taking down a section or two, and the repairs didn't look sturdy. Perhaps he'd been running out of money when he made them. In one place, someone had sawed off and removed a six-foot piece from the middle of a fallen tree, just where it crossed the fence, but repairs hadn't yet begun—the fence had merely been propped up here and there with stakes. In another place, an even larger tree was still lying across the fence, flattening it nearly to the ground.

Randall Shiffley was right. Any reasonably enterprising ante-lope who wanted to leave the Caerphilly Zoo could eventually have found a large enough gap in Lanahan's badly maintained fences. Assuming, of course, that he could escape whatever inner enclosure Lanahan had provided to keep the antelopes from trampling the tourists. For all I knew the whole zoo could be in as ramshackle a state as its outer defenses. At any rate, I didn't think Eric and I would have a problem sneaking in, and neither of us leaped nearly as well as the average antelope.

The farther we went, the more rugged the road became. Eventually, it dead-ended in a small clearing. I saw a "Posted: No Trespassing" sign ahead—presumably the beginning of the Bromley fiefdom—and the zoo fence took a ninety-degree turn and continued off into the woods to our right.

I turned the car around and headed back. I parked near the spot where the tree still lay across the fence, and Eric and I used its trunk to walk across into the zoo as easily as if someone had built us a bridge. And when Eric picked up Spike to carry him across, Spike didn't even try to bite. Clearly I needed to talk with my sister, Pam, about Eric's need for a dog of his own.

I'd brought a small compass, in case we needed to blaze a path through the woods to the main part of the zoo, but after we'd stumbled a few feet through the underbrush, we came across a well-beaten trail. We turned right, more or less at random, and after five minutes of walking we came across an intersection with a signpost. An arrow pointing back the way we'd come showed that we'd been following the perimeter trail. To our left, another trail would take us to the lake. If we continued the way we were going, according to the sign, we'd arrive at the front gate. And even if we were tempted to stray from the paths, a five-foot fence ran alongside both the lake and front-gate branches—presumably a fence that normally enclosed the zoo's less lethal residents.

"Cool!" I said. "We're on the right heading."

Eric looked at me with mild curiosity, as if surprised that there could be any doubt. Obviously he had way too much confidence in my sense of direction.

After a few minutes, we reached a more open area and spotted a series of signs bearing the names and photos of the absent residents. From the positioning of the signs, it looked as if Lanahan had kept all the ungulates in one big enclosure, which meant the creatures shouldn't be too unhappy with their temporary quarters in Dad's pasture.

And had I really mispronounced "ungulates" when talking to Ray Hamlin, or was it possible that he didn't know the word? Of course, I only knew it from hearing Dad and Dr. Blake toss it around while talking about our accidental menagerie, but if I could pick it up that easily, couldn't Hamlin? Did he have any knowledge of zoology? And if he didn't, what qualifications did he have to run a zoo?

I reminded myself to worry about that later. Meanwhile, I pulled out my notebook and began taking notes. Llamas—well, we knew that already. Camels—check. Buffalo. Giraffes. No information on how many he had of each, but at least we knew what species to look for.

Apparently he'd kept the large flightless birds in the same enclosure with the hoofed animals. I spotted a sign for ostriches, and then one for rheas. The ostrich sign noted that "Ostriches are economically the most important species of ratite." I deduced that "ratites" was the jazzy scientific term for large flightless birds, though I made a mental note to check that with Dad before using it in front of Dr. Blake. I had gotten the impression that Blake considered me an intellectual lightweight, and I kept feeling the need to remind him that I wasn't a total idiot.

Eric soon tired of the empty cages and became impatient. So when we found Lanahan's office—a small prefabricated shed with a power line running to it and a "Zoo Administration" sign over the door—we didn't linger long. I rattled the doorknob, but not surprisingly it was locked. I peered through the windows and then moved on, looking for something to entertain Eric.

I lucked out when we hit the koi pond. Eric began amusing himself by dropping leaves onto the surface of the pond and watching the fish come up to investigate them. I suspected their interest in leaves meant that the koi were getting more than a little peckish. I made a note to find out what koi ate and draft someone to bring a supply of it out to them once a day or so, before they all either died or turned to cannibalism. Though perhaps it was too late on the cannibalism angle—the pond contained some awesomely huge koi.

"Don't let Spike fall in," I said, and headed back to Lanahan's office. Eric's occasional shouts of laughter and Spike's more frequent barking reassured me that they were happily occupied.

I spent a longer time peering in through the windows, and took some photos with my digital camera. Then I pulled out the screwdriver and dental picks I'd brought along.

The year I was twelve, Dad had taken a sudden interest in burglary—probably inspired by reading a few too many of Lawrence Block's Bernie Rhodenbarr books. He spent the entire summer trying to learn to pick locks. He always liked to involve a child or two in these educational experiments, and since Rob was too young to be trusted with sharp objects, and my older sister, Pam, considered herself too sophisticated for the project, I spent much of my summer learning along with him. Dad had proved a singularly inept burglar, but I'd gotten good enough to handle reasonably simple locks. I'd kept his burglary tools, just in case. And luckily, Lanahan's door didn't have a complicated lock. I set to work.

Of course, I'd gotten out of practice. One of the drawbacks of living honestly, or at least being organized enough that I rarely misplaced my keys. I poked and prodded for about fifteen minutes without much success, but at least I was beginning to get my

burgling skill back. From time to time, I could hear Spike barking in the distance, as he and Eric continued to explore the zoo.

Victory! I glanced around to make sure no one was watching,
then opened the door and slipped inside.

Lanahan obviously wasn't a minimalist. The office was chock-
full of every kind of clutter: books; office supplies and equipment; foods, both human and animal; assorted veterinary
supplies; toy animals in various sizes; framed photos; enough
rocks, branches, dried flowers, leaves, shells, and other bits of
nature to fill a museum.

Every kind of clutter except one: paper. Lanahan's desktop
was completely paper free. Not too weird—he could have been
one of those people who insist on clearing their desk at the end
of every day. If I cleared my desk, I'd only lose the contents for
the next six months, but some people found it useful.

The desk drawers and the file cabinet were unlocked, but
they contained no files, only a few empty green hanging folders.
But I found several boxes of manila file folders, the top one half
empty, so he must have done filing at some point. And the stack
of green hanging folders was overflowing, as if someone had
piled up two or three boxes' worth on top of the open box.
Putting them back after emptying them, perhaps?

So much for finding files to help me with the animals.

I considered the possibility that the chief had hauled away all
of Lanahan's papers for analysis, but that didn't sound like his
usual procedure. He had so little room down at the station that
he wasn't prone to hauling off huge wholesale lots of evidence.
He'd examine everything in place, then lock it up and go away
again. If there had been anything to examine.

I went outside again, and spotted four industrial metal trash
barrels. I went over and peered inside them, one after another.
No papers. Plenty of drink cans, paper cups, candy wrappers,

soda bottles, empty cigarette packs—the usual detritus you'd pick up if you were cleaning up after the public.

Four trash barrels, and an indentation for a fifth. Not a clean indentation, but a blurred series of overlapping rings, as if the trash barrel had been picked up and put down in much the same place a few hundred times. Each of the remaining four trash barrels was surrounded by a similar set of rings.

And ten feet away was another indentation, this one sharper and surrounded by a slightly scorched area of grass.

At a guess, someone had been burning papers in a trash barrel and then taken the barrel away. Unless I was jumping to conclusions. I'd have to find a way to test my assumptions. Maybe pretend to Horace that I already knew all about the missing files.

Spike's barking interrupted my thoughts. Not that he hadn't been barking intermittently the whole time I'd been snooping in Lanahan's office, but this sounded rather frantic. He'd probably smelled the lingering scent of some animal large enough to make an hors d'oeuvre of him and was boldly issuing challenges to an empty, echoing cage. Silly dog. Eric had brought him; I'd let Eric deal with him.

I had squatted down to study the area of scorching around the trash barrel when Spike's barking hit a new pitch, with a sort of yelping note.

Chill, I told myself. He's with Eric. Eric's a reasonably sensible kid—he'll call for help if something's wrong.

"Aunt Meg! Help!"

I abandoned Lanahan's office and took off in the direction of Eric's cry.

Chapter 26

Eric's voice and Spike's bark seemed to be coming from some place I hadn't been yet, near the back of the zoo. I raced over a small rise and found myself trotting downhill toward an enclosure that was larger and much more elaborate than any I'd seen so far. A short outer fence kept visitors six feet away from a tall inner fence. Inside the inner fence was a ten-foot vertical drop down into the main part of the cage. Opposite me, the ground rose in a series of concrete terraces that were supposed to look like naturally sculpted rock and failed miserably. In two places, large clumps of jungle plants almost hid the cavelike openings in the concrete, though the camouflage would have been more effective if they'd bothered to plant clumps anyplace other than right in front of the cave mouths.

Welded to the outer fence was a sign that said "LION (*Panthera leo*)." And then below that, "Reggie."

No wonder Spike was barking so fiercely. He'd found his way unerringly to the cage occupied, until recently, by the largest, most dangerous animal in the Caerphilly Zoo. He'd probably gotten so frustrated at not receiving any answer to his challenges that he'd fallen in out of pure exasperation. And Eric had fallen or climbed in after him.

I scrambled over the outside fence and peered through the bars of the inner barrier. Yes, Spike and Eric were both standing at the foot of the sheer concrete wall, gazing up at me. They didn't look hurt by their fall.

"Are you all right?" I asked.

"I'm fine," Eric said. "But hurry! What if he comes out!"

I was opening my mouth to remind him that the zoo was empty when a low, rumbling noise echoed through the cage—much like Spike's growl, but three or four octaves lower. It seemed to be coming from one of the openings in the concrete wall at the opposite side of the cage.

Great. A lion in the den. One who probably hadn't been fed since Patrick's death.

"Try to shut Spike up," I said as I looked around for some way to rescue them.

"I've tried," Eric said. "He just bites me and barks even louder."

He sounded scared. Hell, he sounded as if he were hanging by a fingernail over the edge of hysteria, and I understood just how he felt.

Nearby I spotted a coiled garden hose. Just the thing! I ran over, grabbed it, and raced back to the cage.

"Aunt Meg, hurry!"

"I'm lowering a rope," I said as I tied one end of the hose to the bars. Then I flung the hose down into the cage.

"That's a hose," Eric said.

"Pretend it's a rope," I said. "Can you pick Spike up and hold on to it?"

"I can't even reach it."

I peered down. Unfortunately, the hose I'd found wasn't a normal-length hose. It was a mere stump of a hose. Eric was jumping up, trying to reach the end of the hose, but his best efforts were still a foot short.

"Can you find a longer hose?" he called.

Okay, there probably were more hoses around. I was about to go and look for one when the lion roared. Not a big roar, but then we were awfully close to it.

Eric whimpered. Spike shut up. He turned to face the sound, all his fur seeming to stand on end, and uttered one gruff, challenging bark.

Okay, I'd give him top marks for courage, but zero for brains.

"Stand back," I said. "I'm coming down."

Jumping into the lion's den might not have been the smartest move, but I couldn't bring myself to walk away and look for another hose if the lion was about to emerge. I was taller than Eric; I could lift him up to reach the hose, and then climb up myself. So I scrambled up the bars of the inner fence, maneuvered over their curved tops, climbed down the other side, and then slid down the hose. I was in too much of a hurry and landed off-balance, scraping both palms and ripping the knee of my jeans. That was bad, wasn't it? Didn't lions attack when they smelled blood? Or was that only sharks?

My arrival seemed to reassure Eric.

"I can climb up if you lift me up so I can reach the hose," he said. "But how are we going to rescue Spike?"

He got top marks for courage too, I thought, if he could worry about Spike at a time like this.

"We're going to tie him up in your T-shirt," I said. "And then one of us can carry him out."

"I'd probably better do it," Eric said. "He doesn't bite me nearly as much as he bites you." He sounded a little calmer. Maybe worrying about Spike distracted him from his fear. If so, he was welcome to haul the little furball.

To my surprise, my plan worked rather well. We wrapped the suddenly cooperative Spike into a neat little bundle, and then, using the leash and Eric's belt, we rigged a harness that would let one of us sling him over our backs for the climb up. Pretty good, considering how hard it was to keep my hands from shaking every time the lion growled. Thank goodness Reggie seemed to be a lazy, procrastinating lion, taking his own sweet time coming out to devour us. Eric insisted on carrying Spike, and eyeing how high I'd have to jump to grab the rope, I didn't argue.

"Okay, I'm going to lift you up now," I said.

Eric had gotten a lot heavier since the last time I'd lugged him around. I hoisted him up as high as I could, and he could still just barely reach the hose, which meant that getting out wasn't going to be a picnic for me, either. But I breathed a sigh of relief once he grabbed the hose. He scrambled up, nimble as a monkey, and then scaled the tall fence a little more slowly. Now that he was on the way to safety, I began looking around for something I could stand on.

"Don't let Spike loose till I get up there," I called over my shoulder. "We don't want to have to do this all over again."

"Okay," he called down, peering through the fence. "But you'd better hurry!"

The lion growled as if agreeing with him.

I jumped up and tried to grab the end of the hose. No luck. The second time fell short as well. The third time, I grabbed the hose. Success.

Then the hose snapped in the middle, dumping me in a heap at the foot of the wall. I hit my funny bone on the way down and landed on something that knocked the breath out of me.

"Aunt Meg, are you all right?"

I nodded. I didn't have the breath to answer. The lion growled again, and I suddenly felt a wave of fierce irritation at his damned repetitive growling.

"Some king of the beasts," I muttered, with what little breath was returning. "Hiding there in your den, deliberately growling just to scare people."

"What was that?" Eric called.

"Never mind," I said. "You go look for another hose."

"What are you going to do?"

"Wait here for you to come back with a longer hose."

"Okay," Eric said.

The lion's failure to appear had gone beyond luck and was edging into downright weird. Something odd was happening, and I had a hunch what it was. But I waited till I heard Eric's footsteps fade in the distance before moving. If I was wrong, I didn't want Eric to witness what would happen.

I scrambled up from the floor of the cage to the first level of the concrete terraces. There was an opening there, but it wasn't the source of the growling—that was coming from the opening in the second terrace. I climbed up another level, took a deep breath, and began carefully picking my way over to the den's mouth. I heard another growl.

"Aunt Meg, don't! We can find another hose; just wait a little longer!"

We? Eric had returned and was clutching the bars of the cage. Standing by him was Montgomery Blake.

"Get out of there!" Blake shouted.

Did he think I'd jumped in for fun?

"Find me a rope, then," I called back.

"Aunt Meg!" Eric called.

I stuck my head into the mouth of the lion's den.

Chapter 27

Outside, I could hear shouts from Eric and the old naturalist—probably because my arrival at the den coincided with another loud roar. I crawled inside, turned off the tape recorder, unplugged it, and carried it outside. I left behind the timer it had been plugged into.

"It's a fake," I said, holding up the machine. "I don't know what happened to the real Reggie, but he's not here any longer. Just this."

I shoved the tape player back into the den and began climbing down. I checked the other den, just to be sure, but the lion exhibit was definitely empty. Now that I could stop and think, I realized that most of the other cages still smelled as if animals had been living in them recently—a faint, not unpleasant blend of fur or feathers and dung. The lion's cage only smelled dusty.

But it was still a little spooky, and when Montgomery Blake finally came back with a larger, sturdier hose, I wasted no time climbing out.

"Do you realize what would have happened to you if there really had been a lion in there?" he asked, shaking a long, bony finger in my face.

"Do you really think I'd have stuck my head in there if I hadn't been pretty sure there wasn't a real lion?" I asked.

Blake looked shaken, and his face was pale and drawn. He re-

145

ally was over ninety, I realized. Most of the time he was so vigorous you forgot his age. Maybe almost seeing another human being turned into steak tartare upset him. He frowned, and turned to the sign on the cage.

"Reggie," he said. "I suppose that explains it. If the poor old beast really had been still alive, he'd be pushing forty."

"That's old for a lion?"

"Even older for a lion than I am for a human," he said with a harsh bark of a laugh. "Average lifespan in the wild is maybe fifteen, sixteen years. They could easily live another five or ten years in captivity, with proper treatment. But forty? I wasn't surprised the poor old thing stayed in his den growling all the time. That's one of the first things I was going to do, if I'd taken over—have the vet look over Reggie, and more than likely we'd find it was time to put him out of his misery. But still—what the hell were you doing in there?"

"Spike fell in," Eric said. "And I tried to rescue him, and I couldn't get out, so Aunt Meg came to rescue me."

"More guts than sense," Blake grumbled. "Risking your lives for a stupid little runt like that. Completely useless, these overbred toy dogs."

I'd had the same thoughts about Spike myself, when I was annoyed with him, but I'd earned the right to think them—I had the bite scars to prove it. Where did Blake get off, insulting a harmless dog in front of his owners? Well, mostly harmless.

I was about to tell Blake off, when I saw Eric frown at Blake, open his mouth—and stop. He took a couple of deep breaths and closed his mouth again, though he didn't look as if it were easy. Smart kid. I followed his example. What did I care what Blake thought of Spike?

"You said something just now," I said aloud. "If you'd taken over—was that something that might have happened if Patrick hadn't been murdered?"

"Still might happen," he said. "He tried to borrow money from me a year or so ago—some excuse about temporary cash-flow problems. I told him the only way I'd lend him anything was if he opened the books to me and my auditors and followed my instructions on how to solve his problems. He turned me down then, but last month he finally got so desperate that he agreed."

"So he opened the books to you."

"He was going to. That's why I'm here in Caerphilly—seeing whether we can save the zoo or whether we need to close it and find homes somewhere else for the animals."

"Do you know what animals he has?" I asked.

"Supposedly," Blake said. "Of course, the totals might be inflated—he did still have Reggie on the roster. Probably a few other animals who died of old age or possibly inadequate medical care. Though I admit, so far I haven't detected any signs of neglect or mistreatment."

"Could you give me a list of his animals?" I asked.

"Why?"

"Because apparently Lanahan fostered them all out with people who had no idea what they were taking on, or at least no idea how long they'd be stuck with them," I said. "And Dad seems to have extended an open invitation to anyone who can't cope to drop their charges off with me. I'd like to know how bad it's going to get."

Blake hooted with laughter at that.

"I can imagine!"

Then he frowned at me for a few seconds, as if calculating. Was he trying to figure out if I could be trusted with the list? He was definitely up to something.

"I can probably pull a pretty accurate list together," he said. "No idea where they are, of course. I'll be back at the hotel tonight. Bring your father if you like. I'll give you the list, and we can talk about how to cope with your new charges."

"Possible future charges," I said. "And temporary charges at that."

Blake barked his staccato laugh and strode off.

"Where are you going?" Eric called after him.

"To inspect the lagoon," Blake said. He turned around and fixed his hawklike glare on Eric. "Want to see if Patrick got all the animals out of it or if he left a few alligators behind?"

"Alligators?" Eric echoed. "Meg, can we go see the alligators?"

I hesitated. I didn't want to take the time, and I wasn't in the mood to spend more time in Blake's company. But I had just led Eric into serious danger, and I felt guilty about it.

"If you're too busy, he can come with me," Blake said.

I liked that idea even less. What did we really know about Blake? Quite apart from the usual worries one would have about entrusting a child to a stranger, Blake seemed to care more about animals than people. If the alligators were starving and saw Eric as a tempting tidbit, would Blake find their point of view reasonable?

"Aunt Meg, can I go see the alligators? Please!"

Just then a solution appeared.

"There you are." My brother walked around the corner of a nearby building. "Hey, Meg, what are you doing here?"

"Like Dr. Blake, I'm investigating," I said. "What are you doing here?"

"He drove me out here," Blake said. "Confounded doctors took away my license two years ago. Don't see how they expect a body to get around without a car."

"Please," Eric whined.

"Yes, Eric, you may go with your uncle Rob and Dr. Blake to see if there are any alligators in the lagoon," I said. "And your uncle Rob will bring you safely back afterward."

I glared at Rob, attempting to communicate that I expected to get Eric back without any bite marks or missing parts.

"Alligators!" Rob said. "Cool!"

"Come on, then," Blake said. He strode off, with Rob trailing after him. Eric started to follow, then turned back and frowned.

"Aunt Meg? It was really weird what happened with Spike."

"What do you mean?"

"I had to go, so I found the bathrooms—they're down by the lion's cage. That's why I went down there. And I didn't think I should take Spike inside, so I tied his leash really tight to a railing. And while I was inside, he started barking, and I went out and he was gone. And I'm pretty good at knots."

"You think someone untied him?"

Eric shrugged.

"I don't know, but it sure was weird," he said. "And I could hear him barking, and I followed the sound, and he was already down in the cage. How do you suppose he got down there?"

"Through the bars."

"Yeah, except there's this screen—I guess it's to keep little kids out. I didn't think he could jump high enough to get over the screen."

"Never underestimate Spike's ability to get himself in trouble," I said. "After all, he thought there was a lion in there. He probably jumped higher than he'd ever jumped in his life!"

Eric thought about this for a second, then smiled.

"Yeah, I guess he was in a hurry to fight the lion. Come on, Spike."

He turned and ran off, with Spike scampering along beside him.

I returned to the lion's cage and examined the fence. Yes,

there was a heavy wire screen covering the bottom three feet of the fence. Unlike some parts of the zoo, the screen was in good repair—I could find no holes or gaps in it.

So there was no way Spike could have fallen in by mistake. And although I'd pretended to think it possible, to reassure Eric, I also didn't think Spike could possibly have jumped over the wire screen, even with the promise of a lion on the other side. And how had he managed to fall so far without hurting himself?

Someone had deliberately put him in the lion's cage.

Though I often joked about strangling Spike, the idea of someone actually trying to harm him sent me into a cold fury.

Of course, it might not have been Spike they wanted to harm. Anyone who knew us or had been spying on us might have guessed that Eric would try to rescue Spike—and would certainly have expected me to go in after either of them.

Suddenly the day didn't seem nearly as warm and bright, and the silence and emptiness felt ominous.

"Don't be ridiculous," I muttered. Throwing an eight-and-a-half-pound dog into a cage was one thing. Tackling me was quite another.

I'd ask Rob later how he came to be separated from his passenger, and whether they'd seen anyone else at the zoo.

For now, I decided to retrace my steps to the car.

On my way, though, I scoped out the area near the lion's cage—the last part of the zoo I hadn't inventoried. Apparently this was where Lanahan had kept his more dangerous guests. I found the spotted hyenas' cage. It didn't make me feel one bit fonder of them to know that their names were Winken, Blinken, and Allan. I found myself closing the door to the cage marked "Bobcat (*Felis rufus*): Lola." Lola clearly wasn't there, but it still made me nervous, seeing the door to her former lair hanging open.

Though maybe someone had opened it recently. I saw fresh scuffmarks in the dirt inside. Probably Eric, exploring. Maybe I should talk to him about risky behavior. Or, more likely, get someone else to do it—someone who hadn't spent the afternoon leaping into a lion's den. I latched the door cage and moved on.

I stopped by the zoo office to close and lock the door again, then took the perimeter trail, hiked back to the edge of the zoo property again, and used the fallen-tree bridge to cross the fence. But just as I was unlocking my car, I heard an odd thunking noise out in the woods—as if someone were hitting a tree with a hammer. But it wasn't the steady tapping you'd hear if someone was using a hammer—just a single thunk.

I stopped, listened for a few moments.

Thunk! There it was again. Coming from the other side of the road, away from the zoo.

I used my remote to lock the car again, shoved the keys in my back pocket, and went to investigate.

I tried to move quietly, though I suspect that, like Sammy, I could be heard by any real woodsman within a mile. Still, it was a pleasant walk—and not one I would have dared make during the winter, when no amount of bright orange could guarantee that a passing hunter wouldn't mistake me for potential venison.

The thunks continued, at random intervals, and a little louder as I approached their source. I was slowing down, listening for another thunk to make sure I was heading in the right direction, when something whizzed by my head, nicking my cheek before skittering to a stop a few inches away.

I dropped to the ground, clapping a hand to my stinging cheek. Then I pulled my hand away and looked at it.

I was bleeding.

Chapter 28

Only a trickle, but it shook me up—especially since whatever had nicked me had missed my eye by only an inch.

I crawled back a few feet and found the weapon: a crossbow bolt.

I lay on the ground and listened. I heard two more thunks. Then something else skittered through the leaves to my right.

I got up, stuck the bolt in my back pocket, and began running to the left, trying to circle wide before approaching the source of the thunking again.

In a few minutes, I found myself peering out of the shrubbery into a clearing. A young man with the tall, lanky look of the Shiffleys was standing there with his back to me. He held a crossbow. As I watched, he lifted it and released a bolt. It flew toward a tiny target at the other side of the clearing and hit with a loud thunk!

Odds were I'd found young Charlie Shiffley, whiling away the time until hunting season in a rather dangerous manner.

I wondered why he hadn't heard me coming until I noticed the iPod tucked into an armband on his left bicep and the cord that led to the tiny speaker buds in his ears.

I got a better look when he bent down to pick up another bolt from a pile at his feet. Unlike his body, his face was noticeably less angular than Randall's or Vern's. Either his mother's features were softer than his father's, or he hadn't quite lost his baby fat. His face was slightly spotty—only slightly, but remembering how I'd felt about pimples at his age, I suspected he considered himself hopelessly disfigured. Actually, he wouldn't look all that bad if he'd just shave—his upper lip had the slightly soiled look of someone who really shouldn't bother trying to grow a mustache. Still, not bad for a teenager. He was probably quite a hit with the girls at Caerphilly High.

His face was also a lot more expressive than those of the older Shiffleys. His lips moved from time to time, though from a distance I couldn't tell if he was mumbling the words to a song under his breath or cursing quietly. And after observing him for a few minutes, I realized that his expression didn't vary much. Most of the time, he wore a glum look of abject misery. Occasionally he'd frown, and even more rarely, when he made a particularly good shot, a swift, triumphant smile would flicker across his features.

So was this the face of a careless but essentially well-meaning young man who'd accidentally shot an exotic animal, or the face of a cruel and deliberate poacher? More important, was it the face of a lucky young man feeling a combination of relief and guilt because Lanahan's death had had ended a persecution that threatened his future? Or a ruthless killer who'd made his own luck with the very crossbow he was holding?

I waited till he put down the bow and walked over to the target to retrieve his bolts before stepping out into the clearing.

"Practicing for anything in particular?" I asked.

How annoying that my dramatic entrance went completely unnoticed, thanks to his trusty iPod. I watched as he pulled the bolts out of the target, and then, when he turned to walk back across the clearing, he noticed me and jumped a foot.

"What are you doing here?" he asked, detaching himself from his headphones.

"You do realize that if you miss that target, you could skewer anything or anyone who happens to be passing back there?" I asked.

"It's posted no trespassing!" he said. He sounded fierce, but his face looked scared.

"Oh, and that makes it all right to shoot passersby?" I said, gesturing at the gash on my cheek.

"It's posted," he said, but from the way he hunched his shoulders slightly I could see he was backing down.

"And I heard a suspicious noise over here and came to investigate," I said. "What if you'd been a poacher? If I spotted a poacher on your father's land, what would you want me to do—ignore it?"

"If you spotted a poacher, smart thing to do would be run away as fast as you could," Charlie said. "You don't want to mess with those guys."

"Good point," I said. "I'll tell your uncle Randall he should have warned me about that while he was showing me the back way into the zoo."

The mention of his uncle seemed to reassure him a little, as I'd hoped it would. He nodded, and stood, slouched, looking as if he wished I'd go away.

"You should put a bandage on that," he said, looking at my cheek.

"Do you have one?" I asked.

He shook his head.

"I'll probably live," I said.

He hunched his shoulders again. I fished in my pocket and found a tissue. I used it to blot my wound while Charlie shifted from foot to foot.

"So you're keeping in practice for the hunting season?" I asked.

He shrugged.

"Just letting off steam, really," he said. "I mean, everything's so screwed up now."

"Like what?"

"Like my scholarship."

"That's right," I said. "Your uncle Randall told me about that. Congratulations."

"Thanks," he said. "Except with everything that's happened they'll probably take it away."

"What do you mean by 'everything that's happened'?"

"You haven't heard about Mr. Lanahan from the zoo trying to get me arrested for shooting one of his animals? I thought the whole town knew."

"I hadn't until yesterday, when your uncle told me something about it."

"Yeah," he said, kicking at a tree root. "And the people from the university weren't too happy about the whole thing. I thought it would be okay once Chief Burke refused to charge me with anything, but then it seemed like the university still might take my scholarship away because of Mr. Lanahan suing me. That doesn't seem fair!"

"No," I said. "But colleges are like that—they hate bad PR. My fiancé teaches at Caerphilly College, and I'm beginning to realize that anything I do to get myself in trouble could hurt his career."

"Yeah," he said. "So I guess when they hear I'm a suspect in a murder, that'll kill it for sure."

"Not necessarily," I said. "Being a suspect isn't so much a problem—we're all suspects. Getting arrested wouldn't be so good. Mainly it's getting convicted that would really mess up your football career."

"It could happen," he said gloomily. "I mean, Chief Burke's a good cop, don't get me wrong, but he's a city cop. Doesn't know beans about hunting or crossbows or anything."

"Not many people do," I said. "Why hunt with a crossbow, anyway?"

"It's more challenging," he said. "Just as challenging as with a bow and arrow, in spite of what all the purists say."

"Purists?"

"Lot of bow-and-arrow hunters look down on crossbows. Say there's no skill involved, which is bull. Or that it's not fair because crossbows have a longer range, which isn't really true, either." His voice had risen, though he sounded more upset than angry or threatening.

"How far you can shoot an arrow or a bolt in target practice doesn't mean anything," he continued. "They've both got about the same effective range when you're hunting—maybe forty yards max. And when they talk about crossbow hunters not making clean kills, that just—"

"Chill!" I said, backing away slightly. Clearly Charlie hadn't yet acquired the typical Shiffley imperturbability. "I'm not arguing with you. Just asking."

"Sorry," he said. "It's just that I get in a lot of arguments about this with the traditional bow-and-arrow guys. Like the people over at the Sherwood Archery Range. Bunch of yuppies from the college, really. No crossbows allowed."

"Which is why you're practicing here in your own woods."

"Well, there's a range over in Clay County that allows crossbows, but it costs as much as the Sherwood place does for nothing more than a big field. Cheaper and easier to practice here."

"Show me how it works."

He looked surprised for a second, and then shrugged.

"Sure."

As he loaded the crossbow and demonstrated how to hold it, I was astonished at the transformation. With the crossbow in his hand, Charlie was a different person. More confident, more articulate, and even slightly taller, since he stopped slouching and stood up straight when holding his weapon.

The crossbow surprised me, too. I was expecting something sturdy and wooden—a mechanical version of Robin Hood's longbow. Instead, Charlie's crossbow looked as if you'd sawed off the front foot or so of a rifle and replaced it with a small bow stuck sideways at the end of the truncated barrel. Everything was metal or some sort of composite material.

"Want to try it?" he said.

I hesitated for a moment, then took it, trying not to show how uneasy it made me.

"Don't point it at anything you don't want to shoot," he said.

"Like a firearm; right," I said. I noticed that he was keeping a careful eye on the crossbow. I'd gone to watch my cousin Horace take his annual marksmanship test once, and the range master had shown that same watchfulness around the shooters, even though they were all law enforcement officers and theoretically trained in handling firearms. A reminder, just in case I needed one, that this odd plastic-and-metal contraption was a lethal weapon, not a toy.

Charlie corrected my grip on the bow and guided my fingers to the trigger. I lifted it and looked for a sight, then realized that it had a little telescopic sight mounted on top. I peered into the sight and moved the bow a little, and the distant target appeared, startlingly distinct. I could see how many deep scars and holes the bolts had left in it.

I tried to imagine how it would look to have something alive in the scope. I couldn't summon the image of a deer—they vanished from my mind as rapidly as they would flee through the woods if they'd spotted us. But I could call up Patrick Lanahan's face and figure easily. Too easily, in fact.

"Just pull the trigger," Charlie said. He didn't sound impatient. Just calm and reassuring, as if he'd talked a hundred newbies past their fear that the crossbow would explode if they pulled the trigger.

"Okay," I said. But I waited a few seconds until I could banish Lanahan's face from my mind and saw only the battered wooden target. Then I pulled the trigger.

The surge of power that followed surprised me—that and the loud thunk as the bolt struck the target.

"Good shot," Charlie said. I'd hit one of the rings, the third from the center.

"Accidental, I'm sure," I said. "And the telescopic sight makes it pretty easy."

"Not as easy as you'd think," he said. "That's another thing the bow-and-arrow hunters are always on about. How unfair the sights are. Still takes a good eye. You want easy—try this."

He took the crossbow from me, set it down on the ground, and twirled a couple of screws a few turns until he could remove the telescopic sight. He placed it carefully in a nearby canvas case, pulled out another, slightly different piece of metal, and screwed it into place atop the crossbow.

"Check this out," he said, handing the crossbow back to me.

I aimed at the target again. The new scope seemed a lot like the old—maybe with a little less magnification. Then Charlie touched something on the sight and a little red dot appeared on the target.

"Laser sight," he said. "Aiming for idiots."

"So you don't use this too often?" I said. As I moved the crossbow, the little dot moved with it, darting across a tree trunk, disappearing into a tangle of shrubbery, and then reappearing on the next tree trunk.

"Never for hunting, actually," he said. "But it's pretty cool for paintball. Psyches your opponent out. Guy thinks he's safe in the bushes, and then he looks down and sees that little red dot on his leg and splat!"

He laughed. I managed a weak smile in response, but I kept seeing the little red dot dancing across Patrick Lanahan's chest.

"Want me to reload it for you?" Charlie asked.

"No thanks," I said, handing him the crossbow. "I should be getting back. Give me five minutes to get back to my car before you start up again, will you?"

"Okay," he said, nodding.

I still set off at a slight angle rather than straight past his target. And I set a brisk pace, all the while wondering if I was stupid to trust him or stupid to worry.

Still, I was glad when I reached the car, clicked the door open, and sat down. Then I jumped up again with a yelp that was more surprise than pain. I pulled the crossbow bolt out of my back pocket and tossed it into the backseat before climbing in again and slamming the door closed.

I didn't start the car immediately. I pulled out the first-aid kit I kept in the car, did a more thorough job of cleaning the blood off my cheek, and applied a bandage. And all the while I was listening to hear the thunking start up again.

Charlie waited a lot longer than five minutes. Probably more like fifteen. He wasn't a stupid kid. And when you came right down to it, he was rather likable.

Neither of which ruled him out as a murderer. And it definitely wasn't just Vern and Randall who blamed Lanahan for endangering Charlie's football scholarship. Charlie had the same idea.

I sighed with exasperation. I hated thinking that such a likable kid might be a murderer, but nothing he'd said or done ruled him out. I needed to check him out.

Chapter 29

When I came to the intersection with the main road I turned left, toward Caerphilly, rather than right to go home. I had quite a few unanswered questions about Charlie Shiffley, and for that matter about Patrick Lanahan and Montgomery Blake. I thought I could find a few answers online, and I didn't want to wait until my nephew, Kevin, arrived to get our computers in working order again.

I left my car in the shade of a huge oak in the parking lot of the Caerphilly Library and strolled inside. Ellie Draper, the librarian, was reading to a group of rowdy toddlers in the children's room, so I waved at her and headed for the computer area. Luckily, it was at the other end of the library, but the din from story hour was still clearly audible. Of course, the noise level was probably the reason that only one of the library's two public-access computers was occupied. I snagged the other.

The cut on my cheek was throbbing a bit, so I muttered a few uncomplimentary things about Charlie Shiffley and went to check him out in the online archives of the *Caerphilly Clarion*. Lots of headlines from the sports section. Apparently Charlie was the mainstay of the high school football team—article after article credited him with scoring the winning points and beating school records that had stood since the fifties. My knowledge of football would fit nicely in a thimble, so most of the technical stuff was incomprehensible to me, but both local sportswriters seemed to agree that Charlie was something special—more than just this year's star athlete. Much rejoicing in print when Virginia Tech showed the good taste to offer him a football scholarship. Nice human-interest article, painting Charlie in a positive light—a B student, quiet and well-behaved. Active in the 4-H club. Spent his spring vacation volunteering on the Gulf Coast with Habitat for Humanity. The very model of a modern high school athlete. Nice picture of him surrounded by a dozen or so proud members of the Shiffley clan.

Nothing about the unfortunate slaying of Lanahan's stray antelope, though. Maybe the *Clarion* didn't want to tarnish the local hero's halo.

I Googled him, and found much the same information, plus a lot of Virginia Tech football fan sites discussing his high school record and college prospects in mind-numbing detail. So much for the scoop on Charlie.

I returned to the Google search page, typed in "Patrick Lanahan," and got thirty-nine thousand entries. The first twenty didn't seem to have anything to do with our zookeeper. I tried again, adding "Caerphilly" after Lanahan's name, and hit pay dirt.

First in the queue was the Caerphilly Zoo's Web site. I should have looked for that in the first place, I thought as I clicked the link. Maybe I could find out about Lanahan and get a list of the animals in the zoo at the same time.

The home page had a large picture of Lanahan clowning around with a chimpanzee. I winced as I wrote, "Chimpanzee(s)?" at the top of a blank page in my notebook. I had the feeling chimps were high maintenance and dangerously mischievous.

Lanahan looked much as he had when I'd seen him in our

basement. He had a little more hair in the photo, and looked a lot more animated, but it was definitely the same guy I'd seen. I shook my head and moved on.

Unfortunately, the site was reticent about precisely what animals lived at the zoo. Pictures of all kinds of exotic species decorated the pages, but most of the photos hadn't been taken at the Caerphilly Zoo—I could tell from the elaborate enclosures and lush vegetation. It was mostly a puff piece to get people to come to the zoo. Not useful for my purposes.

Lanahan's biography was more informative. Apparently his father had made a fortune in the chicken-farming business before selling out to one of the large national chicken-processing companies. Patrick had received his Ph.D. in wildlife science from Virginia Tech fifteen years ago, and then five years back he'd used part of his inheritance to establish the Caerphilly Zoo. Nothing about what he'd been doing in the intervening ten years. Perhaps none of the positions he'd held were sufficiently distinguished to grace the résumé of the executive director of the Caerphilly Zoo.

Of course, in the current job market, a lot of Ph.D.'s ended up driving cabs and flipping burgers. I Googled his father's name and came across an obituary from seven years ago. Okay, that fit. The old man dies; Patrick gets his hands on the family fortune, and two years later, the Caerphilly Zoo is born. Allowing for the time needed to probate the will and hunt down a suitable tract of land, that sounded perfect.

And five years to run through his inheritance and find himself and his charges at the brink of bankruptcy.

I printed out a couple of pages from the site, just in case, but I had a feeling I'd exhausted the information to be found online about Lanahan.

Unlike the Caerphilly Zoo, the Clay County Zoo didn't have a Web site. I did find an address, though, and checked one of the mapping sites to make sure I knew how to get there if need be. It wasn't hard—there were only three roads in Clay County large enough to have state route numbers, and luckily the zoo was on one of them. Not far from the courthouse, by the look of it, and I knew how to get there, thanks to Michael's and my sneak visit to get the marriage license.

I sighed, and tried to wiggle into a more comfortable position. But the library's computer chairs weren't designed for long-term comfort. Perhaps that was deliberate. The computers were supposed to benefit as many patrons as possible, and the chairs helped ensure that no one monopolized them. Already I could see an elderly man sitting at a nearby table, glancing up from his magazine from time to time to frown at me and look pointedly at his watch.

I returned to Google's main search page and typed in "Montgomery Blake."

The first entry was Blake's own Web site. I decided to check it out.

It was much as I'd expected. Reports on what the Montgomery Blake Foundation was doing to preserve the environment on six or seven continents. Pictures of Blake with birds, animals, and reptiles of all kinds—presumably grateful members of species that were considerably less endangered as a result of his efforts. Though most of them didn't look particularly grateful. The snow leopard cub was trying to sink his tiny, sharp fangs into Blake's hand. The monkey's bare teeth suggested that he was planning a similar attempt. The ten-foot snake draped like a stole around Blake's shoulders had lifted its head and turned it toward Blake, and was gazing at his face with calm, reptilian interest, as if trying to determine if he was edible. Or perhaps he was recognizing a soul mate.

A sudden wave of nostalgia hit me. Many of my fondest childhood memories were of Dad strolling into the kitchen or the living room holding a wild creature, dead or alive, to give us an impromptu biology lesson. Mice, voles, shrews, snakes, snapping turtles, rabbits, and bats from the backyard or the nearby woods, and an apparently endless supply of slightly flattened possums plucked from the highway. Most of the live animals would be trying to escape or to bite Dad—sometimes both at once—and invariably, if Mother was home, Dad's lectures would be punctuated by shrieks of "Get it out! Get that thing out of my house! Now!"

Once Dad had rounded up the largest possible audience—preferably all three kids plus any stray cousins or neighbors visiting that day—he'd adjourn to the backyard to continue his lesson, which invariably ended with someone taking a picture of Dad with his catch, followed by a trek to the woods to bury the dead animals or release the wild animals at a safe distance from any busy roads.

Apparently Montgomery Blake enjoyed similar amusements with the far more varied and exotic creatures he found in his travels, with the added advantage of a full-time professional camera crew.

But as I clicked and moused my way through Blake's Web site, I couldn't see any indication that he'd previously taken an interest in any small-town zoos.

Perhaps Patrick Lanahan had acquired an unusual specimen—some rare exotic or endangered animal hiding in plain sight among the more ordinary llamas and penguins. Once I finally got an inventory of the zoo's animals, I'd try to find out.

I was about to leave the site when, near the bottom of one page, I noticed a link to the Anthony Blake Memorial Fellowship. His father, perhaps? At any rate, it seemed like the first bit of personal information on the site, so I clicked the link.

"Checking up on our distinguished visitor?"

Chapter 30

I started, and turned to find Ellie Draper, the librarian, looking over my shoulder. As usual, her ensemble combined formality and practicality. She wore a conservative gray suit with a long, pleated skirt. A purple silk scarf tied around her neck added a note of color, as did her purple running shoes.

"Trying to see if he's really a suitable associate for Dad," I said. "Am I the only one who finds it a little strange for a world-famous naturalist to show up here in Caerphilly, worrying about the problems of a dinky little private zoo?"

"No, I have a suspicious nature too, but I think we're in the minority," she said. "Most proud Caerphilly residents are probably wondering what took him so long."

"So what do you think he's up to?"

She pondered for a few moments.

"Securing his legacy, perhaps?"

"He's got his foundation for that."

"Maybe he's decided he wants a more tangible legacy," she said.

"He could endow a building someplace," I suggested. "The college is always looking for people willing to buy it a building."

"Yes, but so many people have buildings. He's a big name— maybe he wants something bigger. The Montgomery Blake Zoological Park. The existing zoo isn't that large, of course, but he could be hoping to buy up some of the surrounding land and expand it."

"Yeah, that sounds like his style," I agreed. "Of course, that's assuming Patrick Lanahan was cool with turning his creation into Blake's legacy. What if he wasn't?"

"That might be something Chief Burke would find interesting," she said, with her usual enigmatic smile. Then she glanced at the screen and frowned slightly. "Then again, you do have to feel sorry for Blake. Losing his only son to cancer, and then his only grandson to that tragic accident."

I glanced back at the screen myself. The Anthony Blake Memorial Fellowship was given each year to the most deserving graduate student in zoology, conservation, or wildlife studies at Virginia Tech, where Blake himself had received his doctorate. Okay, so maybe he really was a zoologist, though I wouldn't take it as gospel till I'd checked with someone at Virginia Tech.

I skimmed the paragraphs on eligibility for his scholarship and how to apply, but the last paragraph seemed more relevant. Blake had created the scholarship after Anthony, the grandson, died in a car accident a few days before he was due to receive his Ph.D. in wildlife management from Virginia Tech.

"Only grandson or only grandchild?" I asked aloud. "Blake could be the old-fashioned kind of guy who wouldn't care nearly as much about descendants who can't perpetuate the family name."

"Possibly," Ms. Ellie said, chuckling. "But apparently the boy was his only grandchild as well."

"And how do you happen to know so much about Montgomery Blake?" I asked, raising one eyebrow at her.

"I have a suspicious nature, remember?" she said, returning my raised eyebrow. "I did my homework. Looked him up when he came to town."

Was she implying I had been remiss in not doing the same?

"I only found out yesterday he was here, when he showed up on our doorstep," I said, trying not to sound too defensive. "The move and all. How long has he been around?"

"About a week, that I know of. He's installed down at the Caerphilly Inn."

"Damn," I said. "If he'd just given Patrick what he's been spending on his hotel, the zoo would probably be out of debt by now."

"Are you finished with that?" Ms. Ellie said, gesturing at the computer.

"I will be after I see what I can find about Anthony Blake's tragic death."

"You won't find anything about that online," she told me. "It was fifteen years ago. I've got printouts from the microfilm. Why not come look at them, and give poor Mr. Hughes a chance to track his stock portfolio?"

I collected my printouts, yielded my seat to the impatient senior citizen, and followed Ms. Ellie through the door marked "Staff Only."

Her office was a stark contrast to the serene order that reigned out in the public areas of the library, and also a testament to the amount of work needed to create that order. The shelves were overflowing with books, catalogs, magazines, and stacks of paper, all bulging with bookmarks and paper clips. I removed a stack of magazines from her guest chair—recent issues of *Booklist* and *Library Journal*—and sat down. Ms. Ellie studied the chaos on her desk for a few moments, then unerringly pulled a manila folder out of one stack of papers and handed it to me.

I flipped the folder open. At the front, I found printouts of many of the pages I'd just scanned on Blake's Web site, followed by printouts or photocopies of a number of articles about him. A

Time magazine profile. A *Wall Street Journal* feature. Several Op-Ed pieces on environmental issues that he'd had published in the *Washington Post*. Nothing particularly new or enlightening.

Toward the back, I found two printouts that were obviously taken from microfilm. Both were from the *Collegiate Times,* Virginia Tech's student-run newspaper. The first was a short news article about the tragic accident in which the driver, Anthony M. Blake, had died at the scene. Two other students, passengers in Blake's car, had been seriously injured. Henry C. Carfield and James P. Lanahan.

"James P. Lanahan?" I said aloud. "That's Patrick, isn't it? That's the year he graduated from Virginia Tech."

"Yes," Ms. Ellie said. "Goes by J. Patrick these days, but it's him. Makes you wonder how likely it was that Blake would be helping him out now."

I flipped to the next article. This one had pictures. Blake's grandson had been a good-looking kid. Lanahan's picture was minus the interesting scar, so I assumed he'd acquired that in the accident.

"It says Blake's grandson was driving," I said, perusing the article. "Maybe the crash was his fault, and the other two were lucky to have escaped with their lives, and Blake wants to help them out."

"If that was the case, he could have helped Lanahan find a better job anytime over the last fifteen years," Ms. Ellie said. "I think he's up to something."

"Like what?"

She shook her head.

"And Dad thinks Blake's going to rescue the zoo."

"Maybe," Ms. Ellie said. "But I wouldn't count on it."

I brooded on this for a few moments. I found I was more upset over the prospect of Blake disappointing Dad than I was over the possibility that he'd killed Lanahan. Shallow of me, perhaps, but that was how I felt.

"Should be interesting to see how long he keeps up the pretense, then," I said. "If he has a clean conscience over Lanahan's death, he'll probably pack up and leave immediately. But if he stays around—"

"Could mean he's guilty," Ms. Ellie said. "Or just that he's afraid someone will suspect him."

"Mind if I make copies of these articles?" I asked, holding up the folder.

"You can borrow the whole file if you like," Ms. Ellie said. "Just promise you'll make good use of it."

"I will," I said.

I'd planned on going home, but as I drew near the road to the Caerphilly Zoo, it occurred to me that if I took it and kept on past the zoo, I'd eventually come to Clay Hill, the county seat of Clay County. In fact, Clay Hill was the only place in Clay County that even vaguely resembled a town. And if the mapping site I'd consulted at the library was correct, a mile or so before I came to Clay Hill, I'd find the Clay County Zoo.

Maybe it was time I checked up on Ray Hamlin.

Chapter 31

No protesters outside the Caerphilly Zoo. No hostile Clay County natives patrolling the borders. The peaceful rural vistas of Caerphilly County blended seamlessly into the peaceful rural vistas of Clay County. All very soothing until about two miles outside town, where what Michael and I called the seamy industrial district of Clay County began—a series of sprawling rural businesses. Most of them looked unprosperous, and all of them would have been on my target list for demolition if someone had put me in charge of the "Keep Clay County Beautiful" campaign. The Clay County Farmers' Market—converted at some point from a drive-in theater—didn't have much produce on sale. But from the number of pickups in its parking lot, the nearby Clay County Bait and Ammo shop across the street was thriving. It also seemed to serve as the headquarters for the nearby Clay County Gun and Archery Range. The Clay County Antique and Junque Market seemed to focus more on the junk side of the business, judging from the sprawling delta of merchandise strewn over the brown grass in front of it. In smaller letters at the bottom of the sign I saw the words "R. Hamlin, Prop." Ray Hamlin, the owner of the Clay County Zoo, or a relative?

Next to the antique and junk store was a small off-brand filling station and mini-mart—no sign, but I deduced this was probably the Clay County Service Station and quite possibly the

Clay County Supermarket. Between the gas station and Hamlin's Used Autos was a small dirt road with a sign pointing the way to the Clay County Zoo.

About half a mile along, the road dead-ended at a gate with a barbed-wire fence. On the left side of the gate was a small wooden shack, looking rather like the temporary fireworks shacks that spring up by the side of the roads throughout Virginia in the weeks leading up to the Fourth of July. To the right was an unpaved parking lot, its muddy, rutted expanse nearly empty. I stowed my car in a spot where I thought I could escape the mud without a tow and went to the ticket shack, where a bored young woman in a NASCAR T-shirt took my five-dollar admission fee and handed me a ticket, all without looking up from the supermarket tabloid she was reading.

I was tucking the ticket and my wallet back into my purse when a pickup careened up the road. I recognized the driver—Ray Hamlin.

"Well, hello there!" he called as he pulled up beside the ticket shack. From his tone, you'd think my visit was the most exciting thing that had happened in the history of the zoo. "What brings you to our neck of the woods? Checking out whether we're fit to take on your animals?"

"And curious about what your zoo is like," I said.

"You give her back her money," he said to the ticket seller, in a tone that implied that she should have known better than to charge me in the first place. The girl rolled her eyes and then glued them back on her magazine while she opened her cash box and extracted my five-dollar bill.

"There's no need—" I began.

"Nonsense," he said. "Professional courtesy—one zookeeper to another, right?"

He wheezed with laughter at this, and I chuckled politely.

"Let me show you around," he said.

"Sid wants to see you over at the range," the ticket seller said.

Range? I tried not to show how interesting I found the word.

"Right, right," Hamlin said. "If he calls again, tell him I'll drop by later. My brother, Sid," he said to me. "You see the shooting range on your way in? Sid runs it."

I nodded, and followed him into the zoo. Interesting. Maybe I hadn't kept my face as deadpan as I'd thought when I heard the word "range." Or maybe, if he was as much of an animal lover as he claimed, he was sensitive about any kind of association with the gun-toting hunters who probably did their out-of-season target practice at the range. Or just maybe, if he was one of the few people who knew how Lanahan had died, his tie to the archery range, not the gun range, made him anxious. I'd have to keep my eye on Ray.

But for now, I concentrated on seeing the sights at the Clay County Zoo. What few there were. Sheila Flugleman had been right—it wasn't much more than a petting zoo. Hamlin had a scattering of native animals that most of us could spot in our backyards for free—half a dozen Virginia white-tailed deer, some opossums, and a mixed collection of pheasant, wild turkeys, and grouse. But most of the inhabitants were familiar barnyard creatures, housed in easily accessible pens just inside the gate. Hamlin grabbed a small container of gray-brown pellets and handed another to me, and we strolled up and down the pens dispensing handfuls to the animals. Generic zoo kibble of some kind. The stuff didn't look particularly appetizing, but it must have tasted all right. When they saw us, the animals all crowded against the fence, sticking their heads over it if they were tall enough, and baahed, bleated, oinked, mooed, or whatevered for a taste of the stuff.

"Like I said, we don't have the range of animals Patrick had," Hamlin said, rattling his kibble container at a Shetland pony.

"Still interesting for city kids," I said. I held out a handful of kibble to the pony, which snuffled it up with velvety lips and then turned to Hamlin and whickered softly.

"Yeah," Hamlin said as he fed the pony. "Too bad there's a shortage of those in Clay County. Most of the kids here raise some kind of animals for 4-H."

"So Patrick's zoo was probably pretty tough competition," I said as we moved on to the next pen. The llamas who occupied it seemed just as eager for kibble as the pony.

"Not really," Hamlin said as we fed the llamas. "We get most of our business off tourists who follow the signs to the antique mart. Mom shops, Dad brings the kids here to keep them busy. Caerphilly's too far away to be competition for that."

"But if you had more exotic animals, you might get some people coming here primarily for the zoo," I suggested. "And—yikes!"

The smaller of the two llamas, not contented with his handful of kibble, had grabbed my purse strap with his teeth and was trying to drag me back. Hamlin had to distract him with a heaping handful of kibble to get him to let go.

"Sorry about that," he said when we'd gotten safely out of range. "Sneaky, those llamas. Try the goats."

The goats were evidently too eager to be sneaky. There were about a dozen of them, in various sizes and colors, and most of them were standing on their hind legs, their front feet propped up on the fence of their pen, bleating. They reminded me oddly of a painting by Manet, the one in which a sad-faced barmaid leans on the bar with both arms, her pose reflected by the mirror behind her. The goats, with their oddly glum faces, could have been competing to see who got to pose for a new, more rural version. By contrast, the few too short to follow their example were wriggling through the forest of legs to stick their heads out between the top and second rails.

"If I did start taking on Patrick's more exotic animals on a permanent basis, we'd probably sell the range," Hamlin said.

We? So he wasn't just related to the owner. He was the owner. Or at least the co-owner.

He chucked a handful of kibble into the goats' pen and watched most of them abandon the fence to fight over it.

"No sense asking for trouble," he said as he dusted the remaining fragments of kibble off his hand.

"What kind of trouble? Animals wandering over by mistake from the zoo to the range?"

"What?" Hamlin said, startled. "Hell no. That's Patrick's game. No, I meant trouble from those animal-rights activists."

"Oh, right."

" 'Cause you don't want to get those SOBs from the SOB mad at you," Hamlin said, wheezing again at his own joke. " 'Specially not that Che guy who leads them."

"Shea," I corrected.

"Yeah. Human pit bull, that guy."

"But he only cares about the rights of exotic animals?"

"Dunno. Maybe he cares about animals like mine, but he's smart enough to know he can't get much publicity out of them. They're not rare, they're not cute, they're obviously not starving, and most of them are animals people are too used to seeing on their dinner plates. No one wants a story like that. So they picket the Caerphilly Zoo and leave me alone."

"That makes sense."

"But it would all be different if I had a bunch of cute animals—those leemings of Lanahan's, for example.

"Leemings?" I said. "Oh—you mean lemmings. He had lemmings?"

We didn't have any lemmings yet, and I found myself visualizing a vast quantity of them swarming inexorably toward our house.

"Yeah, like the one Blake was carrying around on his shoulder on TV. Those monkey things with the long tails."

"Lemurs," I corrected.

"Whatever," Hamlin said. "Look, I'm not a fancy animal zoologist like Lanahan and Blake. I'm just a guy who loves animals. You tell me what I have to do to keep 'em happy and healthy, and I can do it, no problem. Can and will. I'm also a businessman. I know how to keep my budget balanced. Won't find me selling off the animals to devil knows who, just to pay the feed-store bill."

"Is that what Lanahan was doing?"

"I got no proof, but the way animals seemed to come and go . . ."

He let his voice trail off and shrugged. He tossed another handful of kibble to the goats and moved on to the sheep pen. The sheep were all looking in the other direction, apparently oblivious to the frantic excitement of the goats. As the kibble disappeared, the goats returned to the fence, one by one, and propped their front feet on it. Several of them were making reasonably good efforts to crawl over it. The sheep continued to gaze serenely into the distance.

"So you think Lanahan was involved in canned hunting?"

"I can't imagine he was involved in it," Hamlin said. "It's illegal in Virginia, you know."

"Involved at least by selling animals to the people who did organize canned hunts?"

"Could be," he said. "Selling's not illegal, you know. Wouldn't set well with most people around here, I imagine, but there's nothing illegal about selling animals. And I suppose if it came out he was doing it, he could always claim he didn't know what they were doing. If Chief Burke's smart, he'll go over Lanahan's papers with a fine-tooth comb. You find who Lanahan's been selling to, maybe you'll find his killer."

The sheep finally noticed our presence and shuffled over to beg for kibble. Hamlin had used up all his kibble on the goats. I dumped the last of mine into the sheep's pen. There were other enclosures, but what few animals I could spot were at the far ends, so I decided to skip them.

"Thanks for the tour," I said. "I gather anything that lives in a field you could probably take almost anytime, but you'd need time to find a home for anything that needs a special cage."

"That's about the size of it," he said. "And I bet it's the very ones we'd have to build something for that you're most interested in getting rid of. Those hyenas, for example. Bet you'd be happy to see the back of them."

"You have no idea," I said. "When I've got a list, I'll get in touch. Where can I reach you?"

"Hang on," he said. He pulled a wad of assorted papers out of his shirt pocket and shuffled through them for a few moments, glancing at several business cards until he came across the one he wanted.

"You can reach me here most days," he said. A card for the Antique and Junque Market. "I own a couple of other businesses—in fact, between me and my brothers, we own just about everything in Clay County that isn't a farm. But me, I'm trying to get out of the low-rent businesses. Used cars, bait and tackle, the shooting range—they're all very well right now, but you can see the writing on the wall with them. You get more of your gentrification going on, more rich commuters moving in, and your upscale businesses, like the antique market, are going to take off."

"Sounds like you have a plan," I said.

"I do indeed," he said.

Of course, to me it sounded like a flawed plan, if not a downright demented one. About the only sign of gentrification I'd seen in Clay County was the petition they'd been circulating to have the county's first traffic light installed in Clay Hill—and they were doing that only because they didn't want to be the last county in the state without one, not because more than three cars had ever reached the intersection at the same time.

But maybe I was being short-sighted, and Ray Hamlin was a man of vision, in touch with the pulse of his community. I wished him a good afternoon and went to extract my car from the muddy parking lot.

I stopped for gas at the service station on the corner—it was a good ten cents cheaper than in Caerphilly. Of course, odds were it would turn out to be so low-test that even my faithful Toyota would balk at consuming it, but I could still hope. I was frowning as I watched how rapidly the dollars rolled by and how slowly the gallons crept, even at this cheaper rate, and wondering if Ray Hamlin also owned the gas station, and whether there was any point to going in to find out. I could buy a soda from the grocery end of the little office. Yes, and then—

"Not you too!"

Chapter 32

I looked away from the gas gauge to see Sheila Flugleman standing in front of me with her hands on her hips and an expression of righteous indignation on her face.

"Not me too what?" I asked.

"So you're going to sell your dung to him too!" she said. "First Patrick and now you! Of all the low-down, sneaky things!"

"I'm not selling anything to anyone right now," I said. I glanced over at the gauge. Should I leave now, before Sheila really lost it, or stick around for the last couple of cheap gallons?

"Oh, so you just came all the way over to the Clay County Zoo to pet the goats," she said. "Explain this, then!"

She held up one of the little brightly colored bags she sold the zoo dung in. At least it looked like one of her bags, though I noticed that the product name had been changed from Zooper-Poop! to Dung-ho! A catchier name, but the quality of the printed package had gone downhill.

"Ah," I said. "Is this a rebranding effort or—?"

"That snake in the grass! Ray Hamlin! He pretended he was going to let me collect his dung, and all the time, he was planning this!"

She shook the Dung-ho! package in my face. Its contents rattled unappealingly. I backed up as far as I could without abandoning the gas hose.

"Well, for your information, I wasn't here to negotiate selling the zoo animals' dung to Hamlin," I said. To my relief, the gas pump clicked off, and I pulled the nozzle out of my tank.

"So you say!" she said, shaking her finger at me. "I'll have you both in court if—"

"Shut up and listen!" I said, gesticulating with the nozzle of the gas hose for emphasis. "I did not come over here to sell dung to Ray Hamlin! I had no idea he was in the market for it, and now that I know, I don't care. I came to see if his zoo was a suitable place to house the animals that are currently living in highly unsuitable quarters in our backyard!"

She began backing away slightly. I wasn't sure if she was cowed by the fierceness of my tone, or my waving the gas hose about.

"And we'll be making that decision based on the animals' welfare, not on what happens to their dung. And if you want to keep collecting the dung in our yard while the animals are there, go away and leave me alone!"

I hung up the hose with a flourish, ripped the receipt out of the slot, and threw myself into my Toyota. She stepped out of the way, and I pulled out of the gas station a little faster than was quite safe. Fortunately, the road was as empty in both directions as most of the roads usually were in Clay County, and after a mile or two, I calmed down.

And then it hit me. "First Patrick and now you," she'd said. Had Sheila found out that Patrick was planning to sell his zoo's dung to Ray Hamlin?

Of course, dung seemed an unlikely motive for a murder. But Sheila had been genuinely angry. Livid. If she'd run into Lanahan when she was that mad at him . . .

Of course, given the peculiar circumstances of the murder, she'd not only have to be mad at Lanahan when she ran into him, she'd also need to have a loaded crossbow in her hands. Still, probably a good idea to let Chief Burke know that there was bad blood between Sheila and the victim.

And probably an even better idea to see what was going on back at the house.

The cars were the first clue that things had gotten out of hand in my absence. As I neared home, I found myself in a pack of six cars following a tractor for the last several miles of the trip. Normally the tractors and I had the road to ourselves. And cars lined the road for the last half mile leading up to our house. Near the house, a young police officer was standing in the road, directing traffic. Not someone I recognized, so I deduced that Chief Burke had called nearby counties for reinforcements.

Well, that was a first. We'd never previously needed a police presence at the beginning of a party.

Of course, it wasn't just the party. I pulled up beside the young officer to convince him that I had the right to enter the driveway.

"You'll have to move along, ma'am, and park down the road," the young officer said.

"It's all right," Dad said, strolling up to the car. "She's family."

"They all claim to be family," the officer said, frowning.

"They are," I said. "But I actually live here." I reached down to fish out my driver's license. "This is my driveway, and—what the dickens is that?"

Shea and the rest of the SOBs were marching up and down in front of our house, carrying their "Let My Creatures Go" and "Animals Are People Too" signs and singing "We Shall Overcome."

"The chief told them they had to stay out of your yard and not block the road, or he'd arrest them," Dad said. "So far they're being very careful."

"That's nice," I said. "But I'd rather have them very gone.

Why are they picketing us, anyway? Do they think we're running a game ranch here?"

"Perhaps they're associating us with Patrick's misdeeds."

"Alleged misdeeds," I said. "And if you ask me, they're just too lazy to make new signs. And what's with the singing?"

"Oh, don't you like it?" Dad said. "That was my idea, really. For the longest time they were just trudging up and down in silence— not a very picturesque protest at all. So I taught them the song. I thought it would make a nice note of historical continuity."

I felt sure Michael's film student appreciated Dad's effort. He was standing on a stepladder across the road, filming busily.

"That's nice," I said. I handed my driver's license to the young officer. He peered suspiciously at it, and then, when he'd verified my address, he stood aside to let me pull into my own driveway. But he was still staring at me suspiciously.

No wonder. I was, theoretically, the hostess. He probably thought I'd planned everything that was happening.

In my absence, a prototypical Hollingworth family party not only had begun but had hit its stride earlier than usual for such events.

Apparently Michael had given in to the temptation to use the Sprockets' excavations as the starting point for a swimming pool. Dad had always had a sneaking fondness for water features of all kinds—ponds, lakes, streams, fountains, even fishbowls. Mother had spent much of her married life discouraging Dad's repeated efforts to irrigate the landscape around him. Perhaps I shouldn't have been surprised that Michael had caught the bug. He and a mixed crew of Shiffleys and Hollingworths were crouched over one of the tables, arguing and dropping bits of relish and potato salad onto some rough sketches. A work crew was busy filling in some of the ditches and joining others together, in a plan known only to themselves. Or perhaps there wasn't a plan at all; perhaps it was a free-form earthmoving event, with everyone pitching in to create or fill holes, according to his or her impulse of the moment. Perhaps I should suggest that at least one of the pool planners keep an eye on them.

But the hole fillers appeared to be in the minority, and their efforts were somewhat hampered by the fact that various other picnic guests found the trenches so interesting or useful. A quartet of uncles had decided that they would work splendidly for pit-roasting an entire pig. Many of the younger kids were playing an elaborate game, rather like a cross between tag and Whack-a-Mole, that required them to scramble in and out of the trenches with much squealing.

And a number of slightly older relatives, not realizing that Dr. Smoot's vampire guise was a form of therapy, had decided to join in the fun. I couldn't walk ten feet without having a figure in a black cape leap out of the shrubbery or pop up from a pit to laugh sepulchrally at me. Dr. Smoot was in his element— probably the first time in his life that he'd been a trendsetter.

Of course, it was a little incongruous, seeing vampires slinking about the yard on an afternoon so warm and sunny that many of the undead were wearing shades and sipping lemonade. Perhaps the incongruity was a key part of Rose Noire's therapeutic plan.

Rob sidled up and held out a tray of hors d'oeuvres.

"Squames de chats?" he murmured.

"Yuck," I said. "You're not going around saying that to everyone, I hope."

"Mais oui!" he said. "Evidently you're the only Francophone in the family. Everyone else just smiles, helps himself, and says thank you."

"Just don't get carried away and say it anywhere near Mother," I said as I helped myself to a couple of prosciutto-wrapped melon balls.

"Do you think I'm a total idiot?" Rob said. "Never mind; don't answer that."

He strolled away to offer the tray to another group of guests. I spotted a flurry of activity at the other end of the lawn and went to see what was up.

Dr. Blake was performing for the cameras again, presenting a pro-zoo case to counter the protesters out front—at the moment, he was holding forth on the important contribution zoos could make to conservation and the preservation of endangered species. He was speaking eloquently, and I approved of every word he said, but I suspected it wasn't playing as well as he wanted it to. Yesterday, he'd charmed the reporters with the lemur, but today's living prop, the baby possum, wasn't working as well. Why had he chosen the possum anyway—surely he knew better than anyone that the term "playing possum" had been coined to describe what possums do under stress. Apparently the baby possum had gone limp shortly after the cameras began rolling, and it looked rather as if Blake were posing for the cameras with a large dead rat draped over one shoulder.

While I was watching, he figured this out, and gestured to Dad to come and take the possum. The reporters all breathed a visible sigh of relief, and the cameramen, who had been focusing tightly on Blake's face, pulled back to show the rich panorama of activity around him—to the great delight of all my family members who wanted to lurk just behind Blake, making a V-sign behind his head and waving to people at home. The only people not happy with the situation were a couple of protesters in SOB T-shirts lurking at the back of the crowd, leaning on their battered placards and scowling disapproval at all comers.

I wondered if the demonstration had ended or if Shea had merely declared a break until Blake was finished and the SOBs could reclaim the spotlight.

185

Not my problem. I needed to find Chief Burke and tell him
the various things I'd learned today without giving him the impression that I was butting into his investigation. Probably not an
easy task.

Then again, maybe I didn't need to tell the chief everything.
Maybe I should find a middleman. I looked around till I spotted
my cousin Horace, leaning against the fence around the penguin
pen, digging into a plate of food.

Horace. Not only could I enlist him to communicate what I'd
learned to the chief, I might be able to get some useful or at least
interesting information out of him at the same time.

Chapter 33

I cruised by the buffet table, grabbed a burger, and joined Horace.

"You know I can't talk to you about the case," he said when I leaned against the fence beside him.

Apparently Horace knew me too well.

"Fine," I said. "We can talk about something else. Want to know what I've been doing today?"

"You mean you haven't been running around prying into the murder investigation?"

"I've been running around trying to do something about the zoo animals' plight," I said.

"That's nice."

"Of course, since the murder and the plight of the zoo animals aren't entirely unrelated—"

"Thought so."

"Never mind, then," I said. "I don't suppose the chief wants to know that Sheila Flugleman was furious with Patrick Lanahan because he was ruining her ZooperPoop! business. Or that both his fellow zookeeper, Ray Hamlin, and Shea Bailey, the temperamental head of the SOBs, suspected Lanahan of involvement in canned hunting. Or that fifteen years ago Lanahan survived the car accident in which Dr. Blake's only grandson died. I don't suppose any of that's of interest."

Horace's face didn't give away much, but I gathered at least one of my bits of information was news to him.

"I have no idea," he said. "But if you like, I'll ask him."

He took another bite of his corn on the cob.

"Sometime today, maybe?" I said.

"What's the rush? It's not like you're going anywhere."

Except I was, assuming nothing dire happened to cancel Michael's and my Plan.

"Oh, no rush at all," I said. "It's not as if a murderer were running around loose or anything."

"Everyone's so impatient," he said. "You almost never solve a murder this quickly, you know. The forensic work takes time. I'll tell the chief as soon as I finish my dinner."

I bit into my own burger, but curiosity got the better of me.

"So how easy or hard is it to do forensics on a crossbow bolt?" I asked. "To prove whose crossbow made the shot, for example?"

"We're trying to withhold the bit about the crossbow," Horace said. "You can't go—"

"I know that. That's why I'm asking you instead of, say, going to see Ms. Ellie at the library, or wandering down to the gun store and pretending I want to buy one."

"Okay," Horace said, slightly mollified. "We don't really know yet. It's not like you get a whole lot of calls for crossbow forensics. With firearms, it's mainly the rifling that lets you tie a bullet to a specific gun. That and the firing pin. Crossbows don't have either."

"So there's no point in testing them?"

"We're still going to test them, yes," Horace said. "The gun shop's lending us half a dozen brand-new crossbows that couldn't possibly have been used for the murder, and we're going to take them over to the Clay County bow range and test-shoot them and see what we can learn. And if we find out that shooting leaves some kind of markings on the bolt that we can tie back to a particular crossbow, then maybe there will be some point in seizing every crossbow in the county."

"That makes sense," I said. "And explains why Charlie Shiffley still has his crossbow to use for target practice, instead of having to turn it over to Chief Burke."

"When we find Charlie Shiffley, I think we'll be seizing his crossbow even if we don't yet know what to do with it," Horace said.

"You haven't found him yet?"

"No—and what's this about target practice? Have you seen him?"

"Yes, he was—"

"We've got to tell the chief."

He put down his plate and practically dragged me into the house. The chief was now sharing his makeshift office in the dining room with three overhead sloths and a cage full of exotic rabbits. He didn't seem particularly pleased with the company. Or, for that matter, particularly grateful to hear my news.

"Why the devil didn't you come straight back and tell us?" he snapped.

"Because I had no idea you were still looking for Charlie," I said. "He lives only a couple of miles from here, and his uncle and his father have been hanging around here most of the last day or so, and they knew you were looking for him. I assumed you'd already talked to him."

"Where exactly did you see him?" the chief asked.

I described the dirt road and the place where the tree had fallen over the fence. The chief turned down my offer to show them, which was just as well. If I went along, once I got to the place where I'd parked, the only thing I could do was wander around in the woods, hoping to hit on the clearing where Charlie had been doing his target practice, and they could do that much for themselves.

So as the chief and most of his officers drove off, sirens blaring, I watched from the front porch.

"Cool," Rob said from the rocking chair where he was lounging. "Something up?"

The thought of explaining my day made me feel suddenly tired.

"Who knows?" I said, sitting down on the top step.

I heard a gruff bark and looked down to see Spike, tethered to the porch railings.

"Here, Spike," Rob said. "Have another *squames de chats*."

He tossed something off the porch onto the ground beside Spike, who pounced on it and devoured it in a single gulp. I leaned against the railing and closed my eyes, enjoying the relative peace and quiet of the front yard.

"Where are they going in such an all-fired hurry?"

I looked around to see Vern Shiffley frowning at the departing police convoy.

"They're off to find Charlie," I said. "I'm afraid I let it slip that I'd seen him in the woods."

"Damn fool kid," Vern muttered. "Don't know what he thinks he's doing."

I could see a curious range of emotions on his face—not just the usual exasperation and protectiveness of a parent who sees his child doing something stupid, but a faint hint of fear.

"Does he even know the police are after him?" I asked.

"Course he knows," Vern said. "Chief Burke said he wanted to see the boy, so I told him."

"You're sure?"

"Of course! What kind of—"

"What exactly did you say?"

Vern thought about it for a second.

"He came in a couple of minutes after his curfew last night," he said. "He has a ten p.m. curfew on a school night, and midnight on weekends, and lately, more often than not, he's been careless about it, so I was a little short with him, maybe. I asked if he'd heard the news about Patrick Lanahan, and he said he had. And then I said that the chief wanted to talk to him, on account of the bad blood between us and Lanahan, and did he want me to go down to the station with him tomorrow. And he said no."

"Just no?"

"He said 'No, sir,'" Vern said. "I raised my boys to have manners. And I asked if he was sure, and he said 'Yes, sir.' I figured that was it."

"You were just going to let him go down to the police station by himself?" I asked.

"He's not a child anymore—he's eighteen. Old enough to make his own decisions, even if they're stupid ones."

I considered suggesting that maybe Charlie was old enough to do without a curfew, but I didn't want to get into an argument.

"No one should ever talk to the cops without a lawyer," Rob said, shaking his head. I was glad to know that Rob had absorbed that much wisdom from his time at law school. Given Rob's ability to get into trouble, it was probably worth the whole three years he'd spent learning it, even though he'd never gotten around to taking the bar exam so he could practice law.

"I can't believe he hasn't gone down there yet," Vern said.

"I can," I said.

"The hell you can," Vern snapped. "He didn't kill Lanahan. He's a decent kid."

"A decent kid, yes," I said. "But he's also a teenage boy. Based on my close observation of the species—"

"She means me, obviously," Rob said, nodding.

"And several of our nephews who actually are teenagers," I said. "Unless we're talking mental age, in which case you still qualify—"

Rob stuck out his tongue at me.

"Anyway, based on my observation of the species, you blew it. Left him an out."

"How do you see that?" Vern asked.

"You told him the chief wanted to see him," I said. "And you asked him if he wanted you to go down with him. But you didn't say to get himself down there today or else. So he's been procrastinating."

"She's got a point," Rob said. "When I was his age, that's exactly the kind of stupid thing I'd do."

Actually, I thought it was more than an even chance that Charlie was dodging Chief Burke, but I wasn't about to say that to his father.

"You could be right," Vern admitted. "Eighteen or not, I just might tan his hide when I catch up with him. Of all the stupid—"

"Maybe you can help make up for it," I suggested. "If you find him before the chief does, and convince him to turn himself in—"

"Right," Vern said. "I'll set the whole family on him."

He strode out, pulling his cell phone out of his pocket as he went. I sat down on the top step, leaned against one of the railings, and closed my eyes. Peace. Quiet. Bliss.

"Poor kid," Rob said after a moment.

"You mean the poor kid who still might be a murderer, no matter what his doting father thinks?"

"Typical," Rob said. "Just because—whoa! Where'd he come from?"

I opened my eyes to see a wolf standing at the bottom of the porch steps, staring at me.

Chapter 34

I might have mistaken him for a large dog if not for the eyes. They were bright yellow and unsettlingly alien. Not like a dog's at all.

"Aren't they supposed to be in cages?" Rob whispered.

"Yes," I said. "But they're not completely vicious. Remember, Rose Noire and Horace were taking them for a walk this morning."

Of course, I suspected the wolves' outing had taken place immediately after they'd been fed, and with close supervision from Dad and Dr. Blake. And I didn't have Rose Noire's ability to co-exist with all creatures, great and small.

I remembered, suddenly, something I'd read about wolves—that they interpreted staring as a form of aggression. So maybe it wasn't quite the smartest thing in the world to be sitting here, exchanging stares with an unfettered wolf.

Except he wasn't really staring at me, but at something near my feet.

Spike chose that moment to utter a low, threatening growl. Absolutely no sense of self-preservation whatsoever. The wolf lowered its head slightly.

I reached behind me and scrambled for something to use as a weapon. The wolf flicked its eyes at me, decided I wasn't a threat, and focused back on Spike. My hands found something—Mrs. Fenniman had left her enormous black umbrella on the porch. It was three feet long and had a pointy end—it would have to do.

I grabbed the umbrella and whipped it around in front of me, leaping to my feet as I did so.

"Go away!" I shouted.

Then I jumped down between Spike and the wolf. I'm not sure the umbrella would have worked all that well as a weapon, but while I was jumping and waving it around, I accidentally hit the button to unfurl it. The black fabric expanded with a whoosh and a thump, startling the wolf. Startling me and Spike, too. He began barking, and thanks to the umbrella, I had no idea what the wolf was up to. I bent down and snatched Spike up. He tried to bite me, but was too busy barking at the umbrella to aim well. I shoved him behind me.

"Take Spike inside and get help!" I shouted. Rob grabbed Spike, yelped—which probably meant Spike's aim had improved—and fled inside. I shook the umbrella menacingly at the wolf, and then peered over the top to see if it was doing any good.

The wolf had retreated to the edge of the yard. Or maybe it wasn't a retreat—just a change in plans. I saw two other wolves join him, and the three of them loped toward the break in the hedge that led to the road.

The road that separated us from Mr. Early's sheep pasture.

I reached in my pocket for my cell phone and dialed 911. Debbie Anne, the dispatcher, answered on the second ring.

"Meg, is this really an emergency? Because the chief is—"

"The wolves are loose," I said. "And for all I know, the hyenas could be next."

"I'll put it out to all cars," Debbie Anne said, her tone suddenly businesslike. She hung up.

I was torn. Should I follow the wolves? Or run to the backyard to recruit help and see what else was happening?

Screaming erupted from the backyard, making the decision for me. I furled the umbrella and ran through the hall toward the kitchen.

When I flung open the back door, it smacked a wolf in the rump. He snarled, dropped the turkey carcass he'd been holding, and whirled to face me. I shoved the point of the umbrella at him, pressing the button to open it as I did. I heard a yelp of surprise, and when I peered over the umbrella again, I saw the wolf fleeing across the yard.

Toward the llama pasture. Great.

Of course the llamas weren't in their pasture anymore. Two of them were at the far end of the yard, standing protectively in front of a small cluster of Mr. Early's sheep. The rest were wandering about as if enjoying the commotion, except for the smallest one, who was standing about halfway between the house and the pasture, digging in his heels and refusing to move while a man in an SOB T-shirt tugged at a rope tied to his halter. Foolhardy man: as I watched, the llama spat a large wad of green goop at him.

"Eeeeuuwww!" the man shrieked. "Gross."

The llama curled his lip and wrinkled his nose, as if not all that happy with the smell, either. The man dropped the rope and abandoned his efforts to move the llama. Instead, he ripped off his T-shirt and scrubbed at his face with it.

A lot of the animals were loose. The lemurs had retreated up to the top of one of the sheds and were looking anxious and sorrowful, but then lemurs' faces always did to me. Perhaps if I read lemur expressions better I would have known that they were inwardly laughing.

I saw a troop of spider monkeys running up and down the picnic tables, snatching food and throwing it at each other and anyone who came near. One of the stouter aunts was shouting,

"Bad monkey!" and trying to whack them with a plastic spatula, but they were a lot more agile than she was.

The camels were pacing slowly across the yard, grumbling to themselves and snapping at anyone who came near.

Several family dogs who'd been brought along to enjoy the party were either running around barking furiously or dragging their owners off their feet in their eagerness to join the party.

From the corner of my eye, I could see small animals fleeing into various hiding places from which we'd have the devil's own time extricating them later.

"Meg! One of the wolves is loose!" Dad shouted, running up to me. "He's heading for the penguin pen!"

"They're all four loose!" I shouted back. "And the other three are heading for Mr. Early's sheep pasture."

Dr. Blake appeared.

"You see to the sheep!" he shouted to Dad. "I'll rescue the penguins."

They dashed off in opposite directions, each recruiting volunteers as he went.

I realized there was one animal group I hadn't seen yet. The hyenas. But I could hear their sinister faux laughter coming from the barn. I ran that way.

I dashed into the barn just as Shea Bailey clicked open the padlock that kept the latch to the hyenas' cage secure.

"Don't you dare!" I shouted, running toward him.

He smirked, stuck his own screwdriver and dental pick in his pocket, and reached for the latch.

I tackled him.

He was a big guy—five or six inches taller than me and solidly built—but I had momentum and surprise on my side. We landed in a heap on the barn floor.

"Don't you dare let them out, you moron!" I shouted. "You'll only—"

He punched me in the face. Hard.

And then he leaped up and ran over to the hyena's cage.

After a couple of seconds of lying on the barn floor, stunned with pain and anger, I jumped up with a scream of pure fury and went for Shea. Luckily Michael and Sammy ran in just as I got my hands around his throat. Michael dragged me away, and Sammy restrained Shea—which didn't take much of an effort. I suspected he wasn't trying to break away from Sammy so much as hide behind him.

"Get that harpy away from me!" Shea shouted.

"Are you all right?" Michael asked.

"He punched me in the face," I said. I was mopping my bloody nose with the bottom of my shirt and blinking back involuntary tears.

"He what?" Michael whirled and took a step toward Shea.

"She started it!" Shea whined, backing slightly. I didn't blame him. Michael didn't often lose his temper, but when he did, watch out.

"Never mind that now," I said. "He was trying to set the hyenas loose. Let's make sure he doesn't succeed. Someone check to make sure their cage door is securely closed."

Sammy hurried to do so. Shea backed away, glancing from me to Michael, as if not sure which of us was more likely to strike.

"Wow, a little push and they'd have been loose!" Sammy said. He pushed the latch more securely closed. Then he bent over to retrieve the padlock.

Shea kicked him in the rear, and sprinted for the barn door. Sammy fell against the cage, to the great delight of the hyenas, and then landed on the ground with the padlock still in his hand.

"Damn!" Michael exclaimed. With a visible effort, he turned away from the door through which Shea was fleeing, and restored the padlock to the hyenas' cage. I raced to the barn door, pulling out my cell phone as I ran.

"Just let him go!" Sammy said.

"I'm not chasing him," I said. "But I'm checking out which way he's heading, so I can tell the chief when I report that Shea was trespassing and turned the animals loose."

"Good idea," Michael said. "I'm sure the chief can think of all sorts of other interesting things to charge him with."

"Assault and battery, maybe," Sammy suggested. "Doesn't look as if the nose is broken, but you're going to have a really impressive black eye."

"And maybe the chief should take a close look at what Shea was up to Friday night," I said. "Because as an animal-rights protest gesture, letting the animals go seems pretty stupid. But it would make a pretty good diversionary tactic, wouldn't it?"

"I guess," Michael said. "But I'm not sure I see what he's diverting our attention from."

"Neither do I," I said. "That's why I said it was a pretty good diversionary tactic. As soon as we get all the animals back— hello, Debbie Anne? Sorry to bother you again so soon. . . ."

Chapter 35

It took several hours to round up the fugitive animals.

The wolves were our first priority. Fortunately, none of them seemed to be alpha wolves, or even particularly bloodthirsty—though when they suddenly appeared out on the road, where the protesters were still diligently marching and singing, they made quite an impression. About half of the protesters fled, screaming, while the other half valiantly leaped to the rescue of the sheep that they assumed the wolves were after. Not that the sheep were in immediate danger. Some of them were loitering in our backyard, under the protective eyes of the llamas. The few still in the pasture spotted the wolves within seconds and fled in the direction of their barn. Any ambition the wolves might have had to nibble on the fleeing sheep or the protesters vanished after they'd been whacked a few times with a "Let My Creatures Go" placard. They seemed almost happy to see Dr. Blake when he showed up with crates to ferry them back to their enclosure. Especially the lone wolf who'd been dashing about in the backyard. After escaping from my attack umbrella, he'd spent the rest of his brief spell of freedom dodging kicks from the two largest llamas.

Mrs. Fenniman gathered up most of the meat that had been on the picnic tables during the monkeys' rampage and slung it into the wolves' cage.

"They're on carefully controlled diets!" Dr. Blake protested.

"Time they had some fun, then," Mrs. Fenniman muttered as she tossed a monkey-gnawed roast of beef into the cage.

Once the wolves were locked up and happily devouring Mrs. Fenniman's bounty, many of the mild-mannered animals appeared almost immediately out of whatever hiding places they'd found, as if eager to return to the safety of captivity. The main exceptions were the monkeys and the llamas. The monkeys retreated from the buffet tables to the trees and led squads of my relatives a merry chase for hours.

Apparently their valiant defense of the sheep had fired up the llamas, and they seemed determined to remain a part of the party. They spat gobs of foul-smelling green stuff on people who tried to lead them to the pasture, until everyone got the message and left them alone.

Through it all, the party continued unabated. The Shiffleys were notably absent—presumably they were all out looking for young Charlie—as were the police, who were pursuing both Charlie and Shea Bailey. And at any given time, several dozen of my relatives would be off in some remote part of the yard coaxing lemurs off roofs, convincing stubborn camels to stand up and walk, recklessly grabbing irritated porcupines, and managing to get bitten and scratched in such large numbers that Dad found himself operating an impromptu field hospital.

Meanwhile, Mother's troops were scurrying around to replace the food the monkeys had eaten or spoiled. I pointed out, several times, that only a small portion of the assembled provisions had been out on the picnic table during the monkeys' raid—probably less food had been spoiled than we usually had left over after one of my family's bashes. But no one paid the slightest attention to me, so I eventually gave up.

Anyway, perhaps they had a better handle than I did on how much food would be needed for this particular party. Apart from more than the usual number of relatives, we also had quite a few visitors. About twenty of the SOBs were still around. Apparently the animal prison break had been the work of Shea and a small hard-core cadre within the organization. The rest, after assisting in the wolves' recapture, stayed around to eat and apologize repeatedly for their leader's misdeeds.

"I mean, what a stupid thing to do," I overheard one of them saying. "Like turning a bunch of wolves loose at a picnic is striking a big blow for animals' rights."

"He yelled at me last week for getting a cat from the animal shelter," another one said. "As if keeping a pet were something really immoral."

"You know, I don't think he really likes animals all that much," the first one said.

And many Caerphilly residents seemed to be turning up—ostensibly to help with the animal roundup, though I didn't see many of them leaving when they found out that the roundup was complete.

Practically the only people I didn't see were the Sprockets. And that worried me. I'd been surprised how easily they'd let me evict them earlier, and I'd fully expected them to show up and try to resume their digging, under cover of the party. The fact that they hadn't seemed to indicate that they had something sneakier and more annoying planned. Like showing up in the middle of the night and beginning to dig with ponderous and unsuccessful efforts at silence.

So at dusk, with the animal roundup mostly complete and the party definitely hitting its stride, I was sitting in Dr. Smoot's Adirondack chair with an ice pack on my black eye, scanning the crowd with my good one, and fretting.

"Don't worry," Michael said, dropping by to check on me for the twentieth time. "We won't be taking any pictures tomorrow."

"Speak for yourself," Rob said. "I plan on taking millions."

"But not of Meg," Michael said.

"Aw, come on," Rob said. "I've never seen such an awesome black eye."

I glared at him, and he snapped yet another picture of me with the ice pack over my eye and nose.

"I think the ice pack's probably done all the good it's going to," Dad said.

"Better safe than sorry," I said. "Besides, it's soothing."

Actually, the ice pack was almost as annoying as Rob, and the intense cold was giving me a headache, and I might have abandoned it, except that Rob's annoying determination to take a picture of me with my eye swollen half shut had brought out my stubborn side.

"Dr. Langslow!" One of the off-duty protesters came running up, looking agitated. "They need you over in the trenches. Someone fell in, and we think he's hurt himself."

I followed Dad to the side of the house where the trenches were still in active use. A crowd had gathered around one of the trenches near the barn, and when I had wormed my way to the front of it, I saw Barchester Sprocket lying at the bottom. Rutherford Sprocket was standing directly across from me on the other edge of the trench, holding a shovel and frowning down at his fallen comrade.

"Ah," I said. "I was wondering when they'd show up. Is he all right?"

"We could sue," Rutherford said. "Incredibly dangerous, just leaving trenches lying around like that."

"There's caution tape around it," I said. "And in case you hadn't noticed, he fell in one of the trenches the two of you dug."

"Poetic justice," Rob said.

"Hoist by his own petard," Michael added.

"We could still sue," Rutherford said.

"I wouldn't," I said. "We have lawyers in the family."

"So do we."

"Lots of lawyers," I said. I looked around at the assembled crowd, about a hundred of them, most of them relatives. "Will all the family attorneys present please raise your hand?"

Seventy or eighty hands went up. In fact, about the only people who didn't raise their hands were the SOBs and Rose Noire, and I could tell she was tempted. For some things, like playing fast and loose with the truth when convenient, I could always count on my family. And at least a dozen of them weren't lying. I wasn't sure if Rutherford believed it, but he stopped muttering about suing.

"How is he?" he asked, looking down at Dad and Barchester.

"I think his leg's broken," Dad said.

"I didn't realize we'd been digging over there," Barchester said.

"I think we need to mark the trenches more clearly," Dad said. "Or we're going to have more casualties by the end of the evening."

"No we're not," I said. "That's it! Party called on account of darkness!"

Chapter 36

"Meg, be reasonable," Dad said.

"Darkness and excessive excavation. I *am* being reasonable. It's too dangerous to have a bunch of people partying in the dark with all these holes and trenches."

"But, Meg," Mother said. "Everyone's come so far, and they only want to have a nice time. You can't just send them home."

"Okay," I said. I climbed up on a picnic bench and took a deep breath.

"Party moving to Mother and Dad's farm!" I shouted. "Everyone grab the food and drink and head on over to the farm!"

To my amazement, it worked. People began packing up the dishes of food and the coolers of beverages and swarming, lemminglike, out to the parked cars.

"What a splendid idea!" Dad exclaimed. "I'm heading over to the hospital right now with poor Barchester, but I'll get over to the farm as soon as I can."

He trotted off beside the stretcher, looking cheerful, as he always did when someone was obliging enough to break a limb, slice an artery, or provide some other reasonably engrossing medical drama. Mother looked less than thrilled.

"Don't worry," I said to her. "If it's still going on when you're ready for bed, you and Dad are welcome to come back here. You can have your pick of the guest rooms."

"I suppose," she said.

"And didn't you say you had lots of odd jobs that needed doing around the farmhouse?" I asked. "While you've got everyone there, you can start recruiting people to do them."

"Now that's a thought," Mother said. She turned and walked toward the back door. On her way to the front yard to catch a ride, I hoped. But just as she was reaching for the doorknob, something caught her eye. She turned and stood on the back porch watching as Sheila Flugleman scuttled by with another bucket full of raw material.

"Meg," Mother said, in what the family called her grand duchess tone of voice. "Who is that . . . person?"

Oops. "Person" was bad. "Lady" would have meant that she was impressed and wanted a suitably formal introduction. "Woman" would have been neutral. "Person," with that slight pause, was as close as Mother ever came to using a four-letter word.

"Sheila D. Flugleman," I said. "Her family owns the Farm and Garden Emporium."

"Ah, the feed store," Mother said, nodding. Apparently she was not in a mood to cut Sheila any slack.

"What's she done?" I asked.

"She's been circulating through the crowd passing out flyers," Mother said. She reached into her purse and pulled out a sheet of paper, holding it by one corner as if it were made of Zooper-Poop! "And . . . collecting at the same time."

"Well, someone has to clean up after the animals."

"Not the sort of thing I expect to see at my parties. And not the sort of thing you want at yours, either, I should think," she added hastily when she remembered that she wasn't in her own garden.

"You know how hard small business owners have to work to

get the word out," I said. Mother frowned at this. After years of threatening, she was finally launching her own small decorating business. Launching it in both Yorktown and Caerphilly, in all probability. Surely she wouldn't condemn Sheila Flugleman for what she herself might soon be forced to do?

"Hmph," she said, pulling something else out of her purse. "If this is true, I hardly think she needs to waste her time bothering my—our guests."

She handed me a copy of that week's *Caerphilly Clarion*, folded open to an article about Sheila Flugleman, complete with a smiling picture of her holding a bag of ZooperPoop! next to her ear.

"It's the local rag, and her family's store is probably a big advertiser," I said.

"Yes, but according to that, she's going to be featured on Martha Stewart's show."

I winced. Mother had a love-hate relationship with Martha Stewart—not that they'd ever met. Mother admired Martha for doing things "properly"—which as far as I could see meant by hand in as old-fashioned, labor-intensive, nitpicking a manner as possible. But I could tell sometimes that she couldn't quite understand how Martha had gotten to be such a celebrity simply by doing things properly, when other people of equal taste and fastidiousness languished in obscurity.

"Maybe Sheila could introduce you to Martha," I said. "Good boost for the shop, once you open it."

Mother drew herself up to her full height. Which was exactly the same as my height, five ten—why did it look so much more impressive on her?

"I hardly care to be introduced to Martha Stewart by a purveyor of designer manure," she said, in her most glacial tone.

Oops.

"Just as well," I said. "After all, she's a suspect in Lanahan's murder."

"Do you think she did it?"

"Who knows?" I said. "But even being a suspect could spoil her chances of being on television. I suspect Martha prefers her guests squeaky clean these days. Legally speaking, of course."

"How unfortunate," Mother said. But she was smiling as she walked off.

Within minutes the yard was empty, except for the odd stray sheep and Michael.

"Good riddance," I said.

"Well, it was a nice party while it lasted," Michael said. "But we don't want to knock off too many guests the first day we're officially moved in. I'd go over to the farm to help out, but it's time I took off to pick up Mom."

"Now? I thought she wasn't coming in till evening."

"It will be evening by the time I get to the airport—she's flying into BWI instead of Dulles, apparently. Adds at least an hour to the drive, and I bet she saved maybe fifty dollars."

"Two hours, round-trip," I said. I thought of several other things I could add, but decided that none of them was something you wanted to say about a woman who was about to become your mother-in-law, so I bit them back. With an effort.

"Next time, I'm making the damned reservations," Michael said. "And any other time, I'd just hire a limo service to pick her up."

"Do you want me to come with you?" I asked.

"Do you want to come?" He sounded surprised.

"To be perfectly honest, no," I said. "Right now the last thing I want to do is drive a couple of hours and sit around in an airport. But I figure it's probably the last thing you want to do, too, and we haven't spent much time together the last couple of days, and maybe you'd like some company on the way up."

"I'd love company on the way up, but maybe I should go it alone. Spend some one-on-one time with Mom, to make up for the fact that we're going to abandon her on Monday."

"Good idea," I said.

"And when I get back," he said as he leaned over to kiss me good-bye, "I'll tell you all about orgling."

"Orgling?"

He made an odd gurgling noise.

"That's orgling," he said. "Part of the llama's mating ritual."

"Yuck," I said. "Let's stick to champagne and roses."

"If you were a lady llama, that would drive you wild."

"You've been watching the llamas mate?"

"No, all our llamas are geldings. But Dr. Blake has been telling me all about llamas."

"If he's been advising you to orgle at me, he's been spending too much time with his animals," I said. "I prefer human mating rituals, thank you."

"Hold that thought until I get back from BWI."

"I will," I said. "And meanwhile, speaking of Dr. Blake, I'm going to visit him. See if I can get some accurate information from him on the zoo's population."

"And maybe a confession to murder?"

"Unlikely," I said, shaking my head.

"I thought you suspected him."

"I do," I said. "But he's too sharp to confess."

"You've tried to get him to?"

"Well, no," I said. "He just doesn't seem like the confessing kind. Maybe I should try."

"Just be careful," Michael said.

"I'll make sure the staff at the Inn sees me arriving," I said.

"Do that," he said. "Or maybe you should just stay home and rest. Do you really expect you can solve the murder and the zoo's problems before we take off?"

"No," I said. "And when we take off tomorrow for wherever it is we're going, I'll gladly leave the murder investigation to Chief Burke and the fate of the zoo to Dad and Dr. Blake. But until then—"

"Until then, you're going to give it one last shot. Fire away, but be careful."

"Will do."

Of course, as I pushed my way through the departing crowds to my car, I wondered if being seen by the Inn's staff would offer much protection if I were seriously worried about Blake. The Inn was notorious as a place people went when they didn't want to be seen having lunch, dinner, or breakfast with someone other than their spouses. What if their guest services extended to providing alibis to special guests?

Or, for that matter, disposal of inconvenient bodies. Did the Inn's concierge have an alibi for the murder?

Okay, maybe that thought was a little too paranoid, but I'd certainly watch my back at the Inn. I was venturing onto Blake's turf.

I should make a point of letting Blake know that people knew where I was. Mention the fact that Michael might be calling the Inn to talk to me.

Just because the chief was busy chasing Charlie Shiffley and Shea Bailey didn't mean that either of them was definitely the killer. I still had the uneasy feeling that Blake's sudden appearance in Caerphilly hadn't been explained by the interest he was taking in the zoo.

Chapter 37

I had to drive a mile or so through the Caerphilly Golf Course to get to the Inn. I kept expecting a sleek, unmarked security vehicle to pull out from behind one of the well-manicured hedges or copses to bar the road, but I made my way unchallenged to a parking lot made of white gravel that gleamed like polished marble. I stashed my battered blue Toyota between a brand new Rolls-Royce Corniche and a Hummer that still had the dealer's suggested retail price sticker on it. The only other car in the lot that wasn't brand-new was a vintage BMW that looked as if it had been washed and polished daily by an army of chauffeurs. With my luck, the Toyota would develop an inferiority complex after an hour or two at the Inn, and refuse to start when I wanted to leave.

I crunched across the spotless white stone toward the front door, which was ostentatiously unobtrusive—in fact, almost hidden between wisteria vines dripping with lush purple flowers. The doorman's manner was scrupulously polite, and I resisted the temptation to explain that my jeans and T-shirt were absolutely clean.

"Meg! What are you doing here?"

I turned to find Dad strolling away from the registration desk. His jeans and shirt weren't the least bit clean—it looked as if he'd come straight from putting the penguins to bed. But he seemed completely at home, and a porter murmured, "Evening, sir," while passing him. Leave it to Dad to make himself at home anywhere.

"I came to see Dr. Blake," I said.

"Aha!" Dad exclaimed. Then he glanced around the lobby for possible eavesdroppers. When he spotted none, his face fell slightly, but he still lowered his voice to a suspiciously conspiratorial stage whisper.

"You suspect him of being the killer?" he asked.

The desk clerk looked up from his computer, ears almost visibly cocked to hear my answer.

"More important than that," I said, in my normal voice. "I suspect him of knowing precisely how many and what kind of animals there were in the Caerphilly Zoo."

"But I could—" Dad began, before realizing what he'd been about to say.

The desk clerk lost interest as soon as we stopped whispering.

"Yes, I know you could tell me if you had the time to sit down and make a list," I said. "But you've been rather busy caring for the animals. So I thought I'd bother Blake. And while we're both here, maybe we can pin Blake down on what, if anything, he's going to do about the zoo."

Not that I'd object to getting in a little prying about Blake's motive, means, and opportunity for committing the murder, given the chance. But I didn't want to set Dad off. Still, I was relieved that his presence meant that someone other than the staff of the Caerphilly Inn knew where I was.

"Great idea," Dad said. "And it gives you a wonderful chance to see the Inn!"

"Wonderful," I echoed. I glanced around uneasily. I'd been to the Caerphilly Inn before, but it never failed to intimidate me. Its brochure claimed that the building was a modern interpretation of a colonial-era mansion, inspired in part by Monticello, Mount Vernon, and other architectural masterpieces from the Old Dominion's more gracious eras. To me, it looked more as if Martha Stewart and the architect of Caesars Palace had gone ten rounds to see who got to have the last say in the decor.

Martha had won on a technicality in the lobby, which was filled with acres of chintz and enough distressed wood to gladden the heart of an army of termites. Rumor had it that Las Vegas ruled in the less public areas, especially the bathrooms, which were larger than most people's living rooms and equipped with both saunas and Jacuzzis. Or so they said—since the all-in price of a weekend at the Inn would have exceeded our monthly mortgage payment, Michael and I had spent our occasional romantic getaways in less rarefied quarters.

Dad, however, was charmed.

"What a lovely place!" he exclaimed as we strolled through the lobby. "Did you see the wisteria outside?"

"It's an alien invasive species, you know," I said. Normally he'd have been the first to point this out, but apparently he was still dazzled by everything associated with Blake. "And can you imagine how much water they use to keep the golf course that green? Not to mention the toxic chemicals. I can't understand how an environmental activist like Blake could tolerate a place like this."

"Well, he's a rich environmental activist," Dad said with a shrug. "You can't expect him to stay at the Super 8."

"Here's the elevator," I said, pausing by the call button. "You got Blake's room number, right?"

"Oh, he's not in one of the rooms," Dad said, breezing past the elevators toward a pair of enormous French doors beyond. "He's in the Washington Cottage."

Wonderful. Blake couldn't be content with an over-the-top

room in the main part of the Inn—he had to have one of the cottages.

Was I perhaps feeling a little jealous of someone who could afford the Inn's most expensive quarters? No—I was feeling a lot jealous. But at least I'd finally get to satisfy my curiosity about the cottages.

The Inn had three cottages—Washington, Jefferson, and Madison—each with its own private patio and a view of the Caerphilly Golf Course. When nearby Caerphilly College sponsored executive retreats and high-level economic think tanks, it always housed the most distinguished international economists and the richest robber barons in the cottages. For that matter, any really distinguished guest of the college could usually count on staying at a cottage—alumni who had given whacking great sums of money, or were expected to do so in future, for example. Michael always joked that if you could get a guest list for the cottages, the names would probably be the same as you'd find on most of the newer campus buildings.

"Why doesn't Blake take a few animals?" I muttered as we followed the quaint cobblestone path to his cottage. "He's probably got more room than we do. And he could turn the llamas loose on the fairways and save the Inn a little money on groundskeeping."

"I'm not sure the Inn allows pets," Dad said. "This is it."

We had arrived at the Washington Cottage, and were standing under a tall white veranda designed to echo Mount Vernon—although there were only four white pillars, not eight, and they were only about a story and a half tall. Still, it looked as if it might grow up to be Mount Vernon if you watered and fertilized it enough.

Through the door I could see parts of the interior. More chintz and old wood. The real Mount Vernon probably didn't contain a sleek modern laptop, but even that was perched atop a Chippendale writing desk.

Blake answered the door seconds after Dad knocked. "There you are," he said. "My, that is a spectacular black eye you've got."

I forced a smile, and reminded myself to be polite. No matter how irritating I found Blake, or how much I suspected him, he was a distinguished scientist, and a guest in town, and our best hope for getting the animals out of our backyard.

"Food's already here," Blake said as he turned to lead us in.

And an impressive array of food indeed. The table in the cottage's dining room was covered with every cold item on the Inn's menu—meats, cheeses, fruits, vegetables with dip, assorted salads, and a bowl of gigantic shrimp in which someone had already made a considerable dent.

Dad began heaping a plate with food. I followed Blake out to the patio, where I discovered that the shrimp-loving someone was Rob. He was already ensconced in a chaise longue with a glass of red wine on the wrought-iron table at his elbow and a heaping plate of food in his lap. On the glass tabletop, the shrimp tails were beginning to overflow the plate on which he'd been piling them.

"Cheers!" he said, raising his glass to us and then taking a healthy sip. "Damn, I wish I'd brought my camera. The eye's getting even more picturesque."

"What are you doing here?" I said. "Apart from the obvious."

"I brought Dr. Blake back here," Rob said. "He can't drive, you know."

"I can drive just fine," Blake said. "I just don't have a license right now. If those imbeciles down at the DMV knew how to administer an eye test properly—but never mind that. Help yourself." He waved his hand back at the French doors that led to the dining room. "What we don't eat only gets thrown away."

I studied his plate for a few seconds, then went in to help my-self to the same things he was eating. Not that I could think of any logical reason for Blake to poison us, but he was rather push-ing the food. He could just be one of those people who judges his success as a host by his guests' food intake. Still, better safe than sorry.

I took my time loading my plate, so I could study the interior of the cottage. Either Blake was naturally tidy or the hotel housekeeping staff had been in recently. Apart from the food, the only sign of occupancy I could see was the neat little office set up just inside the front door. The Chippendale writing desk held not only the laptop, but also a small high-tech printer. Nearby was a piece of luggage that looked like a cross between a large briefcase and a small filing cabinet. I spotted a small stack of expensive-looking Montgomery Blake Foundation letterhead. A traveling office for the rich and famous. The screen saver on Blake's laptop was flipping slowly through a gallery of photos of Blake posing with assorted animals, birds, and reptiles.

Nothing suspicious, alas. But I hadn't yet seen the bedroom or the bathroom. I made a mental note to visit the bathroom before I left, whether I needed to or not.

"Red or white?" Blake asked when I returned to the patio.

"White," I said. I normally preferred red wine, but Blake was drinking white. I had to admit, though, that it was an amazingly good white wine.

"So," I said. "Have you come up with an inventory of animals that might be turning up on our doorstep?"

"Not much on wasting time with useless social chitchat, are you?" Blake said with a chuckle. "Yes, here's your list."

The list was neatly printed on pale cream paper that looked as if it would match the letterhead.

"Of course, it's only what I pulled together, based on what I saw on my first visit last month, and the discussions I had with Patrick," Blake said.

"And your visit to the zoo this afternoon," I added.

"Yes," Blake said. "Though I didn't learn much from strolling around outside, and his office was locked. By the police, I presume. If I could just convince Chief Burke to let me see the zoo's files, I'd feel a lot more confident that the list was accurate."

Was Blake really badgering the chief to see the files? Even if he was, that didn't clear him of destroying Lanahan's files. If I'd burned the files, I'd make a point of demanding to see them.

As I scanned the list, I started to feel relieved. I didn't see many animals that I didn't already know about from my own trip to the zoo—and, of course, my observation of the creatures that had arrived in our yard. If Blake's list was at all accurate, we already had the lion's share of the zoo's population. I pulled out my notebook and flipped it open to a fresh page.

"Impalas, twelve," I said. "I gather we're not talking about the Chevrolets."

"Ah, impalas," Blake exclaimed. "The McDonald's of the African plains!"

"The what?"

"We already have them," Dad said. "In the pasture with the llamas. You know, those antelopes with the rounded M-shaped markings on their rump. Looks like the McDonald's logo. That's how they got the nickname."

"Well, that and the fact that they're the main staple in the diet of so many predators," Blake said. "Lions, cheetahs, jackals, hyenas—"

"Let's make sure we still have all twelve of them, then," I said, making some notes on the list. "Reeves's muntjacs, three. What and where are they?"

"Small deer," Blake said. "Also known as barking deer. Interesting species, though not particularly rare."

"Dr. Gruber's keeping them," Dad said. "He has a big fenced area where he used to keep his St. Bernard before the poor old thing died. I don't think we'll be seeing the muntjacs—Dr. Gruber says he rather likes hearing the occasional bark from the yard again."

"Check. Norwegian feral sheep?"

"They're over at Seth Early's, with his herd," Dad said. "Since they really are just exotic sheep themselves."

"Check. Emerald tree boa?"

"Oh, all the snakes and lizards are down at my office," Rob said. "They're fine there indefinitely. The guys like the company."

"They would," I said. "Have the guys figured out yet why you have such trouble recruiting and retaining women employees?"

"That was a problem long before the snakes arrived."

"The snakes are only symptomatic," I said.

As our inventory continued, I was relieved to see that most of the animals not already in our backyard or Dad's pasture were happily ensconced with people who seemed content to have them stay indefinitely. This could be a problem if and when the zoo tried to retrieve all its inhabitants—what if some of the foster families tried to assert squatters' rights? But that wasn't my problem. Eventually, we accounted for all of the missing animals except for a family of naked mole rats and Lola, the elderly bobcat. I suspected if we searched all the cubicles down at Rob's office, we'd find that his wayward band of programmers had taken in the naked mole rats, on the theory that they were the next best thing to reptiles—Though I hoped they realized that the naked mole rats were occupants of the zoo, and not provisions.

Blake wasn't sure Lola the bobcat was still alive.

"I expect you'll find Lola succumbed to old age, like poor old Reggie," he said.

"If that's the case, then we can probably account for all the animals," I said.

"That's a relief," Blake said. "Though I confess, I wasn't all that worried about the animals that are left. It's the ones that disappeared before Patrick died that concern me."

Chapter 38

"What do you mean 'disappeared'?" I asked. "I thought this was a complete list of animals in the zoo."

"As of the time I showed up," Blake said. "But from the cursory review I'd been able to make of Patrick's records last week, I found there was an extraordinary amount of attrition over the last two years."

"Attrition?" I repeated. "What kind of attrition."

"Animals he sold, animals who died, and animals simply unaccounted for," Blake said. "And all three worry me. Take the animals who died. Sounded to me as if the mortality rate was a little high."

"Could that just be a statistical anomaly?" I asked.

"Possibly. Or it could be reasonable—Patrick did say that the animals he'd been able to afford were often relatively mature when they arrived at the zoo. That's probably understandable, given his financial situation."

"Like Reggie, the invisible lion," I said. "In other words, he was buying over-the-hill animals at cut-rate prices to fill the zoo."

"In a nutshell, yes," Blake said. "And I don't see a problem with that. Geriatric animals need a place to live, too. And from the size of his outstanding veterinary bills, it doesn't look as if he stinted on their medical care. But I wanted to review each animal's case in detail. See if they all sounded reasonable. And I'm even more worried about the animals he sold. An unusually large number of animals, most of them relatively young, healthy animals that would be in high demand."

"Isn't that the flip side of buying over-the-hill animals?" I asked. "Not that I particularly like this business of buying and selling animals like groceries or something, but doesn't it make sense that if he was too broke to buy anything but geriatric animals, he was probably too broke to resist selling off the more valuable animals? To buy food for the rest?"

"After all, selling them's so much less messy than feeding the gazelles to the wolves," Rob said.

"Yes," Blake said to me. He was pointedly ignoring Rob. "But he doesn't seem to have good records showing where he sold them. And it makes a difference. Did he sell them to other reputable zoos? That's fine. To private individuals? Much more dubious. Or to one of those so-called game ranches?"

"The places that run the canned hunts," I said. "Yeah, that would be bad."

"I don't yet know he did that," Blake said. "We were supposed to sit down and go over his records in excruciating detail this coming week. Medical records for the animals that died, sales records for the ones he sold, and whatever the hell kind of records he had for the animals who were missing. Animals don't just go missing from zoos. Not often."

"What kind of animals went missing?" Dad asked, sounding concerned. I wondered if the visions his imagination was tossing out were as interesting as mine. Emerald tree boas turning up on people's rose arbors. Water buffalo devastating the backyards of the Caerphilly Garden Society members. Rogue hyenas lurking behind the freshman dorms.

"Various kinds of exotic deer and antelope," Blake said. "Wild sheep, goats, and boars. In fact, that's also the kind of animal he sold."

"From what I can see, those were the mainstays of the zoo," I said. "Animals he could just turn loose in a pasture to graze."

"They also happen to be the mainstays of these canned-hunting places," Blake said.

"So you already suspected him of some kind of involvement in canned hunting," Dad said, sounding shocked.

"No," Blake said. "But I was starting to worry about whether he was really responsible enough to be running a zoo, even a small one. It wasn't till Meg mentioned it that the pieces fell in place. Maybe I should have realized it sooner, but I didn't really want to believe it. A trained zoologist. A friend of my grandson's."

He shook his head and took a big swallow of his white wine.

"But before you could sit down to give Lanahan the third degree about his missing animals, he turned up dead."

"Which means I still have to figure out what happened at the zoo, and I don't even have Patrick to interrogate," Blake said.

"Weird," Rob said, refilling his wineglass. "If you were the murder victim, it would all make sense now. Lanahan would have killed you to keep you from finding out his crimes. But this doesn't help us figure out who offed Lanahan."

"Those animal-rights activists who've been marching up and down outside Meg's house all day," Blake said. "Their leader's a nutcase, if you ask me. Trying to turn the hyenas loose with all those prey animals at large."

"I don't usually think of my family as prey animals, but I see your point," I said.

"Chief Burke seems to have focused more on poor young Charlie Shiffley," Dad said. "Can't say I understand that."

"He's probably got some forensic evidence," I suggested. "Unlike us. All we have is our imaginations, so we're wasting our time making wild, inaccurate guesses."

"I doubt if your guesses are particularly wild or inaccurate," Blake said. "But then, I don't expect you to share them with someone who's probably one of your suspects."

"Oh, I'm sure Meg doesn't suspect you!" Dad said with a nervous laugh.

"The hell she doesn't," Blake said. He sat back with an annoyingly enigmatic smile on his face. Was it the smile of a murderer who knows he's unlikely to be caught? Or the smile of a consummate egotist who has to be the center of every conversation, even at the cost of being a murder suspect?

"I suspect everyone, of course," I said.

"But especially me," Blake said, as if egging me on. "Go ahead; tell them why. You've checked up on me, I presume?"

"Yes," I said. I thought of giving Ms. Ellie credit, but decided maybe I was in a better position to take care of myself if Blake resented the snooping. "You have no living family."

Blake frowned, almost imperceptibly.

"Yes," he said. "I lost my only child to cancer seventeen years ago, and then, a few years later, my only grandson to a car accident."

"A car accident in which Patrick Lanahan was a passenger," I said. "Did you hold a grudge against Lanahan? Maybe because you thought he was to blame for the accident?"

"And killed him in revenge?" Blake said. "No, Tony dug his own grave. Drinking. Not the first car he'd totaled."

"You had nothing against Lanahan?" I said.

"I admit, I resented Patrick for years," Blake said. "Not because of anything he'd done, but because he lived when Tony died. But that had faded, and by the time he contacted me, asking for help with his zoo, I was feeling guilty about having lost touch. I thought it was a good way to reconnect with a happier time in my life."

Whatever discomfort Blake had felt when I'd brought up the subject of his grandson had vanished now. Or maybe I'd only imagined it.

"Why are you so interested in the Caerphilly Zoo?" I asked. "Because of your guilt about having neglected Lanahan?"

"I think it's important for young people to learn about the natural world," Blake said. "There are people today who've never seen an animal larger than a cocker spaniel."

"There's the National Zoo, in Washington," I said. "And for that matter, Richmond and Norfolk have pretty decent zoos."

"Yes, but they're all at least a hundred miles away. It's so much better having the wild animals nearby—practically in your backyard."

"On the contrary, I'd much rather have several hundred miles between me and the animals currently occupying our backyard," I said. "Have you ever tried to sleep with a troop of bored hyenas laughing maniacally in your barn all night? Never mind, you probably have. So you feel strongly about the importance of small local zoos?"

"That's right," Blake said. He was sitting back with his hands laced across his stomach, smiling enigmatically.

"I don't recall seeing anything on your Web site about supporting worthy small zoos," I said. "It's a new interest, then?"

"Not a new interest," Blake said. "But one I've only recently made the time to pursue. When I turned ninety, it hit me that I should start thinking about posterity."

"Supporting the Caerphilly Zoo's your way of thinking about posterity?"

"It's a start," Blake said. "It's got potential."

I nodded. I was tempted to point out that when older men

started talking about posterity they usually turned to trophy wives and Viagra, not penguins and llamas, but I stifled the impulse.

"So when are you going to make some kind of decision about whether you're going to help the zoo?" I asked aloud.

"I'll probably have to wait until the police let me see the files," Blake said. "I'll need to study what I'm taking on."

"What do you need to study, apart from the animals, most of which are out at our place, and the physical facility, which you've already inspected today?"

"There's the financial situation."

"The bank's already seized the property," I said. I was having trouble keeping my voice light—all his reasons sounded like so many lame excuses. "I bet they'd be ecstatic if you made an offer on it."

"We do need to find out what Patrick's heirs want."

"Whoever they are, I bet they can't wait to get rid of the zoo and all its inhabitants as soon as possible. Why not just tell us if you plan to save the zoo?"

I could think of more, but I stopped myself and took one of those deep breaths Rose Noire was always recommending. It helped about as little as it usually did.

Blake chuckled.

"Not very subtle, are you?" he said.

"Sorry," I said, trying to look apologetic.

"Don't be," he said with a guffaw. "I wouldn't even recognize subtlety if it came up and bit me on the rear. And for your information, I already have my staff at the foundation working on a plan for bailing out the zoo. Assuming I get the chance."

"Why wouldn't you?" Dad asked.

"I'm older than dirt," Blake said with a snort. "I could go anytime. And do I look as if I could defend myself if the killer went after me?"

"Oh, I'm sure that's not going to happen!" Dad exclaimed.

"You never know," I said. "Is there some reason the killer would want to?"

"Meg, of course, is trying to figure out if I'm spry enough to have done the deed myself," Blake said. "What's the verdict on that, eh?"

"Jury's still out," I said, smiling as if it were a joke. "You do seem remarkably active for your age."

"I hope I'm half as active when I'm ninety!" Dad exclaimed.

"So I'm a suspect," Blake said. "Excellent!"

He actually did seem quite pleased at the notion that I suspected him. Under other circumstances, I might have found that oddly endearing. He was brusque and a bit arrogant, but I could see coming to like him. Assuming someone else turned out to be the murderer—

Just then, Rob yawned loudly.

"It's getting late," Dad said. "We should go."

"Mind if I use your bathroom before I hit the road?" I asked.

"Be my guest," Blake said. "Though most of the incriminating evidence is probably on my computer. You want me to stay out here and have a cigar while you search it?"

"Takes all the fun out of it," I said, shaking my head. I sipped the last bit of my wine, then stood up and set the glass on a side table. "Right now, I just want to see if the bathrooms in this place are really as outrageous as I've heard."

I left Blake still chuckling as I strolled inside. The bedroom was, as I suspected, neat and largely free of personal touches. The bathroom was almost as large—twice the size of my first apartment. And yes, it did have both a whirlpool tub and a small sauna. The toilet was in its own little closet at the other end of the room—practically in the next county. The vanity counter had two sinks and at least an acre of spotless mirror. Strangely,

Blake's well-worn leather shaving kit looked right at home in these luxurious surroundings. I confess, I snooped. Except for baby aspirin and vitamins, he didn't seem to take any medications. Nor had he hidden a signed confession at the bottom of the shaving kit beneath the deodorant and shampoo.

So he was neat, well organized, and in remarkable good health for a ninety-year-old. That didn't mean he wasn't a murderer.

"Sufficiently sybaritic for your needs?" Blake asked when I reappeared.

"Yeah, except it looks as if they expect guests to supply their own bath salts and masseur." I headed for the door, where Rob was already waiting. I saw Dad outside, hurrying off.

"Very slipshod," Blake said. "I'll be sure to mention that on the evaluation form."

He reached out to shake first Rob's hand, then mine.

Just then I caught a glimpse of something over his shoulder— a picture on the laptop's screen saver. Blake in an odd pose. Was he—but then the screen saver flipped to the next photo, and Blake was holding the door open for us to leave. Before I could come up with an excuse to delay our departure, I was outside, looking at the closed cottage door. Rob was already strolling toward the main hotel. I scrambled to catch up with him.

"Well, that was weird," Rob said. "Do you really suspect him?"

"Yes."

"Then why did you tell him?"

"I didn't tell him—he guessed."

"Weird," Rob said. He was reaching for the front door to the main hotel building.

"Look, come back with me a minute," I said. "I thought I saw something, but I didn't get a chance to check it out. I want to peek in his front window."

"You don't need my help for that."

"I want you to help me create a diversion if he spots me. Pretend to have lost a contact or something."

Rob shrugged and followed me back to the door of the Washington Cottage.

I shoved my way through several large camellia bushes that partially screened the window, until I reached a place where I could see in. Yes, the laptop screen was visible from here.

"Look for your contact, just in case," I said.

Rob bent over and began peering at the brick walk, shuffling along slowly, and occasionally bending down as if trying to pick up something. I watched the photos flicker across the laptop screen. Yes, there it was again.

A picture of Blake standing over the carcass of a lion. Blake's foot was on its neck, and he was holding some kind of firearm.

Chapter 39

What was Blake doing shooting animals? I thought he specialized in rescuing them.

Just then Blake himself came into view. I pulled back into the shelter of the bush. Blake didn't look up at the window. He passed by, and then a few seconds later, he came back again.

He was holding a wineglass, with a small stain of red wine still visible in the bottom. Not holding it normally, but using a paper napkin to grip the stem lightly. He held it up to the light for a few seconds, then put it in a brown paper bag. He pulled out a Sharpie and wrote something on the bag. Then he disappeared from view.

"Weird," I whispered.

"What's weird?" Rob asked.

"Hush up and follow me," I said.

We crept quietly along the side of the cottage until we were crouching in the shrubbery at the edge of the terrace. At least I crept quietly. Rob made more noise than the entire herd of bison combined, but Blake didn't seem to notice, so maybe he was slightly deaf.

The wineglass Rob had been drinking from was still sitting on the glass-topped table, half hidden by the delta of shrimp tails overflowing the plate beside it. As we watched, Blake took another paper napkin, picked up Rob's wineglass, and put it in a second brown paper bag. More scribbling with the Sharpie. Then Blake snagged another napkin and came closer to us. Heading for the side table.

"Isn't that where you were sitting?" Rob whispered.

Yes, and he was bagging my wineglass. Any doubt I might have had vanished when he pulled out the Sharpie again to label the third bag, and printed "Meg Langslow" in large, precise letters.

He picked up the other brown paper bag and carried both inside. I leaned out a little farther so I could see through the French doors to the inside of the cottage. Blake had set the bags down beside the first one on a small marble-topped table just inside the front door. He turned off the living-room light and went into the bedroom. A few minutes later, we heard the shower.

Figuring the show was over, I motioned for Rob to follow me and headed across the golf course.

"What's he up to?" Rob said as we sneaked past the putting green.

"I'm not sure yet."

Rob thought about that for a moment.

"Does that mean that you think you know but you're not sure, or that you have absolutely no idea?"

"I have several ideas," I said. "None of them pleasant."

"You think he suspects us and is going to check us out?"

"Maybe," I said. "Or maybe he's planning to frame us."

"Frame us? Why?"

"Why do people usually frame people?"

"Um . . . because they don't like them?"

"Possibly, though I think a more plausible motive is that they're guilty and desperately need to blame someone else."

"I hope not," Rob said. "I kind of like the old guy."

Apparently, when it came to suspecting the motives of Dr. Blake, I was in the minority. Of course, the minority included

Mother, Dad, and Miss Ellie, so I was in good company. Still, it was a little frustrating that most people took him at face value.

We emerged from the golf course near the parking lot. Dad had already gone. Rob waved and drove off. I was about to follow suit when my cell phone rang.

"So," Michael said when I answered it. "Do you want the good news or the bad news?"

"You pick," I said.

"The good news is that Mom has safely landed."

"Say hi," I said. "What's the bad news?"

"Aunt Daphne's plane hasn't even taken off yet. Bad thunderstorms in the Midwest and heading this way. No word yet whether they're going to cancel all flights or just wait a few hours till it clears."

"Damn," I said. "Are you going to hang around to see?"

"For a little while, at least. Mom and I are going to have a bite to eat and hope they make a decision by the time we finish."

Just then, I spotted someone coming out of the hotel's front door. Blake.

"Keep me posted," I said, craning my neck to see what Blake was up to.

"The good news is that the thunderstorms are supposed to blow over by morning," he said. "Should be no problem with flights leaving tomorrow. Love you."

With that, he hung up.

I probably should have said something in reply, but Blake's actions were distracting me. He had walked over to a car—the vintage BMW. Now he seemed to be starting it up.

Hadn't he said that he didn't have a license?

Of course, why would that stop him if he wanted to go someplace in a hurry? Or unseen? For that matter, how did we know he was telling the truth about having his license taken away?

Maybe he was just scamming Rob so he'd have a volunteer chauffeur for his stay.

The BMW's headlights came on. It backed rather abruptly out of its parking space and took off, spraying bits of spotless white gravel in its wake. I waited until it passed me, and then turned the key of my own car, intending to trail after Blake.

True to my prediction, the Toyota balked. It wouldn't start until the fourth try, stalled out twice before I got out of the parking lot, and only grudgingly settled down to its usual sluggish but steady pace on the Inn's seemingly endless driveway. Was it an inferiority complex, or the inferior Clay County gas? Either way, by the time I reached the main road, the BMW had disappeared.

So much for shadowing Blake. And probably so much for my contribution to the murder investigation or the zoo rescue. In less than twenty-four hours, Michael and I would be winging our way toward whatever destination he'd chosen for our surprise honeymoon.

The most useful thing I could do now was get some sleep. Probably a major faux pas to fall asleep during your wedding. I turned the car toward home.

I found myself thinking as I drove that maybe it would be easier to let go of what was happening here in Caerphilly if I could start visualizing myself someplace else. Lolling on a sunny Hawaiian beach. Strolling down an elegant Parisian street. Tasting chardonnays in California—or Shirazes in Australia. Even cleaning fish in a cabin in West Virginia. Right now my vision of the immediate future ended at the Clay County courthouse. No wonder I was keeping myself distracted with the zoo and the murder investigation. It made me feel as if I were in control of something.

If for any reason tomorrow's events didn't come off as

planned, I was going to insist on taking charge of the rescheduled honeymoon.

I pulled into the driveway, turned the motor off, and sat for a few moments, savoring the peace and quiet. Then my cell phone beeped at me. I pulled it out and looked at the caller ID. Mother. Probably not a call I wanted to ignore.

"Hello, dear," Mother said. "Your father said your meeting with Dr. Blake was over—aren't you coming over to help with the party?"

"Michael's not back from picking up his mother," I said. "And his aunt. I don't want to get the visit off to a bad start by not even being here when they arrive. I thought I'd come over with them."

Of course, odds were that going to a party would be the last thing Michael's mother and aunt would want to do when they finally got to Caerphilly sometime in the wee small hours, but I wasn't about to tell Mother that.

"I suppose you're right," Mother said. "In-laws, even prospective ones, can be such a trial."

"Yes," I said. "Wasn't it thoughtful of Dad not to inflict any on you?"

"Give my best to Mrs. Waterston."

"I will," I said. "Bye now."

I shoved the phone back in my purse and went inside. I resisted the temptation to dump my purse just inside the door. After all, right now the house was about as private as a hotel. Any number of family members could be coming and going at any time tonight as well as all day tomorrow, and who knew how many strangers would tag along? Or show up uninvited, like the Sprockets and the protesters.

I trudged upstairs, put the purse safely away in a drawer

where only the most brazen family snoops and kleptomaniacs would look, and stumbled into the bathroom.

While I was brushing my teeth, I saw something outside. A light.

Chapter 40

I put away my toothbrush and stuck my head out the window to see better. It looked like someone holding a flashlight and walking through Seth Early's sheep pasture across the road. Not just walking—looking for something. The flashlight swung back and forth in tight arcs, and every so often, it would pause for a few seconds before moving on.

Was this something suspicious that I should report? Or could it be Mr. Early, performing some normal farming task that I just hadn't seen before?

My tiredness disappeared as I strode downstairs. I grabbed my own flashlight from the hall table. Not so much for illumination—a first quarter moon gave enough light for me to see. But the flashlight was one of those heavy industrial-sized models, and its weight felt reassuring in my hand.

Of course, no matter how reassuring it felt to have my own blunt instrument in case the intruder in the sheep pasture proved dangerous, it would probably have been wiser to call the police. And I might have, if I hadn't known that the chief probably had every officer in Caerphilly and the surrounding counties scouring the landscape for Charlie Shiffley and Shea Bailey. Interrupting that search would not endear me to the chief. Especially since he'd already had to interrupt it once to deal with our escaped animals. Never mind that the escaped animals were the SOBs' fault, not ours. Right now, I didn't think that was a distinction that would carry much weight with the chief.

And after all, the intruder would probably turn out to be Seth Early, performing some abstruse sheep-related farming chore that had to be done at night. Or some quirky New Age ritual he'd taken up under Rose Noire's influence. Singing the sheep a soothing, wool-centric lullaby, perhaps. Mr. Early still hadn't quite gotten over being annoyed about the time in February when I'd reported a prowler on his property, and two deputies had interrupted him when he was trying to help one of his ewes through a difficult birth.

The intruder's flashlight disappeared behind a small rise, which gave me the perfect opportunity to sneak up on him. I approached from the other side of the hill, walking slightly crouched, and took shelter behind a convenient rock. And when I peered over the rock, I saw that it was, indeed, an intruder.

Sheila D. Flugleman. She was carrying one of her manure buckets and running her flashlight beam over the grass. A sheep turd appeared, and she stopped, pulled a small shovel out of the bucket, scooped up her prize, and then resumed the hunt.

I stood up, pointed my flashlight at her, and clicked it on.

"So does gathering it by moonlight do something special for the sheep manure?" I asked loudly. "Or could you possibly be diluting the purity of ZooperPoop! with the lowly droppings of the ordinary domestic sheep?"

She jumped and uttered a small scream—not much more than a squeak.

"Seth Early has those exotic sheep from the zoo, doesn't he?" she said. "I'm taking their dung."

"The Norwegian feral sheep? Yes," I said. I strolled down the hill toward her. "And you can tell their dung from the rest?"

"I'll mix it all up," she said. "The package says that it contains manure from zoo animals. It doesn't say that's all it contains."

A sudden thought struck me.

"That's why Patrick started charging you for the manure, wasn't it?" I asked. "As long as ZooperPoop! was a small operation that saved him money on cleanup costs, he didn't care. But when he found out what a moneymaker it was, he demanded a share in the profits. And threatened that if you didn't pay, he'd tell everyone that ZooperPoop! was just ordinary farm manure."

A wild guess, but from the sudden look of panic on her face, I suspected it was an accurate one.

"I guess that's not a rumor you want getting out just when you're on the verge of getting some serious national publicity, according to the *Clarion*," I added.

Her expression turned from anxiety to fury. When will I learn to leave well enough alone?

"Not a word of it's true," she said. "And you can't prove it. And anyway, I had nothing to do with his death, and if you tell Martha Stewart a word of this I'll—I'll—aarrgghh!!!"

She threw her bucket of manure at me and sprinted for the road.

"Eeuw! Gross!" I muttered. I'd seen the bucket coming, and dodged it. At least I thought I had. But I wasn't sure she'd completely missed. I inspected myself by flashlight but couldn't tell.

I heard Sheila's car start up—apparently she'd hidden it in a small thicket of trees down the road from our house. I turned to watch as she careened down the road toward town, tires squealing at every turn.

Good riddance. I'd go back to the house and call Chief Burke. Report that she'd assaulted me with a disgusting weapon.

But not until after my shower.

I unstuck Chief Burke's yellow crime-scene tape so I could get into the basement and throw all my clothes directly into the washer. Then I dashed upstairs, naked—luckily the party had lured all the relatives over to Mother and Dad's farm. I used up about half a bar of soap taking a long, hot shower. Then I wrapped myself in a bath towel and sprawled on the bed. The newly assembled bed with its clean sheets and its incredibly comfortable mattress. I was just going to rest a few minutes, and then get dressed, so I was ready to be perky and welcoming when Michael returned with his mother and his aunt. Really I was.

At least that was my plan. I don't think I'd quite dropped off to sleep when I heard a noise outside.

It sounded rather like the ghastly wailing Mother's cat made if you didn't let him into the house the instant he arrived on the back porch. But Boomer was back in Yorktown. This was Caerphilly, and we didn't have any cats. Ducks, penguins, llamas, camels, acouchis, sloths, lemurs, and seventeen other species of zoo animals, yes—but no cats.

Not yet, anyway. Wasn't there some kind of wild feline missing from the zoo? A bobcat. What if whoever had fostered it had chosen now, at—good grief, one in the morning—to drop off his unwanted charge?

There it was again. Lower this time. Closer to a moan than a caterwaul. Even if it wasn't the missing bobcat, something was wrong. What if some ordinary domestic cat had been prowling around and come to grief—creeping too close to the hyenas' cage, for example?

I peered out the front windows. Nothing unusual. I went into the bathroom, which had a window overlooking the backyard. Nothing. Well, not exactly nothing, but the various sheds, shrubs, picnic tables, lawn chairs, and trenches all lay undisturbed in the moonlight.

But I hadn't dreamed that noise.

I threw on sweatpants and a T-shirt, shoved my feet into clogs, grabbed my flashlight again, and went downstairs to investigate.

Nothing suspicious in the backyard. The penguins stirred slightly when I passed their coop, then settled down to sleep again. At one end of the yard, a llama stood, apparently guarding three sheep who had settled down to sleep under the weeping willow. More refugees from Seth Early's pastures—I'd get someone to take them back tomorrow after they'd finished trimming the lawn.

Then I heard the low, moaning noise again. The llama lifted its head and turned slightly toward the source, ears and nostrils twitching.

I was definitely hearing a cat, and not a happy one. The sound seemed to be coming from the side yard.

I headed toward the noise, reminding myself to watch out for the Sprockets' trenches. Which weren't really that hard to spot if you were looking for them.

I heard a soft whine. Definitely coming from one of the trenches. I just couldn't tell which one.

Few of them counted as pure trenches anymore. It would have been easier to search them efficiently if they were. But Mother's digging crew had been at work, filling in the holes in some places, joining two or more trenches in others. I wandered about, scanning the bottoms of the various holes, and wondered if I should just give up till morning.

No, not if an injured animal might be out here.

But I wasn't finding anything. No abandoned bobcat. No hyena-savaged cat lying helpless in the trenches. And no practical-joking humans pretending to be mating cats, either. A couple of my teenage cousins had tried that once, shortly after we moved in, but I was pretty sure my reaction had discouraged repetition.

Then, in the next-to-last trench from the house, I spotted
it—a patch of slightly lighter gray in the shadows at one end of
the trench. I inched a little closer, and the shadows moved until
a pair of eyes stared up at me. They were yellow-green cat eyes,
but farther apart than a house cat's eyes would be. Clearly their
owner was bigger than a house cat.

Evidently Lola the bobcat had arrived. And she didn't sound
happy.

And what if bobcats could jump the way house cats could?
I jerked back from the edge of the trench, expecting to see
twenty or thirty pounds of peeved bobcat emerge, claws whirl-
ing. But nothing happened. All I could hear from the trench was
a soft whine from Lola.

I circled around the end of the trench so I could peer in from
the other side and flicked on my flashlight as I leaned over.

I saw Lola, flinching from the light, her tufted ears flattened
against her skull. She growled at me.

Then I spotted the crossbow bolt protruding from her flank.

"I don't blame you for being ticked off," I said to Lola. "And I
don't suppose there's any way I can convince you that I had
nothing to do with the pain you're feeling."

She hissed at me. I flicked off the flashlight to avoid stress-
ing her.

"I didn't think so," I said. "I'm going to call someone to help
you."

But who? Dad, perhaps, though I wasn't sure his wildlife-
rehabilitation expertise extended to bobcats, and Mother would
never forgive me if I got him involved and he injured himself.
The Caerphilly Animal Welfare Department clearly wasn't up to
the job of dealing with Lola. Montgomery Blake, perhaps—he
certainly claimed to have experience with big cats. If he was
back at his hotel and not still out roaming the county in a suspi-

cious manner. I didn't much like the idea of inviting him over unless I had plenty of witnesses around. Chief Burke. That was the ticket. I'd call the police and then Blake, and—

Something hit me across the backside, knocking me off my feet and into the bobcat-infested trench.

Chapter 41

As I fell, I twisted to avoid landing on Lola. I succeeded, but the effort threw me off balance. I landed hard, doing something to my leg that hurt so badly I almost fainted. But the five razor-sharp claws raking down my side snapped me out of it, and for a few frantic seconds I scrambled to put some distance between myself and Lola. Not that I felt like moving—I was pretty sure my leg was broken. But Lola seemed to want her personal space back. Fine by me. Whatever Lola wants, Lola gets.

When the dirt settled, Lola and I were lying at opposite ends of a ten-foot stretch of trench, glaring at each other. I could see a fresh trickle of blood from the wound on Lola's flank. I felt bad that I might have hurt her on landing, though I suspected it was her efforts to fight me off that had set off the bleeding. At least she seemed too hurt to come after me. A good thing, too. I was also bleeding, from where she'd lacerated my side. And worse, my leg hurt like hell, and lay twisted at an odd angle. I wasn't up to defending myself.

But I might have to. Whoever pushed me into the trench clearly didn't have my best interests at heart.

Lola howled softly at me—an aching sound, half threat and half pain. I wished there were some way I could tell her that I wasn't going to hurt her. I wasn't the enemy—the enemy was still up there. And probably still up to something.

Just then I spotted something on one wall of the trench—a little red dot of light, like the one Charlie Shiffley's laser sight projected onto whatever he was about to shoot. It played over the wall, found Lola, and moved on.

Whoever was using it was behind me. He'd have to circle around the trench to point it at me.

Probably a good idea to play possum. Let whoever pushed me in think I'd been even more seriously injured by the fall. Maybe I could get a clue to his—or her—identity.

I waited, ears straining. Nothing.

It was annoying that I couldn't put a face to the enemy lurking overhead. One moment I expected to see the craggy face of Montgomery Blake peering over the edge, lobbing a few more genial insults down before he finished me off. The next minute I was sure it would be Shea, the SOB leader. I also spared a few thoughts for Sheila D. Flugleman—a normal person might not think manure a sufficient motive for murder, but she definitely wasn't firing on all cylinders. And the Sprockets, who had appeared so conveniently soon after the body was discovered— what if they'd had something to do with putting it there? Even Charlie Shiffley—perhaps Chief Burke was right, and he wasn't the innocent kid I thought he was. And I could think of other candidates for the killer if I tried, and I probably would if the wait went on much longer.

Patience, I told myself. Sooner or later, my attacker had to show himself, right?

Then a few clods of dirt fell on me. It suddenly occurred to me that maybe playing possum wasn't such a good idea after all. I was lying in a six-foot-deep trench, and the person who had pushed me in was probably the killer. A killer who had buried his previous victim in a convenient nearby excavation. Human beings are creatures of habit—what if he was planning on repeating the process?

"Damn," a voice above me said. "I thought sure she'd finish you off by now."

Startled, I looked up to see Ray Hamlin craning his head over the side of the ditch.

"Maybe if you hadn't shot her from behind with a crossbow before throwing her down here she would have," I said.

"If I'd shot her, I'd have finished her off," he said. "Wasn't my lousy shot."

"One of your clients did it, then?"

He chuckled.

"Yeah, one of my clients. Lousy shot, and a sniveling coward to boot. Took off like a bat out of hell as soon as that damned kid showed up and started threatening to call the police. I should have guessed that kid was going to be trouble. Should have guessed a little sooner you were, too. But we'll take care of all that."

His face disappeared. I glanced at Lola. She was looking up at where Hamlin's face had been, snarling silently.

"Good girl," I said. "He's the bad guy. Remember that."

Just then something landed on the dirt between us. A body, with its hands duct-taped behind its back. Lola howled, and I suspected she was swatting at the new arrival with her claws. It was Charlie Shiffley. He didn't react to Lola's attack, so I grabbed his shoulders and pulled him back toward me as far as I could, until he was out of her reach. Then I checked his pulse to make sure I hadn't just rescued a corpse. No, his eyes might be closed, but his pulse was strong and he was breathing fine. His hair was matted with something wet and sticky. Moonlight washed out the color, but I suspected it was blood.

"There now!" Hamlin's face appeared again.

"Great, now you've incapacitated us so you can get out of town before the chief finds out what's up," I said. At least I was hoping that's what his plan was.

"Running away would be so inconvenient," he said. "And I'd rather be around when they discover the terrible tragedy. Don't worry; you'll be the heroine. You bravely put your life on the line to rescue one of the zoo's animals, and did away with the killer. Too bad that you had to sacrifice your own life in the process—falling victim to the same crossbow that killed poor Patrick Lanahan."

He produced a crossbow from behind his back and flourished it.

"Is that the same crossbow?" I asked.

"Course not," he said. "It's young Charlie's crossbow. Mine's back at the range. But the bolts'll match just fine."

He looked at the crossbow and frowned.

"What's wrong?" I asked. Something that would bring his plan to a screeching halt, I hoped.

"He does you in with the crossbow," Hamlin explained. "But I have to figure out how you kill him at the same time."

He scanned the bottom of the trench, frowning as his eyes dwelled on Lola for a few moments, and then shaking his head as if she had sadly disappointed him.

"Just out of curiosity, why did you kill Lanahan?" I asked. "I'd have thought he was useful. Your canned hunting operation's going to take a hit without him to provide the exotic animals, isn't it?"

"Can't be helped," he said. "There's plenty of other places I can buy from. Hell, I should have known it was risky in the first place, buying animals from someone only twenty miles away. First six months or so, I made up fake bills of sales so it looked like I'd resold the animals to zoos in the Midwest or on the West Coast. But he never came by to see how they were doing, so I stopped bothering. After a while, it came to me that I was wasting money buying the animals when I could just rip a few holes in his fences and let him think they wandered off. But that backfired."

"He paid more attention to the animals he still owned?"

"Yeah. The Shiffley kid shooting that fancy antelope was a gift. Took the heat off for a while. As long as Patrick was busy snooping around the Shiffleys' land, looking for traces of his lost critters, I could get away with anything."

"So what happened?"

"I had a hunter who wanted a big cat. Kind of a disappointment that the lion turned out to be a fake, but I convinced him that a bobcat would be good enough. And turns out Patrick was staking out the zoo. Sleeping out in that miserable trailer office."

"He caught you trying to steal Lola, and you killed him."

"I offered to cut him in on the hunting game but he wouldn't deal," Hamlin said, and from his tone, I gathered he thought Lanahan's refusal fully justified killing him.

"Why did you have to bury him in our basement?"

"Wasn't my original plan," he said. "I was going to plant him out in the swamp on old man Bromley's land. But I stopped by Flugleman's to get some quicklime—speed up how fast the body disappears, you know—and when I heard about the ready-made hole your father had dug, it sounded perfect."

"Perfect," I echoed. I knew the trouble had all started with Dad and the penguins. But all would be forgiven if Dad would just show up soon to check on his beloved birds. I thought longingly of my cell phone, which was upstairs, in my purse, carefully hidden away from sneak thieves and kleptomaniacs. If I'd had it, I could have called for help by now. Instead, I had to keep Hamlin talking and hope someone showed up before he figured out how to perfect his scenario.

"And what was that whole business with Spike?" I asked. "Did you really think Reggie was still in his den?"

"No, but that was the day I went back to collect the bobcat," he said. "Only to find you and the old geezer snooping around the zoo. I needed to slow you down long enough to haul her out. Worked, too. Say, I don't suppose it would make sense for you to whack him on the head with the crossbow, would it?"

"No, it wouldn't," I said. "This stinks."

"Try to look at it philosophical like," Hamlin said. "We all gotta go sometime."

"But not like this," I said. "In books and movies, whenever someone's menaced by a deranged killer, they always seem really upset about the possibility that the guy's going to be so sharp that the police can't catch him. That's nonsense."

"How come?" he asked. He seemed genuinely interested.

"Okay, I don't like the idea of you killing me and getting away with it. But you know what I like even less? The thought of you killing me for no good reason. To cover up a crime when you should know you're only going to get caught anyway."

"What makes you think they'll catch me?" Hamlin asked. He sounded smug.

"Because you've screwed up. I was starting to suspect you, so I'm sure it won't take the police that long."

"Not if I give them a nice, neat solution to their case."

"Oh, right," I said. "As if. I know damn well you're just going to screw it up. The minute Chief Burke gets here, he'll take one look at the crime scene and say, 'Confound it! It's that idiot Ray Hamlin! I should have gone ahead and arrested him yesterday.'"

"That's not a very nice thing to say, is it?"

"You want nice, then stop pointing that crossbow at me. Just my luck. I wouldn't be the second victim of that warped mastermind, the uncatchable crossbow killer. Oh, no. I'd be the unlucky victim of a criminal so dense they'd write him up in a *News of the Weird* feature about the stupidest crooks of the year."

"You've got a mouth on you," Hamlin said.

"You want to explain the nice neat solution you're planning on giving the chief?" I said. "How Charlie Shiffley and I both just happened to fall into the trench with an injured bobcat? Or did we jump in—and he with his hands duct-taped behind his back, just to make things more interesting? And even though he'd just shot me with a crossbow, I jumped in to help him?"

"Well, they won't find the duct tape, of course," Hamlin said. "I'll take that off before I leave."

"Even without the duct tape, it's a pretty odd scenario."

"Not odd at all," he said. "Not for around here, anyway. You heard a noise—you came out to find Charlie here had wounded the bobcat with his crossbow. He shot you to keep you quiet— but then he succumbed to the injuries you inflicted on him during the struggle."

"He had a crossbow pointed at me and I was stupid enough to struggle and lucky enough to inflict wounds?" I said. "Already I'm not buying this."

"Maybe with a rock," he said. "You got any big rocks in your garden?"

"You expect me to help with this plan? Which is not only stupid but incredibly bad for my health? Find your own damned rock."

"There's no need to snap at me," Hamlin said. His head disappeared. I heard him whistling a rather monotonous tune as he presumably searched the yard for rocks. Or perhaps the tune was fine and he was simply a rotten whistler.

I made sure the flashlight, which would make a far better weapon for his scenario, was well hidden under Charlie's body.

And then a thought occurred to me. Hamlin's plan called for

shooting me—probably from the safety of the edge of the trench—and then, when he'd gotten me out of commission, bashing Charlie's head in with a rock. Shooting Charlie definitely didn't fit into his scenario. So if I could pull Charlie on top of me to shield all the major body areas where a crossbow shot would be fatal, I'd mess up his plan. He couldn't shoot me without hitting Charlie, and he didn't dare shoot Charlie. And if I could then convince him that I'd passed out, and lure him into coming down into the trench . . .

It didn't do my leg much good, but I dragged Charlie on top of me. Too bad he wasn't stockier. I liked his height, which meant I could get my head and body under his torso, but he was slender enough that Hamlin could probably still shoot me in the rear, and my arms and legs stuck out. But my head and trunk were covered. That was the critical part.

And even better, maybe I could remove the duct tape from Charlie's wrists. Even if I did, there was no guarantee he'd regain consciousness in time to be much use, but at least it gave him a chance. But I hadn't finished pulling the last few layers of tape off when the tuneless whistling stopped. I lay still, hoping the throbbing pain in my leg would subside, and tried to concentrate on what was going on at the surface. I could see a little bit, through the space between Charlie's body and his right arm. Eventually, Hamlin's head appeared.

"What the hell?" he exclaimed.

There was a pause as he studied the tableau in the bottom of the trench. I continued to play possum.

"It won't do you any good, you know."

I didn't answer.

"I can wait," he said.

Waiting was fine with me. If he waited long enough Michael

would come back from fetching his mother, or someone would come back from the party.

"Don't make me come down there!"

I didn't answer. His face appeared and disappeared from my limited field of vision—apparently he was pacing up and down the bank. Then he stopped.

"Look here," he said. "We can do this one of two ways. Either—"

"Mwa-ha-ha!"

A figure in a black cape suddenly loomed up behind Hamlin, its hands raised with melodramatic menace. Hamlin yelped with surprise, and his finger must have hit the crossbow's trigger—I heard a sharp *fwap!* and saw the bolt sail off into the darkness. Hamlin swore, lost his footing, and regained it a little too close to the edge. The dirt crumbled beneath him and he slid in, landing near Lola—near, not on, since she only hissed and growled, instead of squealing in pain. He made a little noise as if the fall had knocked the breath out of him. His back was to me, so I couldn't see if his eyes were open. I heaved Charlie Shiffley off me and picked up my flashlight.

"Oh, dear."

I glanced up to see Dr. Smoot looking down at us.

"Help!" I shouted. "He's trying to kill us."

"I'm not sure I can," he said, pulling his black cloak more tightly around him. "It's so narrow down there—I'm not sure I can make myself go into such a tight little space."

"I don't want you to come down here," I said. "The trench is getting crowded enough as it is. Call 911!"

I was half crawling toward Hamlin, dragging my broken leg behind me, with my trusty Maglite raised to strike.

"I could just go get a ladder."

"Call 911! Bring the cops! He killed Patrick Lanahan, and now he's trying to kill Charlie and Lola and me!"

"Oh!" Dr. Smoot said, and disappeared.

Then I reached Hamlin. I was tempted to cosh him over the head, but reason prevailed. Instead, I stuck the narrow end of the flashlight in the small of his back, as if it were a gun.

"Don't move or I'll use this," I said.

Lola made a noise, half whine and half growl, as if asserting her prior claim to vengeance.

After a couple of minutes, we heard the sirens—distant, but growing louder every second. Hamlin stirred slightly, as if thinking of making a break for it. I heard a slight noise from overhead.

"You can sit back down now," Randall Shiffley said. "I've got him in my sights. One false move and I'll blow his rotten lying head off."

I sat down and passed out.

Chapter 42

"The party's going simply splendidly!" Dad said as he dashed into my hospital room carrying two more huge floral arrangements festooned with get-well cards. "Everyone's looking forward to seeing you—has Dr. Waldron told you when you can go home?"

"I'm supposed to talk to her this afternoon," I said. Actually I'd already talked to my doctor, gotten her okay on flying with my broken leg, and sworn her to secrecy about when I was being released. A little later, she was supposed to storm in, shoo out my visitors, and inform Dad that she needed to keep me for a second night, to run more tests. And once the coast was clear . . .

Where was Dr. Waldron? I hoped she wasn't waiting for my stream of visitors to die down, because that wasn't happening anytime soon. As if to make up for my having to miss the beginning of the day's festivities, my entire family and half the town of Caerphilly had been trooping through my hospital room in shifts, congratulating me. Michael was hovering nearby, trying not to show how impatient he was for all of them to leave.

At least it gave me a chance to find out what had been going on while I was unconscious. Tie up a few loose ends before Michael and I fled for wherever.

At the moment, I was entertaining a delegation of Shiffleys.

"We're much obliged," Vern was saying, for about the seventeenth time. I was running out of things to say—"It's nothing" didn't seem tactful, since they were convinced I'd saved Charlie's life. Worse, I suspected they felt the need to express their gratitude in some tangible way. Ms. Ellie, the last person I knew who had earned the undying gratitude of the Shiffleys, was still finding haunches of venison on her porch every other week during hunting season. And that was five years after she'd done something to earn their gratitude—something probably a lot smaller than saving a life.

"You look a mess," I said to Charlie, in an effort to change the subject. "I hope none of it's serious enough to keep you off the football field."

"I'll be fine by September," he said. "And hey, it was great, you making sure the reporters knew I was trying to save Lola. Really helped with the college people."

"No problem," I said. "It was mainly the chief who talked to the reporters."

"Do they know if Lola's going to be all right?" Charlie asked. "That wound didn't look good."

"Clarence says she'll be fine," Dad said. Clarence was Dr. Rutledge, Spike's vet. I wasn't surprised that they'd taken Lola to him—a wounded bobcat would present no great challenge to a vet who could give Spike his annual shots. "No permanent damage, and she's resting comfortably. And isn't it lucky that she's had her rabies shots?"

"How can they be sure?" I asked. "I thought Lanahan kept lousy records and Ray Hamlin burned them."

"Oh, yes, but Clarence keeps meticulous records of the animals he treats," Dad said. "He's the zoo's regular veterinarian, you know. Why didn't one of us think to ask him about the animals?"

"I can't imagine," I muttered.

"And Hamlin keeps detailed financial records on all his businesses, even the illegal ones," Dad went on.

"He even had a legal contract with old man Bromley for the hunting rights to his land," Randall Shiffley said. "He just never told Bromley what kind of hunts he was running out there."

The Shiffleys all smiled, and I breathed a sigh of relief. I'd bet anything that they'd already made a deal with Mr. Bromley for the hunting rights Ray Hamlin would no longer be at liberty to exercise—which meant they'd probably stop trying to get the hunting rights to Mother and Dad's farm.

"So between Clarence's records and Hamlin's own," Dad was saying, "Chief Burke should have ample evidence to convict him of violating any number of animal-welfare and game laws."

"And murder, I hope," I said. "Murder and attempted murder and kidnapping and—"

"I've got a long list of crimes for Mr. Ray Hamlin to answer to," the chief said, walking through the door with Dr. Blake at his side.

"What about the Sprockets?" I asked.

"Threw a whole bunch of charges at them, too," the chief said. "Gets my goat, having people complicate my life when I'm trying to solve a murder."

I winced, hoping the chief didn't consider my confrontation with Ray Hamlin one of those complications.

"Like Shea Bailey with his trick of letting all the animals loose?" I said aloud.

"Irresponsible," the chief said, shaking his head, as he pulled over a chair for Dr. Blake. "We caught up with him, too. Looks like he won't be leading the SOBs anymore. Seems his dedication to the cause of animal welfare was just an excuse for milking the organization for as much cash as possible. The SOBs are poorer but wiser today."

"Actually, I think they've all voted to disband and join Rose Noire's animal-welfare group," Dad said.

"Splendid," I said. Perhaps Rose would have more than enough people for her animal-massage class and wouldn't need to recruit me.

"And as their first project, they're all going to come out and help take care of the zoo animals until we can get their future sorted out."

"And how long will that be?" I asked.

"Tuesday," Blake said. "Maybe sooner. I've got a couple of my staff down at Virginia Beach, hunting down that fellow from the bank to see if we can wrap it up tonight. But by Tuesday, at the latest, we'll have that zoo back open or I'll know the reason why."

"And I gather you'll be staying around for a while, overseeing the transition."

"Possibly," Blake said. "Why?"

I hesitated. After all, Blake wasn't the killer. Did the suspicious things he'd done still matter?

Yes. After all, he was going to be hanging around, helping take care of our animals.

Now I was doing it too. Not our animals. The zoo's animals. Who would probably all be back in the zoo by the time Michael and I returned from wherever. But either way, it mattered. If he wasn't completely on the up-and-up, we didn't want him anywhere near anyone's animals.

"If you're going to be hanging around, I want a straight answer on something," I said. "In fact, several somethings."

"Now, Meg," Dad said. "We have the killer, remember?"

"Yes, but that doesn't explain the photo I saw of Dr. Blake holding a rifle with one foot on a dead lion. Can you explain it, Dr. Blake?"

"Probably a fake someone Photoshopped to discredit me," Blake said. "Where did you see it?"

"You have it as part of the screen saver on your laptop."

Blake frowned slightly, and then his face cleared and he chuckled.

"I know the one you're talking about. The lion wasn't dead— that's a tranquilizer gun I'm holding, not a rifle. Keen eyes though. I can see why you suspected me."

"Not to mention the fact that last night I saw you bagging up the wineglasses Rob and Dad and I were using, as if they were evidence. I figured you were the killer, and planning to frame one of us if you got the chance."

"You did?" Blake exclaimed. "That's rich!" He threw back his head and laughed vigorously.

"But now I figure you were snooping around, too," I went on. "You were trying to solve the murder and collecting DNA from your suspects. Is that it?"

"Not exactly," Blake said. "I wasn't worried about the murder investigation. I figured it was in good hands."

"Thank you," Chief Burke said. Blake glanced at him with mild surprise, as if he'd forgotten the chief was there.

"But you're right," Blake went on. "I did want your DNA. I want to compare it with mine."

We all stared at him in astonishment. I was the first to get my tongue back.

"You think we're related?"

"I think you're my granddaughter. And my son," he said, turning to Dad.

Dad took a step back.

"I'm a foundling," he said. "No one knows who my parents were."

"Found in the fiction section of the Charlottesville library," Blake said. "That's what the local paper said, am I right?"

"That's right," Dad said.

"Just where my poor Cordelia left you."

"Your poor Cordelia?" I echoed.

"I was . . . um, engaged to one of the librarians there."

" 'Um, engaged'?" I echoed again. "Had you asked her to marry you, or is that just a euphemism for something else?"

"A beautiful young woman," Blake said. "I was planning to ask her to marry me as soon as I was able. But I was a poor graduate student. And I got a chance to go on my first zoological expedition. A six-month trip to the Galápagos. I explained how important it was to my career. I thought she understood."

"And you came back and she'd vanished."

He nodded.

"I assumed she'd grown tired of waiting—the trip went on a little longer than planned."

"How much longer?"

"It was only a year and a half," he said.

"Smart woman," I said. "I'd have sent the Dear Montgomery letter after seven months."

"Very smart," he said. "And very beautiful."

He reached into his pocket and pulled out an old photo in a plastic protector. He looked at it, then handed it to me.

It was like seeing myself in costume from the Roaring Twenties. Like me, Cordelia was a little too busty to carry off the flapper look, but she had a certain panache. I might have liked her if I'd known her, growing up. I wasn't sure I approved of her taste in men, though.

"How old was she, anyway?" I said. She looked about sixteen.

"It's the only picture I have," he said. "Her high school graduation photo. She was a few years older when I met her."

I handed the photo to Dad.

"I came to town to see Lanahan," Blake was saying. "Just a courtesy. Wasn't going to bother with his little zoo, but then I happened to see your picture in the *Caerphilly Clarion*. Did some research on you. Learned that your father was abandoned as an infant in the same library where Cordelia and I used to meet on my trips to Charlottesville."

He and Dad gazed at each other. Blake looked triumphant and happy. Dad looked as if he was beginning, too late, to appreciate the joys of being an orphan.

"Yippee," I said. "So instead of coming up and telling us this, you hung around spying on us."

"I had to figure out if you were people I even wanted to know, much less claim as family."

So if he didn't approve of us, he was just going to sneak off again? I wasn't sure I trusted a paternal—or grandpaternal—feeling that kicked in only after Blake had made sure we met his standards.

"And you decided to claim us after the events of the last few days?" I said aloud. "I'm surprised you didn't run away screaming."

"You lead entertaining lives," Blake said. He leaned back in his chair, crossed his arms, and smiled, as if awaiting the next installment of entertainment.

I stared at him, baffled. I had no idea how I felt about this. I needed time to think it through. I had a sudden frustrating vision of Michael and me, strolling along that romantic beach, Parisian street, vineyard trail, or whatever, talking about Montgomery Blake instead of us.

Not if I could help it.

"Of course, the DNA test's not in yet," I said. "With any luck, the resemblance will turn out to be nothing but a coincidence, and you can go back to saving animals in more exotic climes."

And until the DNA test was in, I resolved, I would shove the whole thing out of my mind.

"We'll see," Blake said. He heaved himself up from the chair. "Got to be going—I want to make sure those crazy in-laws of ours aren't upsetting the animals."

Where did he think he was going? He couldn't just drop a bombshell like that and leave.

So much for my resolution.

"We should stop tiring you out," Randall Shiffley said. "But we just wanted to say thanks again."

"I've got a whole passel of criminals down in the jail," the chief said. "I should be getting back."

Was it something I said? Not that I minded the idea of some peace and quiet, but I'd been trying to get it all day without success.

"Meg, dear." Mother stood in the doorway, smiling at me and pointedly ignoring everyone else. Clearly they were all in her bad graces today.

Everyone murmured greetings and good-byes except for Dad and Michael. Not surprising—I hadn't been awake for it, but I heard that when Mother showed up at the house last night, a few minutes after Chief Burke, she had given him and everyone else in the immediate vicinity an uncharacteristically frank piece of her mind about abandoning me to the mercies of a killer. If even tough-minded people like Dr. Blake, Randall Shiffley, and the chief were still giving her a wide berth, I was probably never going to forgive myself for passing out and missing the whole thing.

"How are things back at the house?" I asked.

"Everyone's asking about you," she said. "And there was such a nice article about the whole thing in the paper."

"The paper? You mean the *Clarion*? It only comes out on Wednesdays."

"They put out a special edition," Mother said. "Isn't that nice?"

I winced at the headline—"Clay County Businessman Arrested for Caerphilly Zookeeper's Murder." So much for good relations between the two rival counties. And I wasn't thrilled with the picture of me, either—waving Mrs. Fenniman's umbrella at a cowering wolf. The good thing was that they'd taken it before I acquired my black eye, but I still looked rather demented. In fact, the whole article made us look like a pack of utter loons. I couldn't figure out why Mother was so cheerful until I spotted the photo of Sheila D. Flugleman. According to the *Clarion,* last night's foray into the sheep pasture wasn't her first, and Seth Early was charging her with trespassing and petit larceny.

"The creator of ZooperPoop! caught trespassing in a common sheep pasture," I said. "Considering what she was taking, I think even petit larceny is stretching it, but I bet it will really hurt ZooperPoop! sales if it gets out."

"Yes, and imagine what would happen if Martha Stewart got a copy of that article," Mother said.

Considering that Mother had probably been strolling around saying that for hours now, I felt sure that within a few days, at least a dozen of her friends and relatives would be sending copies of the *Clarion* to Martha Stewart. So much for Sheila D.'s chances of appearing on the show.

"Anyway, I brought some clothes for you to wear. To the party," she said, handing me a tote bag. "Though if you don't feel up to coming, I'll understand completely."

I frowned. Normally, Mother would never consider a black eye, a bloody nose, a lacerated cheek, several sets of bobcat claw marks on my body, a possible concussion, and a broken leg as grounds for failing to meet a social obligation. Was this really my mother, or a clever impersonator?

I peered into the tote bag.

"That's Rose Noire's blouse," I said, removing a puff of turquoise silk from its depths.

"Yes, dear, but all your own nice things are still packed away somewhere, and she's perfectly happy to let you borrow it."

"This isn't mine either," I said, pulling out a butter-soft honey-colored suede skirt. "And don't tell me it's Rose Noire's. She wouldn't wear suede. She won't even eat fruit leather because of the name."

"It's a present," she said. "I thought you deserved one after all you've been through."

At the bottom of the bag was a shoe—one of a well-broken-in pair I wore when I wanted to be both comfortable and presentable.

"Before you ask, the other shoe's back in your closet. You'll be in the cast for the next few weeks, so you won't need it today."

"That's great," Michael said. From the relief in his voice, I could tell that even if the wardrobe he'd packed for the honeymoon was perfect, he hadn't anticipated the need to hunt down something presentable so I wouldn't have to wear a hospital gown to our wedding.

"I should be getting back to your guests," Mother said. "I'll see you there if you feel up to it. But I'll tell everyone that we should expect to see you when we see you. Whatever the doctor says goes!"

She kissed both of us on the cheek, beamed at us for a few moments, and then sailed out along with Dad.

"Okay, the coast is clear," Michael said, handing me the tote. "And your mother solved the last thing that could slow us down. I'll go let Dr. Waldron know we're going."

It didn't hit me until I'd put on the clothes.

"She knows," I muttered.

"All clear," Michael said, bouncing back into the room. "Let's make tracks."

"He can make tracks," Dr. Waldron said as she pushed a wheelchair into the room. "You have to ride till you're out of the building. Hospital policy."

"Can I wheel her out?" Michael asked.

"No problem," the doctor said. She turned to me. "Keep the cast dry, take the painkillers if the leg bothers you, and call me if you have any problems."

"Roger," I said. She strode out again.

"She knows," I said.

"Dr. Waldron? If she does, she won't tell anyone."

"Mother," I said. "She knows."

"She knows we might not make the party. I got that much." He was bustling around the room, gathering the rest of my belongings and stuffing them into the tote bag. "Doesn't take a rocket scientist to figure out you might not be in the mood for a family party."

"She knows," I said. "Look what clothes she brought."

"Nice," Michael said, with an appreciative smile. "But not exactly white satin."

"Something old—my shoe. Something new—the skirt. Something borrowed, something blue—Rose Noire's blouse. And look what I found in the skirt pocket."

I held up a shiny, brand-new dime.

"I thought it was 'And a sixpence for your shoe,'" he quoted. "It's not a sixpence, and it was in the pocket. Maybe it was just left there."

"A dime's the modern American equivalent of a sixpence, and it's a brand-new skirt—who could possibly have left a dime in it? Inspector number seven bribing me to overlook any flaws in the stitching? She knows."

"Maybe she suspects, but she can hardly know."

"What if she's down at the Clay County courthouse, waiting for us?" I said. "Crashing our elopement? What if they're all down there?"

"If they're down at the courthouse, they're in for a shock. Courthouse is closed. It's Memorial Day, remember?"

My mouth fell open.

"If the courthouse is closed, how are we going to—"

"We have an open appointment with a justice of the peace in Prince William County," Michael said. "Which is right on the way to Dulles Airport. As long as we drop by her house sometime before dark, she'll interrupt her family picnic long enough to perform the ceremony. Now have a seat and let me wheel you down to the car. The JP doesn't care when we get there, but the airline might not be as accommodating."

I hobbled over to the wheelchair and sat down.

"I still say Mother knows. I wouldn't put it past her to follow us."

"If she figures it out, she's welcome to come to the wedding. They're all welcome to come. There's only one thing I insist on."

"What's that?" I asked.

"Just the two of us on the honeymoon. If I spot a single relative when we get to our destination, we're leaving."

"Just the two of us," I echoed.

Even finding the tin cans tied to the back of Michael's convertible didn't spoil my good mood.